THE
DONUT
LEGION

ALSO BY JOE LANSDALE

THE HAP AND LEONARD NOVELS

OTHER NOVELS

SELECTED SHORT STORY COLLECTIONS

THE DONUT LEGION

JOE R. LANSDALE

MULHOLLAND BOOKS

Little, Brown and Company

New York Boston London

Mulholland Books / Little, Brown and Company
Hachette Book Group
1290 Avenue of the Americas, New York, NY 10104
mulhollandbooks.com

First Edition: November 2022

Mulholland Books is an imprint of Little, Brown and Company, a division of Hachette Book Group, Inc. The Mulholland Books name and logo are trademarks of Hachette Book Group, Inc.

The publisher is not responsible for websites (or their content) that are not owned by the publisher.

The Hachette Speakers Bureau provides a wide range of authors for speaking events. To find out more, go to hachettespeakersbureau.com or call (866) 376-6591.

ISBN 978-0-316-54068-1
Library of Congress Control Number: 2022941849

10 9 8 7 6 5 4 3 2 1

MRQ-T

Printed in Canada

For Nicky, finest dog that ever lived

Religion consists in a set of things which the average man thinks he believes, and wishes he was certain.

—Mark Twain, *Mark Twain's Notebooks*

Insanity is contagious.

—Sebastian Haff (Elvis impersonator)

THE
DONUT
LEGION

(1)

It was late at night and I was on my long wraparound porch sitting at my deck table with a cup of hot tea, a blanket thrown over my shoulders, nursing a light headache. The weather had begun to go cool and the greenery of the woods that surrounded my house had died. But the death of summer and the rise of fall had given me another kind of beauty. Brown and gold, red and orange leaves.

Of course, now, in the dark, I couldn't see them. I could hear the soft wind and limbs shaking in the deep of night and could imagine the leaves coming loose of them and coasting to the ground on the north wind. In the morning the leaves would be a multicolored tapestry on the grass, a carpet in the woods.

I sipped the last of my tea using both hands, feeling the warmth of the cup on my palms. I set the cup on the table and walked off the porch with the blanket around me.

I strolled into the backyard, where I had set up a high stool and a telescope on a tripod. I sat on the stool, positioned the blanket tighter around me, and looked through the telescope. There was a glowing circle around the moon, so either I had cataracts forming or, more likely, it was the old farmer's sign of changing weather.

I was starting to reposition the telescope when I heard a motor humming up my long drive. I slid off the stool and stepped around to the side of the house. Soon I could see car lights coasting down the drive. The lights stopped at the gate and were turned off. A door opened and for a moment, in the car's interior light, I saw a woman framed in the glow. She was mostly a shape from that distance, but I knew her shape immediately. I knew how she moved and how she smelled and how she touched me when she had.

It was my ex-wife, Meg, who I used to call, with affection, Megalodon. She closed the door. The car went dark, and she was a moving shadow. She climbed over the gate like a monkey on a mission and walked up the drive toward the house. Using the side steps, I walked back onto the porch and reseated myself in my chair. The hot tea was gone, but for some reason I held the cup in my hands as if it might still have warmth. It did not. In fact, it seemed the night had brought not only my ex-wife to me but with her a greater chill. It had come along sudden-like and in a mean-spirited mood.

Meg had been to my current home a few times to talk about this or that, mostly about us divesting ourselves of shared property, but this place I owned free and clear of past entanglements. Her clothes had never hung in my closets, nor had her makeup and hair spray sprawled over one of the sinks in the bathroom, nor had her shampoos and conditioners been decked on the rack in my shower. She had never had more than coffee at my indoor table and once out here on the porch.

Fact was, I had been lucky. Even young as I was, I wouldn't have to get a job to pay the bills for a couple years to come. Still, in the mornings, I rose and worked on my next book. Sometime soon I would finish it and send it off through the magic of e-mail to my beleaguered agent. I wasn't rich and this book wouldn't make me rich either, but it kept me from doing a nine-to-five.

It was a better life than before, when Meg and I were married. She scattered a person's thoughts. Now I had purpose, and I only thought of Meg about a dozen times daily, not moment to moment.

Meg was coming ever nearer to me, and the closer she came, the more I thought of her husband, Ethan. Him touching her where I had touched her, and her touching him where she had touched me, and the whole thing made me feel sick and foolish at the same time, like a schoolboy whose date had ridden away in another boy's car because it was shiny.

Meg stepped up on the porch. It squeaked as she came along. She sat down across from me at the table. The moon had dipped more to the west and some of its light was sliding under the overhanging roof and onto the porch. The light struck her in a way that for a moment made her seem transparent. Then she shifted slightly, and she looked fine, her long raven-black hair shifting around her shoulders like a cascade of spilled India ink. Her soft skin appeared even softer in the moonlight, at least the one side of her face I could see clearly. She wore a T-shirt, blue-jean shorts, and tennis shoes. She sat and pulled her long legs into the chair and rested her chin on her knees, her arms wrapped around them.

I could see her anklet, a silver chain with a silver heart fastened to it. I recognized that sitting position. She even slept that way on occasion, her hair draped around her face like a hood. I had moved her hair with my fingers on many a night, gently, so that I might see her face and hear her breathe, had touched her as lightly as one might the wings of a butterfly.

"I thought you'd be up," she said. "You always liked staying up late."

"If I don't have to get up early," I said.

"How have you been?"

"Well enough. But I don't think you came out here at what must be about three in the morning to ask about my health and general welfare."

"Came to ask a favor."

"It couldn't wait until tomorrow, maybe a request by phone? E-mail works."

"We're not together anymore, but I wanted to see you."

"All right. You see me."

"Don't be nasty, Charlie."

"Still feel kind of screwed over by you running off with Ethan. I thought you went to the store."

"Then you'll love this. I need your help. It has to do with Ethan and what I think might be murder."

"Murder? Whose murder?"

"Ethan's."

"Ethan's dead?"

"I think so. I think there's a lot going on and not much of it makes much sense, but what I can figure is what is going on isn't over. I feel dislocated."

"That's damn confusing, Meg."

"Don't mean it to be. I know just enough to know I don't know quite enough."

"Why would you come to me?"

"You were a cop."

"For two years. I hated it."

"And a private investigator."

"About a year or so. I hated it."

"But you were good at it."

"The police. Talk to them."

"That won't work, Charlie."

"I'm still confused. Ethan was murdered? I haven't heard a thing about this."

"I have a feeling you pretty well isolate out here."

"Fair enough. But I read the news on the computer, watch TV now and then. Nothing about a dead Ethan Phillips."

"You still look at the stars and the moon, dream about Mars?"

This seemed like a strange response. "I was doing that when I heard your car."

"Always investigating, in a way. Looking into what people do, trying to figure the face of the moon, the mysteries of Mars. I made a mistake when I left you."

"Maybe I'm okay with you going."

"A person can be a fool."

"Which of us are you talking about?"

"Me, I guess."

"Hell, Meg. We were both silly. Young."

"I think I'm more in love with the idea of being in love than in staying in love. I'm looking for that hit of emotion that comes with the next new thing. In my case, the next new romance. New ideas. New beliefs. All of it is like candy to me. Until I chew it."

"Yeah. I was the monkey in the middle. Cassidy, me, and now Ethan. You go through us like shit through a goose. You use marriage like a placeholder."

"I guess I deserve that. My mother was like that. I guess you learn the best from the best and the worst from the worst, and she was kind of both at the same time. Your mother—now, there was a mother. She was my ideal."

"Mine too," I said. "But as for us, it's done and over. We don't matter as a 'we' anymore."

"Not completely true."

"Because you need my help?"

"That's part of it. I need you to look into something for me as private investigator."

"I don't have a license. Haven't in years. You know that. I'm a full-time writer now."

"But license or not, you know how. Right?"

"I do."

Meg shivered slightly. I got up and draped my blanket over her shoulders. As I did, her hand reached up and touched mine. It felt icy and damp, and it was almost as if an electric spark popped in my eyes, and then the spark was gone.

She said, "Watch out for omelets. And beware the great mound within the circle."

"What?" I said, and the blanket collapsed in the chair.

There was no one there.

It was my turn to shiver.

I looked a long time at the empty chair. I walked down to the gate. There was no car there. I took my phone out of my coat pocket and turned on the flashlight. The earth was still damp from a rain the day before. A heavy rain that washed in the ruts and turned sand to mud. It was perfect ground for impressions, but there wasn't a mark on that moist ground from either tires or footsteps.

(2)

I called Meg, but her cell number was no longer working. I wanted to drive over to her apartment but decided I wouldn't. I didn't believe in ghosts, but I certainly believed something was wrong.

Were there signals I had picked up on about Meg and Ethan that would make me imagine such a thing?

I couldn't quite convince myself of that. Meg had seemed so real. And the car? What about the car?

I went to bed, but I didn't sleep right away. I got up twice and went outside on the porch wearing only my underwear. A wonderful reason to live where I did. No neighbors looking out their windows, calling the cops on me for indecent exposure. I wanted, I could take a pee off the steps of my porch, and had.

On the chair where Meg had sat there was only the blanket. I picked it up. I could smell a sweet smell that made me think of her favorite perfume. Lilacs. That bothered me even more. Had she really been there, come and gone, and I had no memory of her departure?

Thinking about it turned my mild headache into a slightly more intense one. I had been having quite a few headaches of late.

Finally, I climbed back in bed, having brought the blanket inside with me. I curled up around it like a child with his security blanket. I went to sleep with the aroma of lilacs in my nose.

I didn't have my usual omelet next morning, due to Meg's strange warning. I couldn't make heads or tails of it, but it worried me. I had toast and a cup of coffee, showered, and dressed. I was convinced I needed to talk to my brother. I wrapped up a package for him.

I had something else to do before we spoke. Maybe then things would change, and we wouldn't need to talk at all. At least not about a ghost and murder.

I climbed in my car and tooled down to the gate, used the device in the car to open it. I got out and looked more closely at the ground, thinking in the morning light I would find evidence.

Still no tire or footprints. Seeing that unmarked mud gave me another shiver. Like Father Death had traced a cold finger up my spine.

I drove through the open gate on into May Town, where Meg lived with her husband, Ethan. Or had lived. I didn't know what to think after last night. Was Ethan alive or dead? And if it had been a ghost on my porch last night, did that mean Meg was dead?

The entrance to the apartment complex where she lived bore a worn sign with magnetic letters missing so that it read OOM O ET instead of ROOMS TO LET. Otherwise, the place was nice, well cared for. I had only been to Meg's apartment once before. It was on the ground floor near a pool and tennis courts.

A long stretch of flower bed had recently been prepared in front of and to the side of the fence around the pool and Meg's apartment. The bed did not yet contain plants. The dirt was brown and rich and smelled musty. There were bits of gravel in the bed, and one of those bits was shiny as glass. A few weeds had started up in patches. If flowers were planted there, bulbs, they had yet to announce themselves. Spring, I figured, they would pop.

A guy on a little garden mower was zooming about on the grassy median that separated rows of apartments. He was a chap with a cap pulled down tight, wearing work clothes and a face that could have passed for a clenched asshole. As he bounced by on the median, flinging damp grass, he looked at me and nodded slowly.

I nodded back, and he bounced on. I slapped the damp grass off my pants.

I knocked on Meg's door after trying the doorbell and discovering it didn't work. At least, I couldn't hear that it worked.

The knock didn't work either. I tried the door for the hell of it, but it was locked up tight as a bank vault. I walked to the window and attempted to look in through parted curtains.

Dark in there.

"They're gone," a voice said.

I turned. It was a woman, perhaps five years older than me, but there was something about her face that made you think that she had lived her life in a dirty room full of cigarette smoke. She was a willowy lady with shoulder-length auburn hair. She was wearing a loose T-shirt and shorts, grimy white tennis shoes. Had a cigarette hanging off her lip like some sort of appendage. She had an unconcerned attractiveness about her in spite of that dingy life impression.

"Gone?" I asked.

"Yep. Left not too long ago. I'm Evelyn, by the way. Evelyn Woods."

"Charlie Garner. Did they pack up and leave? Do you know?"

"Everything they owned is still in there. Well, they may have taken something with them, but given all the stuff inside, it must have been in a shoebox. I've looked. I have a key, of course, I'm the manager here. Who are you?"

"I'm Meg's ex-husband."

"The writer?"

"Sometimes."

"She mentioned you."

"Are you and her friends?"

"Friendly. I don't know about friends. We talked at the pool now and then. She liked to tan. I liked to sit under an umbrella at a table with a tall glass of ice tea."

"Always told her she was going to get skin cancer," I said.

"She might. But she has dark skin, and that helps. She told me once it wasn't about the tan, because she didn't really tan; it was the heat. She liked the heat."

"Sounds like her. What about Ethan?"

"He was kind of a shadow. A worm with a makeover. Had nice hair. Didn't seem to fit with her, not even a little bit. Really jealous kind of guy. Maybe he had reason. Know I resented the way my husband looked at her. You can tell when a man is thinking he'd like to gobble some woman up like a pork chop. She knew it too. Her and those short-ass shorts. That's him on the mower. Cletus the Penis, they used to call him, maybe still do. He'd poke anything that had a crack in it."

We both looked for Cletus. The mower was way down the length of median grass, and Cletus the Penis was bouncing along on the narrow seat.

"Way he looked at her, that made me pissed at her sometimes."

"You were pissed at her instead of Cletus?"

"I was pissed at both of them, but Cletus I got to live with unless I want to go it alone. I don't. We pay the bills better together. Both of us have good jobs here, a place to stay."

"Do you remember when you saw Meg and Ethan last?"

"Not sure when I quit seeing Ethan about, and I saw her only now and then. Last time was at night, late, out by the pool. I remember because me and the old man had a fight. He wanted a little loving, and I didn't have any to give. We argued. I couldn't sleep on account of it. We live in the upper apartment across the way there."

She turned and pointed, then turned back.

"Place looks down on the pool. I like to watch out the window late at night. Not just for young men in tight bathing suits, but to see the night, when the pool's closed and everything is quiet. Rarely is anyone even near the pool after ten thirty. Cletus locks the fence and cuts all but one light inside of it. I looked out, and there she was at the fence, staring at the water."

"When was this?"

"Maybe a week ago."

"Has anyone called the cops? I mean, one day Meg and Ethan are here, and next day they aren't. And all their stuff is still here."

"I did. They came out, looked around, asked if their rent was paid up, wondering if they took a burner so as not to pay. But it is paid up. They got a few more days before it's due again, then I don't know. They don't come back, guess I can auction off their stuff. I'm thinking they may have jumped because of other bills they owed. Meg said they were struggling a bit. The marriage and the finances. Ethan quit his job at the university, then Meg quit hers at the yoga studio. Conflict with the boss, she said. Went to work at one of the donut shops in town. Said she wasn't making that much at the studio anyway, and without Ethan's salary, it was tough sledding. She was all into flying-saucer shit. You know, the peckerwood cult somewhere out there in the woods. Don't know why they can't just be Christians and go on with things."

"Cops had nothing?"

"Not that they told me. They move like glaciers. Meg and Ethan leaving their furniture and goods behind is odd, but in the end, if they're running from bill collectors, it might not mean anything sinister."

I thanked her and drove over to my brother's office. He didn't live in May Town. He lived in Nacogdoches, which was within a few miles of my wooded property. Nacogdoches was larger than May Town. Not that there were skyscrapers poking at the clouds. Downtown it was brick streets, long-standing brick buildings. Elsewhere, some cool old houses from the town's past, as well as aluminum rectangles with all the beauty of a blackened lung.

Once the city had been lined with trees, but people who I supposed really wanted to live in bleak West Texas had cut down a lot of them, burned the trees that couldn't be sold for pulp or lumber, and poured in concrete for parking lots. It was labeled "progress." I called it "sad." When I passed McDonald's on North Street, I always remembered the big tree that had been there where now concrete shimmered in the sunlight. I heard they cut it down because of insurance problems. That the tree might fall on a car or someone, drop a limb like the Sword of Damocles.

The university in Nacogdoches was where Ethan taught folklore and history before he quit, or at least according to Evelyn he'd quit. I guess it wasn't truly my business, since Meg and I were divorced, but I was curious. And worried. Hadn't her ghost asked me for help? Actually, I was uncertain it had. I was pretty uncertain about everything this late, cool morning.

My older brother, Felix Garner, is a former psychiatrist who quit his practice—that's one way to put it—to take over the detective agency I once owned. I had been good at that business, but when I sold my first book, I was ready to give it up. I wrote it on a whim. I had always wanted to do it, and suddenly I wrote it and it did all right. Not a bestseller, but enough to make me think I could make a living of a sort at it. Film sale helped, though the film never got made.

Before I quit the detective business, Felix had come back to Nacogdoches from Houston, worked for me for a while before he took it over. He was the first person I talked to in times of stress. He didn't always have good advice, but he had advice. And sometimes just hearing him talk like he knew something was a comfort.

Felix was a good detective, though, even if what he mostly detected was who was in whose underwear during divorce settlements. He said he felt the job was similar to psychiatry: looking under humanity's hood to see what made it tick, what made the cylinders whirl, what kept the engine oiled, and what caused it to seize up. He'd made more money as a psychiatrist but felt he had a better life as a detective. Most of the time.

I knew this about him: He was the kind of guy that might throw himself a surprise party and be ecstatic if he were the only one that showed up.

He had upstairs digs across from the Boss Light Bookstore. I parked at the curb, put my package under my arm, went up to the top floor.

There was a hall at the top of the stairs, and Felix owned what was on both sides of it. There was a long window at the far end of the hall, without curtains. It looked down on an alley and across the way to a law office.

On the left side, the business side, the closed office door had a buzzer next to it on the wall. It said PUSH ME.

I pushed.

A moment later a door behind me on the other side of the hall opened and Felix came out.

He was a lot bigger than me, tended toward a little fat. But that could fool you. He used to bench-press three hundred and could deadlift a hell of a lot more. His arms looked like old but healthy trees. He still worked out but nowhere near as hard as when he was younger. He was thirty-seven and six foot five. He had our family's red hair and a red, tightly trimmed beard. I never took to beards and I didn't like his. Today he was wearing a T-shirt that made him look like three hundred pounds of meat squeezed into a small condom. The shirt said NACOGDOCHES FILM FESTIVAL on it.

We used to fight when we were young. Fistfight as a pastime. He won until I learned a little bit more about defending myself. Well, he still won. Boxing a bear was still boxing a bear.

Felix grinned his perfect teeth at me, the result of expensive dental work and his constant obsession with products that kept them white.

"Charlie, so good to see you. No loans."

"Funny."

After we embraced, he said, "Come in, I was just cooking breakfast. Got up late. What's with the package?"

"Later."

I followed him through the door he had come out of into another short hallway, then through an opening that led into the kitchen. It was compact but well arranged, with cooking pots and pans hung on hooks on the wall. A frying pan on the electric stove was full of bacon and was popping grease. Felix turned down the heat.

"Can I fix you anything?"

"No. I had some toast."

"Toast? What kind of breakfast is that? Have some fried eggs. An omelet?"

"I'm off omelets."

"What?"

"Partly that's why I'm here."

"Omelets?"

"You got time to give me some psychiatric advice?"

"You're fucked up and crazy. Done."

"Really, Felix. I'm serious."

"Sure. Let me finish cooking."

I went into the dining room and sat, put my package on the table. Felix called out, "Coffee. You're not off coffee, are you?"

"I can do coffee, but if it's your usual, I'll need some milk to thin it."

He finished cooking, brought me a cup of coffee, went back, brought milk, went back again, and brought out his breakfast, four fried eggs and eight pieces of slab bacon, a rack of toast on a plate the size of a hubcap.

"You should write a cookbook," I said. *"Heart Attacks Are Us."*

"Healthy as a horse," he said. "I could lose a few pounds, though. Okay, what is the mysterious business about omelets?"

I told him what had happened last night, about Meg and her warnings, her saying her husband, Ethan, was dead. I told him about going to their apartment, how they had abandoned it and left their goods. The cops had been told but didn't seem too worried about it.

He ate his breakfast while I told him my story. When I finished, my coffee had cooled. I carried it into the kitchen, microwaved it, and came back to the table. I knew him well enough to know he would be thinking about what I had told him for a while.

I sat and sipped the coffee. Even with the milk, it bordered on deadly. "You need a Keurig, man. This pot-and-filter business is like stuff the Flintstones did."

He ignored that. "That's quite a story there. As a brother, I'd say you're full of it, just a dream, but looking at you as a patient, trying to give you psychiatric advice, I'd pretty much say the same thing. Why I'm not a psychiatrist anymore. I lacked bedside manner. Guy comes in, tells me he can't get his life straight because Daddy didn't play ball with him enough. Mama ignored him because she worked two jobs. I think that's your problem. It's not abuse, it's personal obsession with minutiae and yourself. Hubris. Things like that aren't the sort of things that ought to dictate your life, unless you want them to. Anybody over twelve should know that. Our father didn't exactly play ball with us twenty-four/seven, and I think we turned out well enough. As for ghosts, I always dismissed them unless my client was schizophrenic. I recommended drugs."

"So you got nothing?"

"I didn't say that. Just telling you where I stand on ghosts and a lot of silly parent issues. I don't think they matter much in real life."

"I didn't ask you about the parent part."

"One thing leads to another with me. Maybe I have more parent issues than I thought. You know, bringing it up without being asked."

"Ever known me to believe in ghosts before?"

"No, but you were slow in getting over Santa Claus, and I know you were looking for Easter Bunny tracks a little late in life."

"I hated to let go of the fantasy," I said.

"You've always had an overactive imagination. Have you been thinking about Meg?"

"Always."

"Hard girl to get over. Woman, I should say."

"She is."

"Had a kind of thing for her myself. A crush on my sister-in-law. Until she left you. I was mad at her for that. Inability to commit to day-to-day situations and still be in love. She liked drama. Also, come on, bro, you must admit, she had strange moments and strange ideas. There were times when that girl could hear birds singing down in a well. Read astrology and numerology, occult books, and psychic makeovers, no-touch healing. If she divined the future in chicken guts, it wouldn't surprise me. You're imaginative, but you question things. She didn't."

"I do think about her a lot, and at the same time, I'm glad she's gone. That make sense?"

"Yeah. You know, she had the looks, but the thing that was so appealing about her was under all that was a kindness. You know how she treated our mother when she got . . . sick."

"Yeah. She spent more time with her than we did."

"She did," Felix said. "It's like she knew how much we could take, how much we couldn't, and she took up the slack. I walked into that room, Mama in bed not knowing if sounds were farts or bugles, I just fell apart. Never saw Meg do that. You could see pain in her eyes, but she had more strength about something like that than we did."

"She always was kind of a caretaker. I think she might have left me sooner, but she left when Mama no longer knew who I was, who anyone was. She knew that she wasn't going to hurt Mama by leaving. Which, had Mama had her mind right, would have hurt her a lot. She loved Meg like a daughter."

"Humans are full of contradictions. Meg was full of more than most. Here's something to consider: You said you think about Meg, meaning you miss her, at least some of the time, and the time of night you say she came around, you don't do your best critical thinking then. If you were even awake."

"You're saying I imagined her because I wanted to see her? That's all you got?"

"Doesn't mean you didn't see her. Didn't have a conversation with her. Lot of recent clinical research indicates that the eye is always sending messages to the brain but sometimes the brain sends messages to the eye. It can do the same to the ears, creating sounds that aren't there. It can fill your nostrils with smells that don't exist, your taste buds with sensations of things you haven't eaten. That could explain the lilac smell on your blanket. Some people are more subject to that sort of thing. Often, so-called mediums are convinced they are experiencing something supernatural when they are actually experiencing their own desires. If the desires are strong enough, the brain accommodates. Most of those folks are frauds from the get-go, but some truly believe they have powers. Call them abilities. But what they have are intense urges to believe, and something about their makeup makes it more likely they can create images in their minds that are realistic enough to be convincing to them. You may have been worried about Meg. May have picked up body-language signals from her from some time back, signals that all was not well. A hint from this, a hint from that. But you may not have realized it. Your brain took all that in and scrutinized it and came up with results well after the fact. Some people call it intuition, but it's a learned behavior."

"Like a cop's gut instinct."

"Yeah. But again, lot of cops see things about someone that aren't there because they're convinced the person they're dealing with is guilty. Might be. But it may have nothing to do with their intuition, which is just experience multiplied by common sense. It may be simple things like the husband probably killed his wife because there was a lot of life insurance and it's the sort of thing that happens regularly. A common crime, so common sense indicates that's the situation again. But sometimes it's not. You know all that."

"Okay." I picked up the package I had brought in with me. I unwrapped it, handed it to Felix. "The blanket with her smell."

Felix stuck it to his face and sniffed. "Lilacs," he said.

"Let me ask. Are we both having olfactory hallucinations?"

(3)

eg wore a perfume like that," I said. "It was her favorite."

"Did you have this blanket when you two were married?"

"I did."

"Smells can hang around a long time."

"I never noticed the smell before. I had it over my shoulders when she showed up. I draped it over her for only an instant. That smell wasn't there before."

"After your hallucination, because that's what I'm going to call it, you became more aware. You were looking for reasons to believe she was there because it seemed so real. Your nose finally took serious note of the blanket smell, which had been there all along."

"Maybe."

"Look here, baby brother. You go home and forget this business, and I will check with Cherry, see what she can tell me. She's got connections in May Town. Hell, everywhere."

Cherry was Felix's girlfriend. She was also a crack lawyer and knew just about everyone.

"Leave it to me," he said. "I'll get back to you."

We shifted our talk to other things. Felix was obsessed with sports, had played football in high school, a bit of college ball. I didn't have much interest in any sport other than boxing. I didn't mind watching people run track either, if I had nothing good to read and it was a rainy day.

I let him carry on about football for a while. When I could find a hole in his sports talk, I bade him farewell, went to the car, dropped off the blanket, then went around the corner to the Dixie Café for a cup of coffee that I could stomach. I wanted to be alone with my thoughts for a few moments. Felix can be overwhelming.

After that, I drove home. By then I had begun to lose some of the urgency about things. Felix made sense. But still, Meg and Ethan going off and leaving everything? It bothered me a little longer than the ghost business, but finally I decided the apartment manager had been right. They might have skipped out on bills. That sounded like the both of them. The word "flighty" could easily have been their middle names.

(4)

Few days later, very early morning, after a night of wind and unsettled sleep, I was upstairs at the computer checking my bank account. I found it to be looking good.

I thought I would be okay for quite some time if I didn't buy a yacht. I didn't want a yacht.

I had my bills set on automatic payments, and all my credit cards had been paid off. Life was good. I wasn't thinking about Meg or Ethan. I hadn't thought about them much in the past couple of days, and my memory of Meg's visit had faded slightly. Enough that Felix's explanation seemed pretty likely. She and her ghost car hadn't actually come to me late at night.

I tapped around on the computer awhile, bought a book on Amazon, read a few articles, considered trying to work some more on the new book that I had high hopes for, but instead took a stupid online IQ test that involved knowing the answers to the simplest questions possible. None of it had to do with intelligence. It was kind of fun, though.

My phone buzzed. I picked it up. It was the door camera. It had a wide view. An old blue pickup spotted with rust had just arrived.

Felix.

I watched on my phone as the camera showed him climbing out of the truck. He looked a bit like a bear awakening from hibernation and exiting a small cave. I went downstairs and opened the front door.

"Little brother," he said as he neared.

"Big brother. You want some coffee?"

"Not that brown water you drink." He came inside, said, "I got some information for you."

"Okay." I fixed coffee anyway. I wanted a cup, and Felix decided he could stand the Keurig stuff after all.

We sat on the couch in the living room.

"I talked to Cherry, and I went over to May Town as well."

"Yeah?"

"Cherry looked into some things for me. May Town cops were a little pissy with her. Said the chief over there, John Patrick Nelson, wears a pearl-handled six-shooter in a concho-laden holster. Colt Peacemaker. Looks like those old Western revolvers. Struts around like George Patton. Or George C. Scott playing George Patton."

"I don't know him, but I know of him. When I was detecting, both as a cop and investigator, I crossed paths with the cops over there a few times in minor ways."

"Small-town police like that get protective, feel a little inferior, and, frequently, rightfully so. Most of their officers fell off the hay truck and onto their heads."

"That's very narrow of you."

"It's true. Least in May Town. Cherry of the excellent dark skin and more excellent brain feels the same. They are narrow."

"You sound like you're in love."

"Maybe."

"You've dated a lot of women. But this sounds different."

"How so? I'm in love with every beautiful woman who has brains and a lot who have brains and aren't beautiful. Unlike you, baby brother. I lack the shallowness of your emotional and intellectual depth. I exist in a free-falling void of wonder and intelligence and am looking for sex with a variety of smart women."

"And you talk a lot of bullshit."

"Agreed."

"Let's go out on the porch," I said.

We took our coffee with us out to the table where I had sat the night I saw, or thought I saw, Meg. I sat in the same place I had sat then. Felix sat where she had sat. The morning was like a daylight version of the night when Meg came up the drive. The wind blew and the trees swayed, but this time I could see them, and I could see the colorful leaves blowing on the wind, the dry ones making that crispy sound, like someone stepping on crackers. There was the faint smell of something dead in the woods, and when the wind shifted it would go away, but before long, the wind would shift it back.

Felix studied me briefly. "You could see Meg's car too?"

"I told you I could."

"Tell me again, what kind of car was it?"

"You know, that's funny. Don't remember. Don't know if I could have identified it when I was looking at it."

"What color was it?"

"I don't know. Light-colored. You know, white, beige, but I couldn't really tell. I don't think it was a dark color, though."

"That could add to the hallucination theory. A car sometimes in a waking dream is just a car, lacking identifying features. Goes for a sleeping dream as well."

"You're sure of that?"

"Not really. But I think that's right. Was it the kind of car she drove?"

"I hadn't seen her in a while. She was notorious for changing cars, one cheaper than the other."

"Was it an old car, a new one, a somewhat recent one?"

"I wasn't paying attention. It was night and it was all the way at the gate. Could be that I couldn't tell what kind of car it was from here. The lights shining at me and then the lights being turned off, leaving the dark shape of the car and the dark shape of Meg coming down the drive."

"But you recognized her, even in the dark."

"Who wouldn't?"

"You have a point there."

"Being married to her, I know her walk, her presence. You know how that is. I saw you in the night coming up the drive, I'd know you immediately."

"I suppose that's true. I'd know you. We'll consider the possibility that you were asked to do a favor for a ghost. But for now, let's put that in abeyance."

"You haven't actually told me what Cherry told you."

"She found out some things from other sources than the cops, including Evelyn, the manager of the apartment complex. But she didn't find out any more than you did. She met Cletus in passing. Said the way he looked at her, she could feel his eyes in her pants."

"Evelyn said he was a horndog. Seems to think he's a lot more than he is. Did Cherry ask about the abandoned goods at their apartment?"

"Got the same information you did. Lady seems anxious to sell what's there." Felix frowned after sipping a bit of his coffee. "Maybe you could wave a bag of ground coffee over this shit."

"Ha-ha."

Felix sat the cup on the table. "I don't know you remember," he said, "but this bunch Meg is said to be part of, they believe a flying saucer is buried in the ground where their compound is."

"They had pretty much fallen out of my memory until Evelyn mentioned it. I think the Caddo claim that mound is one of the mounds from their culture, dates way back. But it's on some bozo's land, and he says it's not a Caddo mound but a landing site. Says he gets vibrations or some such from it. But I may be misremembering that."

"The group sort of pulled in their tentacles, so to speak, some years back. Authorities think there are a lot of guns up there or stored somewhere in town, but they don't bother them. Don't want a Waco shoot-out. FBI really doesn't have any legitimate reason to go in there, and the local cops don't want to bother. They don't want to get shot. And here's the cork in the pig's ass: Lot of the cops sympathize with the cult, not for the flying saucer but for guns. They think it's a big Second Amendment issue, guns being taken away from groups, no matter what their intent. Around here, you say 'God' or 'guns,' wave the flag or the Bible, you can get away with anything, even if you're waving it while you've got your finger up a chicken's ass. Still, they haven't been an obvious threat, outside of some rumors here and there. Cherry said the cult survives because several of its members have donated big money to its Grand Doodoo, or whatever he's called. Members work outside jobs, cash their paychecks, and give them to this cult shithead. Whole thing sounds like a grift for money and probably sex. Cults always turn into being about sex and money, don't they?"

"Power," I said. "Money and sex are just about keeping score. You know that from your former profession. Or you should."

"Power, then," Felix said, and sipped the last of his coffee like he had to do it. "I've caught you up, and now I assume you plan to go over to May Town and look around, because I know that's not going to satisfy you."

"Correct."

"I'll go with you when you go."

"I plan to go today."

"I prefer tonight. I think we ought to investigate the apartment for ourselves, before all the stuff in there gets hauled away. It's not as if the May Town cops will bother. They mainly drink coffee and buy donuts, shoot a Black guy now and then if he looks suspicious. You remember that shooting last year? Black man left the keys in his truck. It was an older model, and he was trying to jack the lock with a coat hanger that was lying in the truck bed. Someone saw him, called the cops, and one of the cops shot him on the spot without asking questions.

"A warning shot to the back of the head, as they used to say. Amazingly, he lived. There was quite the to-do about it. Cops were clearly in the wrong, but nothing was done to them. I think the man got shot ended up with a bit of money as a settlement. Bet he sees a coat hanger, he shits himself. I tell you all this to warn you: Go now or go with me tonight, you're facing the possibility of coming across those same trigger-happy assholes who watch too many cowboy movies. Course, we're not Black, so they might not shoot us right away. They might give us white guys a warning, say, 'Take off running,' and nail us then."

"I'm still going, and tonight is fine."

"Very well, little brother. And you buy us some dinner when it's done."

(5)

We ended up parking Felix's truck down the block from the apartments and walking over. I hoped there were no security cameras.

There was light, but it wasn't much light. A lot of it rested on the concrete walk and the fresh flower beds that Cletus had recently dug. A sickly light was coming from the pool area. Someone needed to make friends with Reddy Kilowatt.

Felix had his lockpicks with him. He told me the lock on Meg's apartment would be a piece of cake. It was. He was through that door faster than a cheetah could run down an antelope.

Inside, we looked around with the lights on our phones. There was furniture, and all the rooms except the living room were stacked with moving boxes. We checked and found they were filled to the brim with clothes and the usual paraphernalia people collect over the years. It wasn't so much stuff, though, they couldn't have moved it out in a day or two, toted it off to their new abode.

Did they have a new abode?

"Doesn't look to me like they just walked off and left things,"

Felix said. "Why bother to pack if you're walking away and leaving the goods? Maybe you're onto something, Charlie."

"So a ghost did visit me?"

"To tell you to be wary of omelets. I don't think so."

"Don't forget the mound within the circle."

"Yeah, that too. I've seen enough. They were planning on moving this junk. But where were they moving? Why were they moving? And what happened to make them leave their stuff?"

"What I've been saying."

Through the living-room window, I could see a light outside between the apartment sections, swinging back and forth. I thought it might be the landlady, but a moment later there was a hard knock on the unlocked door, then the door opened without giving us time to respond, and a beam from a flashlight that must have been as big as an antiaircraft gun shone on us.

"Police," a voice said.

———

We were hauled down to the police station without being shot.

At the station, Felix said, "Looks to me you won't be buying us dinner, and maybe we won't even have any dinner. Don't mention the ghost business to anyone or we may be here a lot longer than is already planned by our friends the police."

"They let you call your lawyer," I said. "That's a step in the right direction. What is it you always call Cherry? 'She Who Makes Grown Men Cry and Grown Women Agree.'"

"These days I just call her the Shark."

We had briefly visited with the chief of police. He'd studied us when we came into the station. He was on his way home, so there wasn't any time for the rubber-hose treatment. He was a little fat guy with a cowboy hat and that pearl-handled revolver looking almost too large for the holster that held it. The chief had a flushed face and looked as if he might blow a major hose at any moment.

"You boys are in some serious trouble," he said to us. "And you're stupid to boot."

This was hard to argue with.

He said to one of the cops that had brought us in, "Clink them up. I'm going out for pizza."

"Clink" turned out to be the sound the cell made when they closed the door behind us. But there was a nice concrete bench for us to sit on. Even a classic barred window. A dead roach lay on its back in one corner with its legs sticking up.

If only I had a harmonica and knew how to play "Nobody Knows the Trouble I've Seen." Maybe I could pull a Cool Hand Luke and eat fifty boiled eggs while I was here. Dig a tunnel. There were things to think about.

We could see through the bars an open door and a long hallway. We could hear a TV going somewhere.

The place had the atmosphere of a men's club. I wouldn't have been surprised if one of the cops came in wearing nothing but a jockstrap. We didn't see any female cops, no cops of color, unless you counted the chief's inflamed complexion. It smelled like 1960 in there.

Back at Meg and Ethan's apartment, it had happened pretty quick. Turned out there were two police officers who had come to check on us, and not only did they have massive flashlights, they had massive guns.

It was my first time riding in the back of a police car as a criminal. When I was a cop, I always took the front seat. Looked at the perps through the wire with a snotty attitude. Now I got the chance to look at the back of the cops' heads through wire, and I felt less snotty. They hadn't said any more than they had to, and neither had we. The man driving seemed as if he might like to drop us down a mine shaft. His nameplate read DUNCAN TAYLOR. It was unusual to have both the first and last name on a shirt tag, but then again, this little town was different about a lot of things.

Someone, probably Evelyn looking out her window in the apartment across the way, had seen us go in, or perhaps she had seen the puny lights from our phones moving about in the apartment. Whatever. Someone called it in. And then we had a nice ride in a police car, and now we were at the cop shop in a nice cell.

Me and Felix played I Spy a few times, but there wasn't enough in the room to see and suggest. After noting the bars on the cell door and window, our bunk, and that dead cockroach, we were done.

The door finally opened, and along with Duncan, the cop who had driven us here, was Felix's lawyer and girlfriend. She said, "What in the hell were you thinking?"

The cop leaned against the cell and listened.

Cherry Shires may have had the personality of a shark, but she was a very attractive lady in her mid-thirties. Her hair had been tamed by a generous application of hair spray and what other goods a lady might use. Her clothes hadn't been bought in May Town or Nacogdoches. They fit her just right. Her smooth black skin had been polished and tightened by more than good product and makeup. The faint touch of the surgeon's knife was there.

"It's Charlie's fault," Felix said.

"Hi, Charlie. I didn't figure you for quite the idiot your brother is. For shit's sake, Felix."

"Hi," I said.

Cherry turned and looked at the cop, who took the hint and went away. "All right," Cherry said. "Tell me what went on."

We told her everything, including the part about the ghost. She said, "We'll leave that bit out when I talk to the police."

"I guess that's best," Felix said.

"Listen, boys. You infantile idiots did a bad thing. It could cause you to end up behind bars for a while. Here's how we play it. You tell the truth. Charlie, you were worried about your ex-wife and didn't believe the story about them leaving their furniture, so you asked your brother, in his capacity as a private detective, to check out the apartment to see if that was true. That they had left things. You boys found packed boxes that obviously suggested a planned move that didn't happen. Suspicious business. You did this break-in because you two felt the police had not investigated it properly, had merely taken the landlady's word. How am I doing?"

"All correct," Felix said.

"We throw in that part about the police not doing their job so they can worry about a lawsuit. They've had a few of them. They know they didn't look into this business very well, didn't even go inside the place before arresting you two or they would have seen the boxes packed and should have had the same concerns you two did. Negligence on their part."

"Very unprofessional," Felix said.

"Exactly," she said.

"Will they be giving us toothpaste and a brush?" I said. "I like to brush my teeth before I sleep in a jail cell, or most anywhere."

"Give me a few minutes. I think I can have the charges dropped and walk you boys out of here, and then"—she paused to look at her watch—"you can buy me dinner. Oh, again: We leave the ghost part out. Keep that in mind. You don't do that, Charlie, it might be the electrodes and the rubber diapers."

"Gotcha," I said.

"Though we won't mention the ghost, unlike Felix, I do believe in them. I'll tell you about one of my experiences sometime. Another thing worth mentioning, children: You were on camera at the apartment complex. So we want to tell the exact truth here. They have you entering the complex, picking the door lock, and going inside.

Not that they need any of that. They caught you red-handed. Which means I have to do my lawyer magic."

"I was hoping there was no camera."

"That's where hoping got you," Cherry said.

"Damn technology," Felix said. "I just seriously hate that stuff."

(6)

We did get out of there, and damn quick. I drove Felix's rust-spotted truck, and he rode with Cherry in her gold Mercedes. Felix once told me she told him she liked being conspicuous. On that matter she could claim success.

The restaurant we ended up at was in Lufkin, and it looked to be on its last legs. The food tasted as if it had been in the freezer too long. Perhaps the electricity had bumped off and on a little too often.

After tasting the food, the Shark refused to eat the meal and made sure I refused to pay for it. She threatened a lawsuit, and the owner let the bill go. Back in Nacogdoches, we ended up at a Dairy Queen.

"Being able to eat indoors with people is weird," Cherry said. "Think back. Not so long ago, we were wearing COVID-protection masks."

"Finally, that nightmare is over," Felix said. "At least for now."

"Don't say 'for now,'" I said. "Let's say 'for a long time,' and if we're lucky, forever. Thanks to vaccinations, masks, and the passing of time."

This was, of course, not spoken with great confidence.

We had burgers and fries. The Shark had a chocolate malt with hers. Cherry not only operated like a shark, she ate like one. A petite shark with table manners, but she could put it away. One of those rare and much reviled humans who could eat a lot and not gain pounds. Or, rather, someone who earned her meals because she worked out all the time. I knew her well enough through Felix to know she spent a lot of time at the gym. Me and her had a friendly relationship, but not a close one. I was kind of afraid of her.

We ended up at my place, had some hot tea and a few cookies. We sat out on the porch to have the cookies. Sat at the table where I had sat the night Meg climbed over my fence and then disappeared from the chair Cherry now occupied.

"You said you had a ghost story," I said to the Shark.

"I do."

"Here we go," Felix said.

She gave Felix a look, and even in the dark, I felt the heat from it. I half expected Felix's beard to catch on fire.

"It's simple," she said. "Not a lot to it. Let me preface this by letting you know I do not believe in life after death in the common manner, some soul lost in the ether. I don't believe in heaven and hell, and my idea about God is if He, She, or It is out there, They don't have a thing to do with our lives. Mother Nature is God, in my view. We were created by an accident of nature—"

"Nature should have worn a condom," Felix said.

I said, "Kind of a deist view, I suppose. Not the condom part, but the other."

"I suppose," she said. "This happened one night when I was young—not a child, a grown woman—living on my own in Houston, Texas, and not living in any classic haunted house with drooping trees dangling over the roof or vines growing up the side of it or creaking boards and rattling windows. No racoons in the attic. There was nothing like that to set the mood for a ghost story. I was sleeping tight, no real worries in my life. I was just beginning my law practice, which I eventually moved from Houston to Nacogdoches. But there I was in an apartment in a high-rise, and if I'd pulled back my curtains and looked out, I would have seen a city of sparkling lights. Had I been able to open a window—I could not, they weren't that type—I would have heard the overwhelming clatter of traffic on the interstate, sirens, the usual city sounds.

"So you get the idea. Nothing ghostly about the place in the classic tradition. I'm sleeping, and I started coming out of it slowly, and I thought it must be morning, my body clock kicking in, wanting me to get up. And then I thought I heard a voice calling my name. My grandfather's voice. I sat up in bed, and there at the foot of it stood my grandfather. He was in shadow, but there was a night-light shining in through the cracked-open door that led to the bathroom. The light went through him and his skin looked more the color of cigarette ash than black. He just stood there looking at me, his head turned in the way he did, calling my name over and over. I answered him. He said, 'Take the cutoff at Fifty-Nine and Forty-Five.'

"I said something like, 'What?' but he was gone as soon as I spoke. I got up, grabbed hold of the baseball bat I kept near my bed, went through the apartment looking around."

"You were going to bean Grandpa," I said.

"I couldn't believe it was him. He lived in Mount Enterprise. Nearly four hours away. I didn't believe he had driven a car, taken the elevator up to my swank apartment, picked the lock, and stood at the end of my bed calling my name to tell me to take the cutoff at Fifty-Nine and Forty-Five. He couldn't be in the apartment. And he wasn't. And neither was anyone else.

"Now, here's the thing. Next morning I'm going to work. I had a usual route, but this morning I'm driving along, thinking about the night before, and as I come to where Fifty-Nine cuts off toward Forty-Five, I was overtaken with this strong urge to do as the ghost, or dream, suggested. I fought the idea, because it was farther for me to get to work taking that route. Not a practical way to go at all. In the end, seconds before I would have passed the cutoff, I took it.

"I ended up an hour late to work due to traffic backup, but when I got to the office my boss said they had been worried about me. I apologized for being late, told him I made a choice to take a cutoff that I shouldn't have. He shook his head, said, 'Not because you're late. Don't you know?'

"Turned out there had been an incredible pileup on Fifty-Nine. An eighteen-wheeler had jackknifed for some reason, and car after car slammed into it or into other cars that had already wrecked. Pretty soon there was a chain of wrecks going miles back. There were a number of deaths."

"You think your grandfather was warning you?" I asked.

"I think it's possible. Later that day I got a call from my mother telling me Grandpa had died during the night. What I think is that ghosts are the result of our own energy, our life force, and sometimes, in a moment of trauma, whatever is inside of us—call it a spirit, a soul, energy, what have you—it releases, and it has memories and knowledge that we aren't privy to. I think it flows through time and space and sometimes has a hard time settling. Perhaps as he was dying, his energy went on a walkabout, and he could see what was coming in the future; he was thinking about me, and he warned me."

"Oh, horseshit," Felix said.

"Did Grandpa ever come to you again?"

"No. That was it. Maybe the energy lets go eventually, just becomes part of the greater energy of the universe. Maybe how long that energy exists can vary. Perhaps that's how it was with Meg. I met her only once, through Felix, and she had a strong personality. A little shy of common sense in some ways. I could tell that right off. But powerful in other ways, energy-wise. Her personality might have let her loose and she came to you as a ghost. Maybe it wasn't a ghost. Perhaps she came to you through astral projection."

"Astral projection, my ass," Felix said.

"If it was astral projection, she could well be alive. But I'm not saying she is or isn't. It's late. I'm all over the place. I don't know anything but the story I told you about my grandfather. That's as close as I come to an example of the possible connection between ghosts and prophecy. I'm sure the odds are she's fine, and I'm full of law books and spooky bullshit."

"Hell's bells with my balls for clappers," Felix said. "That's ridiculous."

"I probably imagined Meg showing up," I said. "That makes more sense than a ghost. Maybe she and Ethan went off and meant to come back but got caught up in something or just decided to hell with it. They might have let their old lives go, and they're out there somewhere, rambling around, healthy as horses."

Cherry said, "I don't know all the answers, maybe none, but the story I told you about my grandpa, I believe it happened. He warned me. If I hadn't taken that cutoff, I might have been killed or injured. As for Meg, I don't know anything for sure, but I'm saying I believe you. I don't think you imagined it."

"That gives baby brother something to think about tonight when the wind blows and the trees rattle their limbs in the dark. Like they are now. Sounds like squirrels with maracas in the trees. Man, this weather is weird. We ought to go, girl."

"Sorry if I upset you," Cherry said.

"Sorry" was a rare word from her. I said, "You didn't."

But she had got me thinking.

As we all walked off the porch, out to Felix's truck and her Mercedes, I gave Felix his keys.

He said, "Me and Cherry, when we go to my place and go to bed tonight, I hope her old grandpa doesn't show up to give me instructions, if you know what I mean."

"Thing is," Cherry said, "you really could use them."

(7)

Couple days passed and I played games on my computer, read a little, watched the stars at night. Meg's shade didn't climb over my gate and leave her ghostly car parked in front of it.

That was disappointing.

I tried calling her a few times but got the same lack of results as before. Not even a recorded message. I called the apartment complex in May Town. Got hold of the manager. Evelyn had less to tell me than before. She seemed upset that the furniture and other goods in the apartment wouldn't be sold to cover the unpaid rent. The police had removed everything and, according to her, said they were putting it in storage. There was an investigation. Notes were taken. Officers consumed coffee and donuts on-site.

For the time being, that was it. All the news that was news.

———————

Following my and Felix's ill-advised trip to May Town, I decided to try and give myself a break from my worries about Meg, observe some heavenly wonders through my telescope—gaseous stars and mysterious planets, a few streaking meteors on the edge of the atmosphere.

I actually knew nil about astronomy, but I knew where to look for some things, and I knew how to look, and I enjoyed looking. I had a good telescope and 20/20 vision. It was all so wonderfully enigmatic, the heavens, and it made me think about the whole flying-saucer-cult business. Meg always loved science fiction movies and read books about aliens from way out and beyond our solar system who came to Earth, often in suits that looked to be made of aluminum foil or wrapped up in flowing robes like an escapee from an old biblical movie.

They came to harm us or help us, depending on the narrative, or to be more precise, the personality of the narrator. The Whites, as certain tall, nasty aliens were called, were out to kill humans. There were also the ones who showed up in your bedroom and whisked you away to spread your ass cheeks with salad tongs or some such. Stick a glowing, vibrating screwdriver up the anal canal to take turd samples. Then they returned you home and tucked you in, only to reappear at a future date for another examination. In my imagination, the alien leader was always a bulbous, leathery head with waving octopus's arms tucked under what looked like an enormous, transparent cake cover.

I had seen too many old science fiction movies.

Still, some of it made you wonder. There was such a need for mystery, and the cosmos was the greatest mystery, so turning unexplained things in the night sky into a belief system wasn't that difficult a leap. The more I thought about Meg, the more I knew she was just the kind of person to become a disciple in a saucer cult. She needed mystery. She needed freshness. She needed promise. We all do, but some of us need it more than others. I certainly felt the tug from time to time.

I went online and studied photos that had been taken of the

compound and the enormous house on a hill overlooking the pasture that contained the mound. It belonged to the founder of the cult, or religion—take your pick.

Looking at that house made me realize the flying-saucer business was good. There were other buildings on the property, including a dozen working chicken houses and what looked like bunkhouses, long and low with a lot of doors and a window per room.

The mound in the photos was indeed enormous, had what looked like a plowed ring around it.

What had Meg's ghost said besides beware omelets? Beware the mound within the circle.

I read a little more online about how the Saucer People expected the buried craft at some point to come unburied and take true believers away. More spacecraft were to arrive to assist. A wagon train of saucers would haul true believers away to the stars.

Not so curiously, true believers donated money to the cult. It was necessary for the leader not to have to work and to continue to communicate with the spirit of the celestial astronaut that lived in the saucer underground. That part was a little vague. Apparently, the founder needed quite a bit of alone time to communicate with the alien's life force.

Prophecies were given. An expiration date for life on Earth would eventually be revealed, and all the true believers would need to pack their bags and rendezvous with the alien rescuers. For now, however, keep that money coming.

It was space-age evangelism, and like nearly all evangelical operations, it was pretty much a clever form of con.

I read something about the current organization being run by a group called the Managers. A title given to them by the founder. I read that the cult owned a string of donut shops. All in all, the cult was tolerated by the community if not exactly embraced. But as of recently, there was new and more serious attention given to the cult, as more and more TV shows and so-called documentaries and government revelations had given some credence to the idea of traveling space aliens who were wise beyond their years, helped build pyramids, and might even have contributed their DNA to us and invented the vanilla milkshake.

I was just beginning to read about the founding of the cult in the 1950s, when one Ezra Bacon encountered the spacecraft that came to be buried in the mound, when my cell phone buzzed and did a bit of dance at the edge of my desk.

It was big brother Felix.

(8)

The bright morning was full of chilly wind. Trees were swaying along the road as I left my property, and when I hit Highway 7 and drove east, I could see them on either side of the road, whipping about like frenzied dancers.

Straight in the distance, a darkness hung over the horizon like a bully waiting to put a dark sack over the earth and beat it with a stick.

When I got to town, I found a parking space on Main in front of Felix's home and agency. I got out and pulled my jacket tight around me. The wind had grown even more unfriendly. I was starting up the stairs when Felix appeared at the top of them pulling the hood of his gray sweatshirt over his head.

"Wait," he said. "I'll come down."

We went out and around the corner to Dolly's Diner and ordered some coffee. We were seated in a booth, and as it was late morning, the place was reasonably empty. The breakfast crowd had played out, and the lunch crowd had yet to congregate. We had a cozy spot near the door. The hot coffee felt good after the cold wind.

"You called so we could have coffee? I love you, Felix, but I was reading about the flying-saucer cult out in May Town. It's more interesting than you."

44

"I read about it too. Started last night. I'd heard of that cult before, but there's a lot more to it than I thought. Not just some lone-ass nut who wants to tell everyone how he was taken up by a spacecraft and had a visit with an alien. Fact was, all Bacon's visiting was on the ground. Cherry and the former chief of police of May Town Grover Nunn are coming to my office in an hour. That's why I wanted you here."

"And the exact reason for that is what?"

"It's about Meg, of course. Maybe not directly, but I think it could be about her. Cherry, first thing this morning, set to investigating for me. Well, not first thing. We warmed up the morning first."

"I'll try not to imagine that."

"Cherry called Grover, thinking he might have some old contacts, might convince someone over there to actually look for Meg and Ethan. Part you'll really like is Grover Nunn was once part of the cult. Quit it after a while. When he retired from the cops, he had a security business. Ran it for a few years, then sold it, and is now fully retired.

"Cherry thinks he's a good egg. He's got a degree in criminology and one in philosophy. Interesting guy, she says. She had some dealings with him a few times in the past, before the present chief. Grover left the cops because he felt his position and the department were being undermined by powerful people with lots of money. Boondoggled. Money is a great mover and shaker. Small towns are worse than big cities. Easier to own a town when it's small."

"Couldn't Grover have told what he's got to tell by phone? Or Zoom or something like it?"

"Cherry wants us to be with him when he gives us the lowdown. Thinks she can tell a lot about a person when she's near them. Thinks we can too. Part of being a detective is being a kind of half-ass psychologist. We ought to all work together. You've already been hired by Meg's ghost. Got to give your client due diligence."

"I didn't agree to take the case, if I was taking cases."

"But deep in your itty-bitty heart, you know you want to."

(9)

Full of coffee, we went back to Felix's office, the section on the left side of the stairs. Felix settled in his chair behind his big metal army-surplus desk, leaning back with his feet on it. Where I was sitting, I could see the bottoms of his boots. They were nice soles. They were nice boots. Handmade by a Mexican boot maker across the border. They were blue and red with a Texas flag on the toe. Felix went to that boot maker now and then and had a pair or two made. They were expensive. He could afford it. Felix had done all right in this business. Far better than I had done.

The buzzer near his desk sounded and a little red light lit up on the wall. It let him know someone had opened the door downstairs.

"They're a bit early," Felix said.

We waited for their arrival. We could hear footsteps in the hall. Felix had left the office door open, and a moment later, a big man with a ruddy complexion and a lot of muscles walked inside. Like a shadow, another man, a less muscular version, came in after him. They favored each other.

"I'm getting divorced," Muscles said.

"Congratulations," Felix said.

"My wife had you follow me, and now we're getting divorced."

"This is not who we were expecting," Felix said to me.

I had figured that out, of course. I'm sharper than I look.

Felix turned his attention back to the duo. Muscles seemed angry enough to fart a rain cloud with residual lightning. The other man looked a little nervous, like a supportive brother who was rethinking things about the debt of kinship.

"You should have left private business alone," said Muscles.

"Ah! George Howard, the cheating husband. It's not private business if I'm hired to make it un-private."

"I was getting some on the side, but I didn't have any intention of divorcing. Now I'm being divorced, and it's your fault. I was content."

"Your wife wasn't. And I'll explain this to you so you can understand it: If you've come here to make a ruckus, well, goddamn, you and your backup asshole can get started or hit the street."

Felix swung his feet off the desk and stood up. He and Muscles were the most imposing sights in the room. Two water buffalos sizing each other up. Felix walked around and stood to the side of the desk, not four feet from the duo.

I stood up. I didn't want anything to do with this, but, like Muscles' brother, I knew there was a familial obligation.

"What I think," Muscles said, "is I'm going to give you a good whipping."

For a big boy, Felix could move. And move he did. He went across the four feet between them like it was six inches and he was jet-propelled. He grabbed Muscles by the throat with one hand and by the crotch with the other, lifted him up, and slammed him back into the man I assumed was his brother. Felix drove them through the open door and out into the hall. I darted after them.

Felix shoved Muscles into his brother again. That pinned the backup brother between Muscles and the wall—a brotherly sandwich. The smaller man's arms were waving out behind Muscles like a traffic cop trying to slow a speeder.

And then Felix lifted Muscles over his head as easy as if he were a mannequin and slammed him down on the floor hard enough the place shook. Back in the office, something fell off Felix's desk and clattered onto the floor.

Muscles made a squeaking sound like a dog toy. I thought I smelled shit. Muscles tried to crawl, but all he managed to do was scratch the floor with his nails and stink. He suddenly lay flat like a rug.

Felix reached across the downed Muscles and grabbed the other by the coat lapels, snatched him up, and carried him to the stairs.

"No, Felix," I said.

Felix's dander got up, all the wit and grace and common sense he had took a vacation. Something raw came out in him then.

At the stairs, I repeated Felix's name over and over, grabbed at the back of his hoodie. I might as well have been trying to turn a semi over with a toothpick for a lever.

"I ain't really got no dog in this fight," the smaller man said. He had now been lifted higher in the air by his coat lapels, his toes dangling over the stairs.

Felix took a deep breath. His chest heaved and filled like a dirigible taking on helium, then he blew the air out. He slowly set the man down so that he was standing on the top step. He straightened the man's coat slightly.

"Thank you," the man said. "We won't bother you anymore."

"Never let me see you again," Felix said.

"Done. May I collect my brother? He was merely distraught."

"He is merely a jackass," Felix said. "Am I right, Charlie?"

"Way right," I said. "Let me see if I can nurse Jackass along."

I called him Jackass, but in my mind and heart he would always be Muscles. But for him to mess with my brother, he didn't have enough of them. He needed to pick up his gym work, take some steroids or something. I went over and tried to stir him by pushing at him with my foot.

"You need to be going."

"I'm trying to go," he said.

"Come help him," I said to his companion.

Felix stepped aside, and the other one came across the floor and tried to lift Muscles up. It took some work, so I helped him.

When we finally got Muscles on his feet, I waltzed with them to the edge of the stairs, one of Muscles' arms around my shoulders. His other arm was around his brother, who had just recently missed a short flight down the stairs.

Felix said, "Take him out of here. Wipe his ass. Spray him with some disinfectant and give him a couch to sleep on. But I meant what I said. I never want to see either of you again."

When they were at the bottom of the stairs, Muscles, who had regained enough of himself to move his mouth, said, "I got a gun in my car."

"Good," Felix said. "I got one in my office. Don't make me come down there and see how far I can drive your head into the sidewalk."

"He's just talking," said the brother.

"I'm not," Felix said. "I mean business."

"I know that," the smaller man said and danced his brother through the door at the bottom of the stairs and out onto the sidewalk.

"Always someone's got to be disgruntled. He'd kept his ying-yang in his pants, I couldn't have taken pictures of him and his poke going into a motel room."

"It's all right," I said. "It's done."

In the office, Felix went behind his desk and opened a drawer and took a big revolver out of it. It was Old West–style. He had just pulled it out when the door buzzed, and the red light went on.

"I guess he got that gun," Felix said.

We stepped out into the hall and paused at the stairwell. Cherry and an elderly man in a shirt festooned with cartoonish alligators were on their way up the stairs. The man was carrying a package.

Cherry looked up, saw Felix's gun, said, "Was I that bad last night?"

"Hardly, honey," Felix said. "We were expecting rats."

(10)

I got some folding chairs out of the closet and set them out. Cherry let the man with the alligator shirt have the good client chair. Me and her sat in the foldout chairs I had placed next to the wall. Felix sat behind his desk. I took a good look at our guest.

He was quite old. His nose was large, and his head was too. He was bald except for a circle of hair around his temples that looked like a brown ring inside an uncleaned toilet. I got the impression the brown of his hair was due to hair dye. My take, you got that little bit of hair and you're past fifty, you might as well let it go gray or shave it off. His face looked to have spent too much time in the clothes dryer.

The package was wrapped in brown paper. For him to have carried it upstairs was akin to a donkey with broken legs trying to wiggle his way up a greased playground slide. The skin on his arms shook like a loose suit as he settled himself. If one of his bones broke, he'd probably collapse into a puddle. He was breathing heavy. His legs trembled. Even the alligators on his shirt appeared tired, looked as if they would have preferred to have been hand-fed.

Felix returned the revolver to the drawer. He punched a button next to the front-entrance buzzer. We could hear the door lock click all the way upstairs.

"Privacy," Felix said. "To keep me from killing someone today."

"We had an unpleasant visit due to one of Felix's cases," I said, not offering more explanation. After that, we stood up and introduced ourselves to the man who had already collapsed into the guest chair. We shook hands. I was so glad to be back to shaking hands. I was surprised at how much I had missed it during the height of the COVID business.

"Cherry told me about you two," Grover said.

"Of course," I said, and me and her sat back down and prepared to listen.

"I've known Grover a while," Cherry said.

"Not always on the same side of a legal issue," Grover said, "but it was always good to sit in a courtroom and listen to her. I know it's old-fashioned and the Woke Police might parachute in and whip me, but I'm going to say it: I never minded looking at her either. She's easy on the eye."

"This is true," Cherry said. "And I only defended the innocent."

"Uh-huh," Grover said, and gave her the side-eye.

"We're worried about Meg," I said. "I suppose you know her backstory already?"

"I do," Grover said. "Cherry told me." He took a dark hand-kerchief from his shirt pocket and wiped his forehead. "Specifically, I don't know that I can help you, but generally, I just might. You see, I've been, shall we say, on the inside."

"What we heard," Felix said.

"I was a member of the Donut Legion. They don't call themselves that. But some folks around town do. I'll come to that. Be patient, let me give you the whole enchilada with gravy and a side of steaming bullshit. Then we'll have the donut for dessert. For about five years I was messed up. Disappointed, defeated, and then, finally, happy when I got it all together again. Well, that's not entirely true. I'm happier, but I wouldn't dance and sing about it, even if I could. I should also mention I haven't eaten a donut in five years."

I had no idea where he was going with this, but I held my water.

"Back then, being a member of the Donut Legion, it seemed to make all manner of sense. Now I feel like I was living inside a comic book. My wife, bless her soul, gone now, never really let the cult go. Not really. I haven't told anyone what I'm about to tell you. I mean, anyone with half a brain that knows about the cult can guess it, but talking about it, that's like dropping your drawers in public. I was too embarrassed to talk about it in detail before. Made a bit of a fool out of myself about it all. Thought everyone else was the fool, until I realized I was the one wearing the dunce cap.

"Back in the fifties, when I was a kid, old Ezra Bacon, who was a farmer and rancher of sorts as well as a weekend Baptist preacher, claimed one winter night he was out in the pasture looking for a lost cow and saw something light up the night.

"In fairness to him, a lot of people saw that light burn across the sky. It was reported in the local paper for several days. It was the most exciting thing since the town banker ran off with his secretary and the contents of the bank. He was discovered in Mexico without the secretary or the money. Money was never recovered, nor was the secretary ever heard from again. Rumors are she is somewhere in Ecuador. I tell you this to say how rare exciting news was and still is in May Town. I think that had something to do with why some people got suckered in with this flying-saucer business. They're bored and feel common and devoid of magic. That's my theory because that's the way I felt."

"Seems like an astute enough theory," Felix said. "Continue."

"Also, the fifties were a big flying-saucer time. Like now. Lots of science fiction movies about aliens coming from space and so on.

People saw everything in the sky as a flying saucer packed full of little green men.

"As the story goes, Ezra Bacon had been standing in the pasture near the woods, enjoying the night and looking at the stars, when he saw that light rip out of the sky. He claimed it dove down and hit the earth. Ezra said the impact, those flames, the heat, burned his eyebrows off and curled the hair poking out from under his hat. Even set fire to his shirt, burned holes in, scorched his skin a bit. Said his face had blisters on it.

"When the flames died down, and the smoke was mostly blown away, Ezra walked over to the hole it had made. Keep in mind this pasture was maybe a hundred acres. Ezra owned about five hundred acres then. It got whittled down to three hundred later to pay for some building fees and such.

"The hole was damn near five acres wide and pretty far deep. Ezra could see something large and shiny glowing down in it. Could only make out part of it, the rest of it being covered in dirt from the impact. Thought it must be a meteor. The heat was still uncomfortable, and later he said something to the effect that if he'd stood there too much longer, he'd have been baked like a Christmas ham.

"Said he moved back to the edge of the woods and looked out at the hole in the ground and trembled, full of revelation. It was one of those flying saucers he'd been hearing about. Like the one supposed to have crashed in New Mexico."

"Roswell?" Cherry said.

"Yeah. Silver and shiny, and in this case not broken and not small. Ezra went home and told his wife, and next morning she went out and looked at it. It was much cooler then. She was said to have felt something right away. Like something was speaking to her from afar, like a bad telephone connection, full of static and desperation. I'm talking about the old phones we used to have. You folks may be too young to know about that.

"Ezra said he started to call the authorities and get them out there, but he had a feeling he shouldn't. That night he said dark clouds moved in and brought a rainstorm that would have drowned a water snake. It was so intense, the water spread over the fields and through the trees, flowed under the door of his house, and his house was on a high hill. Not the one that's there now, but a smaller one back then. A barn that was on lower ground washed away.

"Said when they looked out the window, it was like peeking out of a porthole on Noah's ark. It was as if the oceans had joined up with all the creeks and lakes and rivers and ponds and wells and backwoods springs and had covered the Earth. I know about all this, because he wrote it down in what he called the *Saucer Bible*. Isn't that cute? The *Saucer Bible*. I feel like an idiot when I say it out loud."

"No judgment," Felix said. "Go on."

"By midday, the land was seriously damp, but the water was gone, rolled on along or back into the earth. Some of his livestock were floating in the water like balloon animals left over from a pool party. Dead, of course.

"Ezra drove his truck out to the impact hole, or close as he could get to it. He had to walk part of the way through the woods, arrive at a different angle, because the ground was wet and soft. When he looked in the hole, it was full of water, but when he came back late afternoon, the water was mostly absorbed into the ground. He could see something in the hole, poking out of the dirt that had partially covered it. He came back with a shovel and began to dig.

"Over a period of months, he got all the dirt worked off it, could see what was beneath it. A spacecraft. Ezra couldn't figure it for anything else. It was massive, saucer-shaped, shiny as a brand-new dime."

Grover paused, exhausted. He wiped his sweaty forehead again with his handkerchief.

"Would you like a bottle of water?" Felix asked.

Grover nodded. Felix had a small camper-style refrigerator behind his desk. He opened it. It was full of plastic bottles of water and a batch of bananas. Felix picked bottles out for all of us and passed them around. A banana was not offered.

Grover struggled with the cap on his bottle, but in time he got it off and took a swig, drank like a man dying of thirst. His hands quaked. "Ezra went out there a few times to look at it, and one day a side of the saucer was open, like a secret wall panel. The opening was even with the ground. Ezra said he went down into the hole and inside the saucer. It was comfortably cool inside and there were blinking lights, and the interior of the craft seemed larger than it could be. There were elevators of a sort, and you could see into them. Not because they were glass or plastic, but because in the ship you could look right through them. That's the closest Ezra ever came to explaining. He said it just like that. You could look through them.

"He walked around. As he did, the lights blinked even more. Pretty soon he came to a wall. He felt compelled and walked right through it. There was something in the ship that was encouraging him to explore, and the ship gave whoever was inside abilities, he said."

This was beginning to sound a lot like how Hal Jordan got his power ring and charging lamp and became Green Lantern. But I didn't say anything about that.

"He came to a room that was full of lights, and the lights moved, and in the lights, there was something unidentifiable. Not some little green man or some tall, slick-headed critter with big eyes. Nothing like that. Ezra wrote he could feel it more than see it. There were projections coming out of the walls. Not gears or knobs or buttons, but random constructions designed for something other than human hands.

"Ezra said this thing shifted shapes. It was a mist, and then it wasn't. He couldn't truly describe it. It didn't fit the human experience, or even human imagination. Said seeing that thing gave him a feeling like his head was bursting with information, and he said suddenly he was caught up in a revelation. Those were his words. 'Caught up in a revelation.' Right then, he said, he was through being a Baptist."

I was beginning to feel chills hiking up the back of my neck.

"He said he just knew."

Grover paused and worked on the water bottle some more. He pulled it from his lips with reluctance. For a moment, it seemed like he had finished with what he had to say and was starting to think about a light lunch and a long nap back at the house.

"Knew what?" Felix said.

"That the thing he couldn't identify was an alien and that it was dying, except for its soul, and that he, Ezra Bacon, had been chosen to wear that soul like a bodysuit and become the alien's prophet."

I thought: Yeah, a prophet for profit.

(11)

Grover tried to lift the package in his lap and readjust himself in the chair, but it was like a tadpole deciding to leave the pond and take a sweet frog to the movies. It wasn't going to happen.

Cherry walked over and lifted the package from his lap and placed it on the desk.

"Open that," Grover said.

"Would you like to pause your story a moment while we do?" she said.

"I would. I see you have a coffee maker. Might I have a cup?"

"Of course," Felix said. "Cherry, would you mind opening the package?"

Making coffee consisted of water and Keurig pods. Felix didn't use them in the kitchen where he lived, but in his office he did. This was a relatively new addition, and I was glad of it. Big brother was moving out of the Flintstone era. Reluctantly.

Felix poured water from water bottles into the clear plastic container on the side of the coffee maker while Cherry unwrapped the brown paper.

Inside the paper were three fat black books, all identical. The title on the side of each one was in gold and visible to me: FROM A GREAT DISTANCE THEY WILL COME: THE SAUCER BIBLE.

When the water was hot, Felix made us each a cup and put sugar in Cherry's cup without asking and gave the rest of us ours black.

Grover sipped his coffee as if it were the elixir of life. He took a deep breath and sat back in the chair.

"Those books are left over from when my wife and I were true believers. They tell you what I've told you in greater detail. I can almost quote them. I was that much into them. I had been that way about the Bible. I read it nightly. I transferred that energy and interest to this book. Looking back, having been disappointed, I don't read either anymore. I don't believe in much of anything now.

"In a nutshell, Ezra believed he had been given a prophecy by that alien in the ship who was dying or transferring his soul to a higher plane. The prophecy said that within a short time, the world would end. And the Saucer People, who were already en route to Earth, would show up at the site of the buried saucer, as its coordinates were known to them.

"They were coming from far across space and it would take years for them to arrive, but they were close, considering how long they had been traveling. The saucer on Ezra Bacon's property was an advance scout, but things had gone wrong, and the saucer had crashed, and the dying saucer man, whose name was unpronounceable by humans, passed on his knowledge to Ezra, who, as I said, had been chosen to continue the human race by evacuating true believers into the saucers when they arrived. The alien had Ezra enter a rejuvenating machine. A device made of fog and lights and shattered mirrors, is how Ezra described it. The device made him a better example of himself and filled him with knowledge. Why the alien didn't use it remains a mystery. It seemed to prefer a ghostly self.

"Damn. I hear this coming out of my mouth, and I have no idea how I succumbed to such ridiculousness. It's like that stupid

Scientology stuff. Had that bunch hit on me first, I might be hanging out at their Los Angeles headquarters having a beer with all their famous movie star members, taking a day off to go to Disneyland and buy a mouse hat.

"Saucer man told Ezra the fleet of ships would haul all believers away and turn them into pure energy for the trip. It would be like going to sleep. They would arrive on what he called the perfect planet with guns and food and supplies, and they would be made physical again.

"They would defeat the evil aliens on this lost world, because the bad aliens had spirits that caused evil, and their spirits reached across the vastness of space and made humanity on Earth evil. But if the enlightened ones killed them one and all, took over the planet, a paradise would be created, and everyone would become beings of energy again and would coexist with the energy of the good aliens. It would be equivalent to Christianity's heaven.

"It was Ezra's understanding that all religions were based on the impulses of good that came from the good-energy aliens, like the one that had landed in his field, and that the bad in humans came from those that had to be conquered, the bad aliens.

"Those of us here on Earth who didn't believe wouldn't find a place in the fleet of saucers and would die in explosions and flames. Armageddon awaited. I think on it now, and I wonder how turning to energy and back to human form to fight aliens who had the power to send evil across time and space was going to work. Why did we need weapons and food if we could be energy? I supposed it was a test to measure how worthy we were as warriors for all things good, bright, and beautiful. I think I rationalized it that way.

"Ezra predicted the arrival time of the impending saucers by some mysterious mathematical equations he had received from the alien. On that date, in March 1978, he and his true believers, a handful of folks then, gathered in his pasture to stand on the mound. By that time, the mound had been covered in dirt again. To protect the saucer, the book says.

"No aliens arrived. They didn't even send a 'We'll be late' message.

"Ezra reviewed the math and found out he'd messed up. Left out a decimal or something. Forgot to have X equal Y, or some such. He redid his calculations, and damn if he didn't find that missing decimal or whatever, and he set a new time for their arrival. Missed the boat on that one too. Well, missed the saucers. His followers began to drop off, but he had some diehards. Kind of folks who, no matter how wrong their cult leader is, they just double down on the purposeful stupidity it takes to believe in that sort of thing. I know. I was one of the double-down folks. At that point in my life, I would have believed Ezra if he'd said fairies lived up my ass."

"You believed him twice?" Cherry said.

"I was in my twenties then, nearly thirty. I was a young police chief, a husband and father, and the Baptist Church wasn't cutting it anymore. I had a degree, a family, but I had ended up being a boring police chief in a town where the biggest excitement was a trip to the local café and driving over to Nacogdoches to go to the movies. I wanted something more. The Saucer People — that sounded exotic and interesting.

"Both times the arrival of the saucers was announced, believers showed up at Ezra's property with guns, canned goods, lawn chairs, and a good book to read while they waited. The *Saucer Bible*, of course.

"So we waited and waited. The first time, the day went by and the night went by, and the aliens didn't come, and the world didn't destruct. Followers drifted off. Second time was the wake-up call for me. My wife, she left with me, but she always harbored suspicions it was all a math problem. A rogue decimal.

"There were still a handful of people who went out there to listen to Ezra and his revelations. His lectures, or sermons, if you prefer, had become erratic and authoritarian. Demanding.

"By then, Ezra's son, Ben Bacon, had grown up. He took over the cult as his dad aged and then died. Like Moses, never seeing the Promised Land.

"Ben preached and declared end-times. He said his father had made a number of mathematical mistakes, but he was working on the problem and would at some point in the future make a grand prophecy that would not be in error. He claimed that the alien's internal energy, or some such, the business it had given his father had been passed on to him."

"Like swapping baseball cards," Felix said.

"You were gone from the group by this time?" I asked.

"I was. But not totally disconnected. I knew some who had stayed, and they tried from time to time to bring my wife and me back into the fold. It was tempting, truth be told. We'd put a lot of hope and energy into that business. Anyway, they kept us filled in, treating us a bit like we were still part of it.

"Gradually, Ben began to gain new followers from near and far. Ben saw the business potential better than Ezra had. Ezra's wife, Ben's mother, was still alive, but she had checked out. I don't know how much she'd believed in Ezra and the flying saucer to begin with. We only have Ezra's claims and the *Saucer Bible* that says she saw the saucer before it was covered up again.

"Thing about Ezra's wife, Ola, was she could cook. And one thing she could cook up was donuts. Ben started with one donut shop in May Town, and then there were three. The original donut shops had belonged to some Cambodian immigrants. But Ben bought all the sugar from their supplier, effectively putting them out of business and him into business with his mother's donut recipe. She passed on a while back, by the way. In recent years Ben added drive-through windows to his shops. Saucer Donuts was the result. You may have seen them here and there. Those shops are busy as a moth in a mitten.

"The cult is growing again, and they've become more aggressive, dangerous even. A sign of the times, I think. Political fever, fear of change. A rampaging climate. The internet wired to our brains. And listen, I know what you're thinking: You could never be fooled into believing nonsense. But maybe you have already. If you can be groomed to be a Baptist, a Buddhist, a Muslim, a Mormon, or whatever, you can be convinced. Being taken away by a flying saucer, being Raptured out of your clothes to heaven, your spirit rising from the dead—it's all a way to deal with our egotistical idea of being worthy of living forever. Trust me, you want something bad enough, evidence isn't needed. Gets down to it, if you want to, you can believe in teddy-bear shit and unicorn farts."

"I'm happier believing in nothing of that sort," Felix said. "For me, religion is as unfamiliar to my life as wearing Nerf shoes and a fuzzy hat with my name on it in Sanskrit. I don't get it. I believe in me, and I'm not always sure I'm trustworthy."

"I say, with all sincerity, good for you," Grover said. "I think I'm a fellow that wants to believe in something. And now I can't believe in anything. I read a lot and watch old cowboy-show reruns. That's it for me. My wife is gone, and for the most part at my age, so am I."

"What do you know about Meg?" I said.

"Meg was after my time with the Saucer People. She worked at Saucer Donuts, the one just across the street from the bank. You could see her at the drive-through window. Everyone knew who she was. Meg, the beautiful donut lady.

"Always a line of cars at that window, men mostly. She had a kind of glow, you know? Well, guess you do. I understood it right, she's your ex-wife?"

"That's right," I said.

"Saw her, always thought about that old Woody Guthrie song about the Philadelphia lawyer. How he described the Hollywood maid as having a shape so rare and divine."

"She was a lot more than looks," I said.

"I'm sure she was," Grover said. "There's looks, and then there's radiating looks. Something inside that jumps at you. I guess they call that charisma."

"Do you know if you have to be a member of the cult to work at the donut shops?" Cherry asked.

"No. But most employees are part of it. Some are stone-true believers, some are on the cusp of belief, and some believe because they need a job. People are paid a cheap wage, but they are told they are working for the greater good. What's money if the world is going to blow up and you're going to ride away in high gear on a flying saucer to save another world that will be transformed into paradise?"

"Seen Meg lately?" I asked.

"Don't go to the bank that often, but last few times I did, I checked the donut window. She wasn't there. Sometimes, certain believers are picked to live out at the compound. Beautiful ladies seem to have an edge. Ben Bacon likes being surrounded by attractive admirers. Living out there is considered an honor, and the closer you are to the prophet, the earlier you board one of the saucers. Seems there are a lot of front-row seats. Pretty sweet selling something invisible, isn't it?"

"Do you know Meg's husband, Ethan?" Felix asked.

"Didn't know she was married or had been married until Cherry told me about her. I will tell you this, and I want to emphasize what I said before. Those people have grown more dangerous. Ben has developed a hierarchy, and at the top of it, just under him, are the Managers. Thugs, actually. They do his bidding."

"How so?" Felix said.

"Things happen to anyone who speaks out against the Saucer People. Former members are especially despised. I say too much, they hear about it, hell, they'll be after me. No worries about that from me. Old age is trying to kill me, and good for it. I've had enough of this world, and I'm no longer interested in flying-saucer paradise. I look forward to oblivion."

Grover used his hankie to wipe his sweaty face. "Now, you have your background. I hate to impose, and I feel awful asking, but do you have someplace I might lie down for a while? I don't think I could make it down those stairs and out to the car."

"Certainly," Felix said. "Across the hall."

"I can't manage out of this chair without help. Feel like the juice is sucked out of me. It's like that for me from time to time. Then I'll get my strength back for a while. I think just talking about this absurd shit wears me out. Thinking I embraced such foolishness eats at me. My emotions make me physically weak sometimes."

Me and Felix got our arms under his, boosted him out of the chair, mostly carried him across the hall. We toted him into the living room and stretched him out on the couch. I worked off his shoes and placed them on the floor. Felix put a couch pillow under Grover's head, picked up a crocheted cover that was folded on one of the chairs, and spread it over him.

"Is the cover too hot?" Felix asked.

"Comfortable. Please leave it."

"As you like," Felix said.

Felix pulled the curtains so that it was dark, and we left out of there to let Grover rest.

(12)

Back in the office, we closed the door and Felix passed more bottled water around.

"That information doesn't help us much when it comes to Meg," I said. "He saw her. She was good-looking. She worked a drive-through window. Someone told him her name. Then he didn't see her anymore."

"Tells us what her mindset might be," Felix said. "Makes a case for her still being alive. Out there at the Saucer People's compound, perhaps. If she thought there was something good about that shit, she'd latch onto it like a lamprey."

"When you know how people think and what people think about something, it helps you understand what they might do," Cherry said.

"Cherry, honey," Felix said. "You believe in that religious stuff, don't you?"

"Episcopalian with all my heart. We are taught how to transform mental bullshit into mental wine. Maybe all religions aren't the same."

"In my book, they are," Felix said. "At the core. But it's all a matter of degree. Cults of any sort annoy me, from right-wing fanatics to anarchists to the Woke Movement dictating how I should have a checklist for everything I say so it fits into their purity box. My take, right-wing extremism is the same as left-wing extremism. They go far enough in either direction, they meet at the back of the circle where they can fuck each other in orgasmic anger."

"Orgasmic anger?" Cherry said.

"You can use that if you want to," Felix said.

"Way I see it, this means I have to go to May Town and check things out for myself," I said.

Felix shook his head. "It means the two of us have to go to May Town, little brother."

"You two can do that," Cherry said. "Hope it's better than your last trip. I'll go on my own. I work better by using my methods. Lawyers find people too, you know. I always start with the money. Cult has donut shops, and they raise money for guns and food, so they probably have a bank account. I know some people who know some people, so I can get some information on that."

"Good ol' shoe leather," Felix said.

"More like computer-wizard connections."

We continued to let Grover rest while we thumbed through the books he had given us. The *Saucer Bible* wasn't particularly well written, and like the Bible and other religious texts, it contradicted itself a lot. But there was an undeniable enthusiasm there.

About an hour later, with us still reading, Grover walked into the office under his own power, his shoes on, looking a little less like Death on a borrowed crutch. He was apologetic for having to nap. We helped him downstairs, and Cherry drove him home.

Felix had some work he had to do before we went to May Town, so I decided to go home and wait until he called me.

Truth to tell, I wasn't sure what to do. I tried to formulate a plan. I called over to the May Town apartment complex to see if Meg might have shown up. No soap. The manager said I could consider her evicted. And to stop bothering her.

I called the donut shop across from the bank. A man answered. Sounded young. Said his name was Kevin. When I asked about Meg, he asked who I was. I told him. He stewed on that briefly, said he knew Meg and that she had worked there. Said she was nice. Could sugar-powder donuts faster than anyone.

She didn't show up to work one morning. Still hadn't heard from her. Her old position had been filled. Did I have any interest in a Saucer Donuts card? They punched out a spot on it each time you bought a donut. You got six punches, you were eligible for a free one.

I passed.

Kevin seemed disappointed. I think he'd thought I was someone who sounded as if he would want a donut card.

In an offhand way he offered me something else. Kind of snuck up on it and gave it to me: Was I interested in finding out about paradise beyond Earth?

I passed.

He added that I might want to come by sometime and try one of their donuts, and maybe I'd rethink that punch card.

That was it.

Okay, Charlie, I said to myself. What's next to do?

I waited.

Come on, Charlie. Just one little idea.

(13)

Eventually, my inner Charlie came up with something. As my dad used to say, "I'm going to do something, even if it's wrong."

I decided I wouldn't wait around for Felix to finish his business. I coasted into May Town right before noon, parked near the bank, and walked across the street to the donut shop. There was a red OPEN sign made of curlicue neon in the large display window. As I watched, it went out, and one that said CLOSED came on.

By eleven a.m., the donut crowd thinned so much, Saucer Donuts wrapped things up. I knew that much from reading about them online. I hadn't made as good a time driving over as I had hoped to.

The door was not locked.

When I went inside, the door set off a bell. Rubber flying-saucer balloons hung from the ceiling in numerous spots. They briefly swung a little when the air pressure from opening the door went to work. I noticed the bathrooms off to the side said SPACEMEN and SPACEWOMEN. There was a scattering of chairs and tables.

A young man behind the counter was pulling sheets of donuts from racks and pouring them into a large silver trash can. He glanced at me. He was tall and bony, had long blond hair tied back in a ponytail. Some of it had leaked out and was springing over his ears. He wore a white apron over a white shirt and had black pants dusted with powdered sugar and what looked like crusty regions of grease. He looked like a man with a porn collection and a freezer full of TV dinners.

We were the only ones in the place. When I walked over to the counter, he said, "Ah, man, we're done for the day. I'm getting rid of the donuts. They're considered day-old now. Just about to lock the door."

"Are you Kevin?"

He paused in his work. "Yes."

"My name is Charlie Garner. I talked to you on the phone about Meg."

"Oh. I don't have anything else, man. Told you what I know. Look, I can give you a donut before it goes in the can, free of charge, and that's about it. Already poured out the coffee."

"I don't want a donut. Could I buy you lunch? I have some questions about the paradise business after all. You mentioned it on the phone."

"We have some literature here on the coming of Armageddon and the world beyond. I can give you a brochure."

"I don't want a brochure. You were going to talk to me about it on the phone, so let me take you to lunch, ask some questions, and when it's over, I'll slip you a twenty for your time."

"I don't think you are thinking about becoming a convert. I think you really still want to talk about Meg."

"Twenty-five."

"Could you make it thirty?"

We strolled over to a place near the bank that looked like one of those old-time cafés you see in movies that take place in the fifties. It was called Cecil's Eats. It had a clean picture window, and inside were several dining tables and dining chairs from a bygone era, and along the wall were booths with rips in the upholstery and struggling strands of cotton leaking out of them. We were the only ones in there. The lunch crowd had yet to arrive.

I was excited about the place until we got our food. The sandwich was on toasted bread with lots of mayonnaise, some wrinkled lettuce, and tomatoes so thin, you turned them sideways, they were damn near invisible. The meat was limp and a little gray. The crinkle fries were precut and precooked. Warmed up in a microwave. They had a soggy taste, like chewing on the fingers of a drowned man.

Kevin, on the other hand, seemed to relish his meal. I suppose it's all relative. When I was his age, I liked everything, especially if it was free.

"I'm going to come right out and say it," I said. "I got the impression you aren't truly all that excited about this idea of flying saucers taking you off to the Promised Land."

"Got that impression, huh?"

"It was in your voice. Am I right?"

He casually looked left and right. A few people were filing in, being led to their seats by a waitress.

"I have a job to keep," he said. "Every third call in, I got to say something about the saucer stuff and planetary paradise. Sometimes I cheat, go as much as ten calls before I mention it. Depends on who's in there with me. Today, I was just being careful."

"Get much in the way of response?"

"Be surprised. Not everyone you talk to is interested, but there are plenty looking for another way, you know. Ours is the only one of our shops in May Town that discusses the saucer religion. Idea is to keep it out there but not to beat the drum so much we wear customers out. Got to keep those donuts moving and that money coming in."

"I'm going to come back to it: Do I detect some disillusionment with the religion?"

"Shit, man. You aren't one of them, are you?"

"One of who?"

"A Manager. And of course you aren't. I really thought you were, I wouldn't have asked. You can spot those fuckers coming a mile away."

"I'm a private investigator, and I'm looking into something that might help me solve a problem. A mystery, if you will."

"Meg?"

"She hasn't been heard from as of late, and she's moved out of her apartment. No one knows where she or her husband, Ethan, are."

"Ethan, I met him once. He came to the shop with her. I think he dropped her off every day, but that's the only time he came in that I remember. He was way into the Saucer People. He was like a walking billboard for them. He and Meg, they didn't seem to go together, you know? Didn't fit. But who can really know, right? Listen here, I need the donut job. Town isn't full of employment opportunities, you know. Not for a high-school drop-out. I wanted to write comic books. Can you believe that? Me, some small-town kid from Lufkin, Texas, wanting to be a comic-book writer? Wanted to write *Spider-Man* or *Batman* or something like them. Realized snappy-quick I didn't know anything about writing a comic book. And if I did, I had no idea who to give it to. Odd ambition, huh?"

"That's not odd at all. Unlikely you've heard of me, but I've written some articles and a book, working on another. Not self-published, by the way. Got a film option on the first one. Stars I've never heard of are attached."

"Yeah?" he said.

"Yeah. And I was serious when I said I don't think what you want to do is odd at all."

"Did you go to school to learn how to write?"

"I have a degree in criminology, but no creative-writing classes. Learned from experience and reading. What I do isn't the same as comic books, but maybe I can find some contacts. Put you in touch with someone in the know."

"Think so?"

"Yeah."

I didn't actually think that and felt bad dangling false hope to a desperate kid—he was maybe twenty years old, at most—but I was willing to swear true love to an amorous sheep and buy it an engagement ring and give it a fun honeymoon in Vegas if it would get Kevin to give me the information I needed.

Kevin played with a French fry on his plate. He pushed it around with his thumb, sliding it through a mound of ketchup.

"Before I got the donut-shop job, I was so low I could have walked under a snake on stilts wearing a top hat with a feather in it. No money. No real home. Couch-surfing. I needed the donut job, and I don't want to mess that up just yet. Not that it's a dream job. I make minimum wage, get up damn early to help fix donuts with a couple others. They drift by ten a.m., and I man the shop until eleven or so, then close it up. Doing the donkey work. People don't buy many donuts after the morning hours.

"Used to do that with Meg, now it's just me. Job sucks, but the bills, such as I have, get paid. Even rented me a little shit shack over by the railroad track, next to a washateria. No more couches. Place doesn't have any regular hot water. Big wind blows and the lights go out. Train rattles by couple times a day and once at night like clockwork. Shakes the house. Still, it's what I got and it's all I got."

"I understand. I don't want to mess you up."

"Can I see the thirty?"

I pulled out my wallet and placed a twenty and a ten on the table. I set the saltshaker on them. "It awaits your information."

"That's really not much money these days," he said.

"Fair enough." I opened my wallet again and slid another ten under the saltshaker with the other bills. "That's it."

"Ask me," he said. "I don't mean to sound like a money-grubbing asshole, but right now I'm so short on dough, if someone said they'd pay me fifty dollars to shit in a teaspoon, I'd drop my drawers."

"That's not something I want to see. And you aren't getting fifty dollars. How well did you actually know Meg?"

"Like I said, not well. She was a stone-cold fox. She liked to wear blue-jean short-shorts. It was against the rules, but no one was complaining. And that damn anklet, something was sexy as hell about that. Jingled a little when she walked."

I knew about those short-shorts. Meg sometimes didn't know her personal worth and depended on her looks and her shape. But I must admit, I liked the looks and the shape too. In our society, intelligence looks best in a nice wrapper. You can think that's wrong, and you'd be right, but if you think that isn't true, then who's kidding who?

"She's something," he said.

"I know. I was married to her."

"No shit?"

"No shit."

"Damn, man. You shouldn't have let that bird fly away."

"Forgot to close the cage door, I guess. How true a believer was she? I know she was into it."

"Thing was, six months ago, I'd have said she was one of the truer believers. She could really spout the party line, like her husband. While back, so could I. She didn't have the kind of money some of the others had, you know, to tithe, but again, those looks worked about as good as dollars for the Managers. They'd drop by the donut shops now and then. Always dressed in black and wearing sunglasses, their hair cut short and slicked close to their heads. They look like the legendary Men in Black. One of them is a woman. She looks like she could turn over a car. Bodybuilder. Maybe more a weight lifter than bodybuilder. The head Manager, though, he's different. Wears cowboy clothes. You know, a snap-button shirt, pockets in a V shape, with jeans, black cowboy boots with really sharp toes. A black cowboy hat that looks like it's seen some rain. That dude is big. Basketball-player-tall. You know what I mean when I say Men in Black?"

"Supposed to accompany flying-saucer sightings. Sometimes thought to be government men, sometimes thought to be aliens in disguise."

"Yeah. These guys, the Managers, they stand around looking threatening. Just thugs is my guess, now that I'm seeing clearer. Cowboy—that's what everyone calls the tall one—is the head duck. Out at the compound, he walks around with a chimpanzee on a chain."

"You shitting me?"

"Nope. Chimpanzee is like his constant companion out there at the Landing Pad, the compound, or whatever you want to call it. Mostly the chimp is kept out there, but he brought it into the donut shop some. Thing wears diapers and a collar with a gold name tag on it. Mr. Biggs, the collar says. We don't let dogs in, but he brings in this foul-smelling ape. He gives it donuts. The chimp looks at me like any moment it might wig out, leap over the counter, and stuff me in the donut fryer. Creepy thing. I heard Cowboy bought it from a dying carnival. It's as well trained as a wild animal can be. Those things, they are incredibly strong. I bet they're ten times stronger than a man. Dangerous beasts, can turn on you faster than a drunk mother-in-law. Could reach up your ass and pull your face out through it. It's big too. Scarred up from mistreatment in the carnival is my guess. Doesn't look like the ones you always see that are small and cute, lots of shiny hair.

"Cowboy and his men, sometimes just him, come in to check the books—computer spreadsheet, to be more accurate. They pick up the weekly receipts. Though sometimes we drop them off at the bank ourselves. I mean, all you got to do is walk across the street. But it's a kind of surprise drop-in that they do. Making sure we're not eating all the donuts, that we're cleaning the restrooms, and that we aren't pocketing the dough. And I don't mean the donut dough.

"They always check us out, but Cowboy checked Meg out a little more than the rest of us. Cowboy talked to her in a way that indicated she might have a chance to come within the tighter circle. I think that appealed to her. She asked about Ethan joining her. He didn't seem interested in Ethan moving out. I remember one time the chimp came in, she patted it on the head. Chimp looked at her like it was jealous, like she was maybe jockeying for Cowboy."

"Tighter circle?"

"Bacon, our fearless leader, gets the last word out there at the Landing Pad. Bacon likes good-looking women, and maybe he has designs on more than giving them words of wisdom, promising them a front seat on a saucer. His wife, she's like a walking-dead woman. No fun going on there. Cowboy recruits good-looking women for Bacon, though I'm not saying Meg would have gone for that."

"But she caught their eye, and after a bit, she wasn't at the donut shop anymore?"

"All I know is they liked her, had her handling the spreadsheets when they found out she had some college. Next thing, she's gone. Where she is now, I can't say."

"And Ethan?"

"No idea."

"You go out to the compound, this Landing Pad, much?"

"Everyone that's serious about the religion ends up going there. It's expected. Controlled. You go out to the mound at certain times, when it's allowed, and raise your hands to the sky. Money is appreciated. And like I said, some people, picked by the managers, live and work out there. You know, there's a gift shop. You can buy all manner of shit there. None of it worth a tenth of what you pay for it. But there was a time when I would have given my left nut to have been picked to be out there.

"Then, one night, I'm out there at the Landing Pad, looking up at the sky, along with a couple hundred people praying to the stars, and all of a sudden, I'm thinking how I give the Managers ten percent of my monthly earnings, the money I'm paid by them. Just giving it back to them, right off the top.

"Finally, I'm thinking, What have I been thinking? It's all an angle of view. One day you accept looking down a corridor, not seeing anything but what's in front of you, what's laid out for you, and then another day, for some reason or another, you see a crack of light, a window, and you look out of that and realize you're a fucking idiot. That's a hard thing to embrace. Lot of people, even if they look out the window, they been believing so hard for so long and wanting this stuff to be true, they just can't leave the window open. They shut it. I must have shut it a thousand times before I left it open.

"Few months back, I couldn't see a shooting star or a jet at night without thinking it was Bacon's aliens coming to pick us up to do war on a distant planet. Had to look out that window a few times before I climbed out of it. Thinking, too: What chance do I, or a lot of those folks out there, have against bad aliens? I couldn't win a game of Scrabble in a fair fight, let alone whip aliens in an unfair one.

"Been putting a bit of money back since then. Weekly check doesn't have much left after I pay bills and the tithing. Been eating a donut and coffee free at the shop for breakfast. At home I have a potpie for lunch, and for supper I toast some bread, put some margarine on it. Eating like that, I been able to stash back enough to leave. Haven't had the guts yet to make the jump. One day I just won't show up for work. I don't like the idea of giving notice, because I don't like the idea of dealing with them over something like that. Hey, maybe I can keep up with you by e-mail or some such, get a connection to a comic-book company. You know, give it a shot. I got some good stories in my head. Trouble is putting them down, you know?"

"That is the trick, isn't it?"

"I could use a connection, man."

"I can do that. Here's a simple question. Do you think the Managers, the Men in Black, Cowboy, are truly dangerous?"

"Know this much—I'm scared of them. I got no direct reason to feel that way. But indirectly, you know, you get vibes. Hear stories here and there. And they may have an inkling that I'm not enamored with their bullshit anymore.

"Here's another thing. They're supposed to have been gathering food and guns for years for the travel, for the big battle. Lot of ships are supposed to be coming. Even if some of that stuff they've gathered, the food and the guns, are in the warehouse they use outside of town, even big as it is, it should have been filled long ago. A new one would be needed. Think about that. After all these years, they could have filled up the mound, Bacon's house, the chicken houses, and the warehouse, which they claim is the main place for supplies. They talk about it all the time, how the warehouse is full of food and guns for the great journey, the great war. Everything's great, by the way. Nothing is so-so in their universe."

"Do you know for sure that's the only warehouse they have?"

"Pretty sure."

"When were you last at the Landing Pad?"

"Couple months ago. Place is guarded with a gate. There's no fence around it, but there's lots of woods, and the Managers are defending the place. Not many of them, but they're not carrying switches."

"I understand there are tourist visits?"

"They recruit that way. There are times for it, and they're not weekly. They give the tour, which you pay to take, and it doesn't amount to much. Mostly it's just folks interested in seeing the place, hearing from the faithful. They lay on the talk heavy, though. All they need to keep going are a few who believe them and are willing to pay regularly for their seat to heaven. Some people have given their life fortunes for a first-class ticket.

"As for me, another hundred dollars or so and I'm hauling. Got a half-ass car that'll get me away before it breaks down or the tires blow. I can find another job, some place far away from this shithole. Come next Christmas, I'll forget I ever lived here. Just smelling donuts makes me sick, and like I was saying, I have to eat one every day because it's free."

"Don't they have kolaches?"

"Hate them more than the donuts. Sausage in them is greasy as my old car's transmission. Yeah. I think I'm going. I calm down a bit, maybe I'll wait a couple days. I might wait a week or two, stash back the dough. Cheat them on the tithing, pick up my last check, cash it, and go. Yeah. Now that I think about it, I need a couple weeks' pay."

When the bill was brought, I paid it. I lifted the saltshaker, and Kevin took the money under it and put it in his wallet.

"One more thing," I said. "Can you tell me where this warehouse for the goods and such is?"

"Keep in mind that it is way locked up. Security cameras."

"Understood."

He gave me an address and I wrote it down in a little black book with a big black pen I carried in my coat pocket.

I told him my e-mail and he put it directly into his phone, tagging it with my name.

As we were leaving the café, Kevin said, "Watch yourself, boss. Managers don't like folks prying, and they don't like members talking. Maybe I'm making a lot of shit up in my head now that I've seen the light, but then again, maybe not."

On the sidewalk, we shook hands. Kevin walked the opposite way I was going. Walking home, I presumed. Saving gas and the unnecessary balding of the tires on his escape vehicle.

I didn't offer to give him a ride.

I watched him cross the street and pass by the bank, making good time.

I walked back to my car.

(14)

I had a headache again. Headaches had been rare until recently. Or they came only when I had studied all night to pass a test, drunk too much coffee. Allergies. Colds. Flu. Stuff like that.

Other than that, I had been mostly headache-free.

Now, at least once a day, sometimes twice, I was visited by a pain that lasted for an hour or so. A mild throb that grew in intensity, poked a spike through the brain, then faded. Tylenol helped most of the time, but now and again, nothing did. It just had to run its course and go away.

I was waiting for it to go away.

I didn't really know what to do next. I wasn't ready to drive out to the Landing Pad, and I probably couldn't get inside legally anyway. I didn't know when they had tours. I'd look it up.

The storage facility seemed like something I had to check out, but I hadn't forgotten Kevin's warning about the cameras and security. I remembered what he said about the Men in Black too. About Cowboy. Mr. Biggs might even be a problem.

I decided to put that business on the back burner and started home.

I got a text from Felix. I played it out on the Prius screen. It read aloud in its annoying computer voice that Felix couldn't get together with me today. He was finishing up a project, which was what he called cases, and wouldn't be done until tomorrow. There had been complications. He'd be in touch.

That suited me.

When I got home, I plucked a bottle of water from the refrigerator, went upstairs, and tried to write a little, remembering some good advice that I hadn't followed in the past couple of days: Don't wait for the muse, just write, because you are the muse, and the only way the muse shows up is if you show up. I showed up. I got a bit done, and it wasn't bad. But I needed to show up more regularly.

When I finished writing, I did internet research on the cult, found out when they offered tours of the site. One was coming up. I read some of the book Grover had given us. I wondered how people could be taken in by this stuff, but then again, those who believed it probably wondered why those who didn't couldn't see the truth.

That said, I thought they were fucking idiots.

I went downstairs and thought about dinner but discovered I didn't really have much of an appetite. I settled for a glass of milk and a piece of buttered toast on some good nutty bread. I had it outside on the wraparound porch at the table.

Night came. I sat out there in the cool dark and moved thoughts around in my head, and considering I still had a headache, it was a little like trying to move heavy furniture by myself.

What I got out of all of this mental-furniture moving was that there was a good-size cult that had worked money out of people over the years. It had waxed and waned, but it was still there. Doing pretty well right now.

Bacon's son, Ben, had inherited the money and the cult from his father. With that money, he had opened a lot of donut shops to make more money. Had a gift shop, and I was surprised to discover they had not only chicken houses but a sawmill.

I looked up once, thought I saw something moving between

the trees. A shadow that had disengaged itself from its owner and gone rogue.

The shape of the shadow was uncertain. It could have been a lot of things, from a deer to Bigfoot to Men in Black who were keeping an eye on me. It creeped me out a little.

I scrutinized where I had seen the shadow. All I could see now were strips of darkness between the trees, and none of that darkness separated and moved.

I had seen something. I was certain. I hadn't imagined it, but it could have been many things, and all of them natural. Deer. A bobcat. A wild hog. All manner of wildlife. They all had shadows. I was letting my imagination off the hook a little too much. I often did.

Maybe at heart, I was one of the idiots. I wanted to believe the unbelievable. Perhaps that's why I wrote. To get away from the absurdity of life by creating my own absurdity that I could control. It certainly gave me pleasure. Though I didn't miss detecting all that much, I thought about it now and then, because, like writing, you were trying to solve an issue and bring some sort of order into the world and into your own life. Write a mystery story, you put it all together in the end, things are solved. But even then, you always discover you have some plot threads dangling.

I had to find out what had happened to Meg. Not just for the mystery, but because deep down, I had yet to let her go, and there were plenty of times when I thought I might never be able to.

The vision that always came to me of Meg wasn't her in those tight shorts. It wasn't her sans shorts, lying on the bed, legs spread, arms outstretched. The first thought that came to me was what Felix had mentioned, how she had treated our mother. In fact, I think she stayed with me longer than she wanted to so as not to leave Mom dangling. I remembered walking into that hospital room, seeing Meg sitting there beside the bed, holding Mom's hand. We had fought the night before, something silly, but the fights had become constant, and I knew she was trying to find an argument to justify her moving on. Her wave of romance had played out and life had gotten real, with bills to pay and compromises to be made, and she was through. Except for Mom.

The light from a window came through a split in the curtains like a road to heaven, and it lay over her and made her hair shine in such a way, it looked as if she had a halo. I'll never forget that. It took my breath away a little, that halo. And in that moment, I knew how deeply I loved her and how much pain I would soon bear. For I knew it was coming, her departure. And when Mom finally slipped over into a darkness so deep, she didn't know her ass from her elbow, Meg finally gave me up. She still visited Mom for some time after. Until she knew it didn't matter anymore.

But even after she'd gone and quickly taken up with Ethan, she still checked in by phone. "How is your mom?" she would ask, as if anything could change. But I liked that. Thing about Meg, she always thought things could get better, no matter the situation. But she was searching, reaching out for something she couldn't find in the day-to-day, that her personality couldn't latch onto and hold.

I took a deep breath and tried to purge her from my thoughts. It wasn't easy, but I managed it enough to accept it all once again. My mother's situation, and the loss of Meg.

Where was she? How was she?

There'd been a moment in time when I thought she pulled the sun up from the darkness when morning came and tucked it away for moonlight when the day ended.

Some part of me still felt that way. A big part.

I left my saucer and glass for the morning and locked up the house. I used the automatic control for all my living-room blinds and lowered them. I took two Tylenol and got into bed, propped myself up with my pillows mounded on top of one another, read a bit by the light on my nightstand.

It was a good book. I lost myself in it for a while, then I was suddenly overcome with an intense feeling that something was way wrong out there in Saucer Land at the old Landing Pad, and maybe, just maybe, it had something to do with Meg.

If so, I didn't know what to do about it.

I turned off the light, worked my head out of the book, out of those bad thoughts about Meg, and finally fell asleep.

(15)

I t turned cold as polar bear toes that night. I woke early, feeling pretty good. I pulled a heavy robe over my pajamas, slipped on my house shoes, opened all the kitchen and living-room blinds, and went out on the porch. It was raining, so I found a position where I could see the sky and not get wet. All there was to see was the misty gray heavens and the bullet rain. It rattled on the roof of the covered porch.

When I got bored with that, which was damn quick due to the cold, I gathered up last night's dishes, went back inside, made some coffee, and thought about an omelet, then decided against it. I'd trusted the ghost on that one. No omelet. It was toast again.

I sat at the dining-room table, rising only to put another pod in the Keurig, and watched the rain through the windows as I sipped my coffee.

The rain was so intense I couldn't really see the woods just beyond my yard, the spot where I had seen the shadow disengage from between two trees and blend into darkness.

About nine, my cell buzzed. It was Felix.

"Today doesn't seem like a good day to pursue a visit. Cherry has some news, though she says it's not much and she hasn't told me much because she wants to get us together so as not to repeat it. Maybe tomorrow."

"Is she there with you?"

"Spent the night."

"Look, I'm coming in. It's not that terrible a rain."

"Yes, it is."

"I'm coming in anyway. I don't care to hang out here all day and not have the news."

"She can tell you over the phone, and I can sit and listen to her. Smarter move, little brother."

"Might be, but I'd rather be looking at the both of you. Well, Cherry, anyway. You hurt my feelings."

"All right, knothead. Come on in, but drive carefully."

" 'Careful' is my middle name."

"Unfortunately not, little brother."

"Give me about twenty minutes to shower and dress, and another twenty to get there."

"We await your arrival with bated breath that smells of coffee, kippers, and eggs. Great breakfast, by the way. We had it about six a.m., sat at the window seat and watched the rain and a car wreck in front of the bookstore. No one was hurt. However, I have a mild disappointment about that. The car slid on the brick streets and hit a lamp pole, and the driver was that asshole you met the other day at the office."

"Guy with the muscles and his brother?"

"His brother wasn't with him, but it was him. He's been driving by now and then. Looks at my place like he plans to bomb it. I think he's been trying to get his courage up to come see me. He might have helped his marriage if he'd stayed home with his wife instead of chasing women. But he thinks it's my fault. I sort of hope he comes back to see me."

"Where is he now?"

"I called the cops and told them there was a wreck. I doubted I could make a case he was driving by my place with malicious intent. That would be hard to prove. So I didn't mention it. They took him in, and by that I don't mean arrested, just helped. A wrecker arrived about twenty minutes later and hauled his car away. The front end was nearly in the front seat. He's a lucky bastard."

"You should lock your door."

"Oh, it's locked. Haven't unlocked it this morning. Me and Cherry are taking the day off. Call me when you're near, and I'll unlock it. But it would be fine with me if you stayed home and not out in this mess."

"I know you, brother mine. Sounds to me like you and Cherry have further plans for carnal activity."

"That could be."

"Cancel them. Heat it up later, like leftovers in a microwave. I'm going to head your way."

(16)

We had mugs of cocoa that Felix prepared, and we sat on the long window seat that was nestled in front of a long row of windows with gauzy white curtains. There were darker curtains that could be pulled over those, but this way we could look out at the street and see the rain and hear the windowpanes gently rattle against the wind.

I had a blanket over my lap. Felix and Cherry had met me at the top of the stairs with towels. Even walking the short distance between my car and the door to Felix's office left me drenched to the bone. They had been ready for me.

Now I was drier and warmer. The cocoa had marshmallows in it, and they were soon in me. The steam from the cup made my face feel warm, and the smell of the chocolate filled my nostrils. I told Felix and Cherry about my conversation with Kevin.

"Okay, Cherry. Tell us what you got," I said.

"I know people who know people," Cherry said. "And some of those people worked at the bank. Information like that comes with my job as an ace attorney. I have more than once dealt with financial issues in May Town. I thought one of my contacts, Jim Boer, still worked there. But he was gone. Been relieved of his position, as they stated it, a few weeks before."

"Less said about Jim the better," Felix said.

"Me and Jim dated a little," Cherry said. "That's why Felix doesn't like him."

"Exactly," Felix said, looking at Cherry through the mist rising from his cup of cocoa.

"I looked Jim up," Cherry said. "We had lunch yesterday. By the way, if you're over there, never eat at Cecil's."

"Too late," I said. "That's where me and Kevin had lunch."

"That's too bad. We ate at the Mexican restaurant behind the bank. It's better, though microwaving is involved. Some of what you learned dovetails with what Jim told me. Gradually, the bank has replaced tellers and the like. Not an amazing occurrence. It happens. But all those who were replaced were replaced by cult members, or what Jim called sympathizers. Cult owns the bank. They bought out the original owners—it was operated by a small corporation—and now the bank is owned by East Texas Private and Commercial. That's the cult. That's one of their many businesses. Donut shops you know about. Here's something you may not know. They have successful chicken houses, a sawmill, a catfish farm, and a few other odds and ends."

"I didn't know about the catfish farm," I said. "Knew about the others."

"You mentioned this Kevin told you about Cowboy. What I know about him from Jim is he spent some time in Huntsville, and not as part of the cook staff. Got out, tied up with the cult. Pretty much runs the business for Bacon. Provides muscle if it's needed. Like most of this stuff, it starts out with someone believing in something, then seeing the business potential, and finally turning it into a racket."

"Then there's the warehouse," I said. "Supposed to be stuffing it with food and weapons. Cult members pay for all that. Managers take the money and buy the stuff—canned and dry goods, guns—store it there for the forthcoming interplanetary battle."

"I hope they lose," Felix said.

"Kevin brought up the idea that by now it would be overfull," I said. "Unless they have another warehouse, several others, where is all that money going that's supposed to be for the goods? And isn't there some kind of law against having a storehouse of weapons?"

"Law pretty much stays out of that business, even if they shouldn't," Cherry said. "Or at least, it tiptoes around it. East Texas is full of gun fanatics, and it goes beyond hunting and target shooting. They talk about tradition and being hunters, but at heart they are antigovernment or like to play army. Lot of the gun folks, in their own way, are just as fanatic as the cult members. Hell, those kind of gun owners are a cult. Thing is, FBI and, especially, the local police, lot of them sympathize, and they're all scared of another Waco. Scared of militia nuts, men and women who've watched too many movies and own too many camo outfits and have no appropriate place to wear them."

"The whole thing is dopey," Felix said. "I got nothing against owning a gun, but having a ton of guns is not like having a ton of cattle."

"You don't have to feed them," I said.

"That's a valid point, little brother."

"We either need to let this go," I said, "which I will not, or we need to find out what's in the warehouse and pay a visit to the saucer site."

"Question is," Cherry said, "how do we get into the warehouse?"

"I'm working on that," I said.

(17)

When the rain slacked, I drove back home with my brain buzzing. The rain continued for three days, only letting up long enough to let the wind blow awhile before the deluge came back in a loud whooshing wave.

As much as Felix, Cherry, and I wanted to explore the cult business, we had to pause until the worst of it passed.

While we waited, one thing occurred that upset me and made matters worse. One morning, online, I read a piece out of the small Nacogdoches newspaper. The paper didn't run daily, so the report was three days old when I read it. I was surprised it had even made our newspaper. The paper hated to give up ads for news. I followed up by looking at the May Town newspaper's website. There wasn't any mention of the event. Maybe next week.

The upsetting news was Kevin was dead.

His body had been discovered in a ditch near a patch of piney woods that was being cut for lumber. It had been there for a couple days. An anonymous person had phoned the police, and a highway patrol officer was sent out to investigate. She said the body had been burned, wrapped in a rug, and thrown in a ditch.

When the cops unwrapped the rug to take Kevin out, they saw

his arms were torn out of their sockets and tossed into the rug with him. One side of his face had been ripped off like damp, peeling wallpaper. Vital organs had been pulled out. There was a crude castration, as if his business had been jerked off. His knees were snapped and his teeth were knocked out. Somehow the corpse had been identified.

His car was found down a country trail. It had been set on fire and burned out. Investigations were continuing.

I felt a little guilty. I hadn't expected anything like that, but after what he told me and the savagery of his death, it was a logical consideration that the cult was involved.

I took a break from the computer to take a nervous walk inside the house, room to room. I watched the rain through the windows. I didn't see any Men in Black creeping about in the rain. Aliens didn't jump out of the closet with probes for my ass.

Back upstairs with a bottle of water in hand, I went back to the article and read it again. There was still nothing there that enlightened me. There was plenty to darken me.

I checked my e-mail to have something to do besides think about Kevin. I had one from my agent, a simple matter concerning a book sale in Germany. It wasn't anything special or life-changing, but I responded with enthusiasm at the sale. It wasn't exactly free money, because I'd had to work to write the book, but it was money for a book already written. That gave me a tidier bank account.

The next e-mail took me aback. In fact, when I saw who it was from, I hesitated to open it for a long moment. I sat and drank from my bottle of water like a camel preparing for a long trek across the desert.

Eventually, my thirst sated and consumed by curiosity, I opened the message.

(18)

The e-mail message read:

Mr. Garner. I suppose you think I'm writing you about the comic-book connections. But to be honest that is something I have shelved for the time being. I've been talking to someone who asked me a lot of the questions you asked, but they had more money. Her name is Amelia Moon. What a cool last name. Moon. I talked longer with her than you. She asked questions in a way that led me to want to talk more. She looked good and smelled good.

Afterward, Cowboy came to my house. Came straight in. Had the door been locked, which it should have been, he'd have most likely kicked it down. Came in with his chimp on a chain, as if that chain would hold the beast if it decided to ignore it. Mr. Biggs was wearing bright green stretch shorts. Had on a little green derby, like a leprechaun. Pinned there to its fur, I guess. Its stench filled my house. I can still smell it. It turned its head left and right while Cowboy talked to me. It creeped my ass out.

Cowboy said they had concerns about me. Feared I was a dead spirit, threatened me with excommunication from the Saucer People. This dead-spirit shit, it's one of the things the Saucer People say can happen to humans. Dead spirits are left in limbo. Their walking bodies will be taken over by the bad guys, the astral-projected evil spirits of those from the planet where the last war before paradise will be fought. Being a dead spirit is not thought to be a good thing.

I am straight as an arrow when I say I am leaving soon as I can for any place where I think I will be safe. Waiting two weeks is off the table.

I talked to Miss Moon at the same café where we met. I think the people who own the café must be part of the cult, or someone that works there is. Someone I don't know. I know a lot of the members, but not all, and I don't always know what they do. Of course, not all of them are from May Town, but I think this was someone at the café. Doesn't matter. It's all a guess.

Concerns about me have been around for a while, even before they needed to be concerned. It's like they could smell a doubter in the wind.

My old car is being repaired and, if all goes well, should be returned to me later today or early tomorrow. I get it, I'm gone.

You may not hear from me for a while. And unless my desire to write comic books should return, you may not hear from me again. I think when I leave May Town, I will cut all ties and go off the grid for a while.

Cowboy talked around things, but there was a threat in there. The way he came in was threat enough. Way Mr. Biggs looked at me. Cowboy wanted to know if I had a copy of the financial records at the donut shop. Did I have it on a thumb drive? Did I have it printed out? Did I have it up my ass? Those records have become a big concern.

They were scaring me to scare me, but that doesn't mean they won't act on it. Maybe the good-looking lady, Miss Moon, is in cahoots with them. Said she worked for the May Town paper. That's two pages of mostly ads, two headlines, an obituary column, and a half page of funnies. There's one comic strip with a dog I like. Was she really a hard-hitting journalist writing an exposé to be tucked between Brookshire's coupons and an article on forthcoming high-school graduations? I think not. But hell, I wanted to talk to her. I'm shallow and she was cute as a puppy.

Cowboy left a little mark on the door of my house to show I was excommunicated. Kind of dramatic about it. Used a red marker. Lots of people have quit the cult, but of late, Cowboy and the Managers seem a lot more bothered by it. They're like an abusive spouse that's reached the summit on their possessive insanity. What they can't control, they destroy.

There's something else. One last something from me. I chose to put that SOMETHING in the mail. A package. Watch for it. Kevin

P.S. These guys mean business, and you're meddling in theirs. He asked me about you. And about Miss Moon. I didn't say much, but it doesn't matter. They know a lot. They have connections. Watch your ass.

(19)

The "tomorrow" Kevin had spoken about turned out to be couple days ago, and now he was dead. Did they truly fear a little dude like Kevin? Did they believe he would actually throw a wrench in their hyperdrive, and were they seriously concerned about me as well? Was Kevin living a comic-book dream?

And who the hell was Miss Amelia Moon?

And might I add, who the hell goes around with a chimpanzee on a chain dressed up for an Irish weekend?

———

I wondered about the package. What was that about? And did Kevin have my mailing address?

Of course he did. He could find it online if he wanted to. He could see my house from space on Google Earth if he chose to.

I spent a moment remembering where Kevin said he lived. By the railroad tracks next to a washateria. I could have found it online, way he had probably found my address, but I didn't bother. I needed to be in motion. I was itching with curiosity.

Foolishly, I decided to brave the wind and the rain. I needed a look around his place. I needed to know things that might help me figure out what had happened to Meg.

Oh, and Kevin.

I wanted to find out who would do such a thing to Kevin. And who might want to do it to me.

And once again, who the hell was Amelia Moon?

(20)

I put a crowbar, gloves, and a raincoat in my car on the front seat, then pulled out from under the carport and drove into the rain. It was so bad I almost turned around. Then I thought: No. This is just right. I'm less likely to be hassled for what I'm going to do, less likely to be noticed.

There were no other cars on the road because everyone was smarter than me and had stayed home. The reasonably short trip to May Town seemed like an unreasonably long trip to somewhere on the other side of the earth. I had to intensely watch the road, the wipers beating furiously, the headlights on, the beams bouncing off sheets of rain.

I eventually came to May Town, drifted through intersections with dead traffic lights out to where the train tracks crossed, which wasn't too far away from the main part of town. There were no lights anywhere. The electricity was out all over. It was like that in East Texas. Electricity died easy in rain and a high wind. Since we were a place of frequent rain and wind, you'd think someone would have figured out how to make that happen less often. I wondered if my electricity was on. I wondered if a chimp was waiting at my house in a stinky diaper wearing a leprechaun hat and carrying a blackthorn stick.

Going through May Town normally took about the time it would take to lick your lips. With the wind and the rain knocking my car around, it took a little longer.

I turned and drove along a blacktop road that ran next to the railroad tracks, saw a washateria with a yellow house by it. The house looked as if it were sinking into the earth. The wooden steps and small wooden porch that led to the front door looked precarious as a drunk high-wire walker. The house was on about an acre of browned-out grass with one oak tree out to the side that looked ragged and suicidal.

I pulled up the gravel drive and parked. The cops had to have been here to see where their victim lived, but there was no yellow crime tape anywhere. That made me wonder. Maybe they were out of crime-scene tape. Maybe they were out of interest.

Did I have the wrong house, and a moment from now, when I used my crowbar to break open the door, would I find a family of four shivering on the couch with blankets wrapped around them?

I took a deep breath and wrestled into the raincoat. I slipped on my gloves, removed my flashlight from the glove box. I put the flashlight in my coat pocket. Feeling plump as the Pillsbury Doughboy with a thyroid condition, I draped the raincoat hood over my noggin, grabbed my crowbar, and waddled up the drive like I lived there.

There was a leaky overhang over the shaky porch, and it threatened to collapse at any moment. There were gaps in it, and the rain came through in small waterfalls that splashed on the porch and my rain hood. I looked up and saw a bird's nest in one corner of the overhang. It was leaking water. No birds seemed to be home. The suicidal tree clicked its branches together in the wind. I noticed a large red mark, more of a slash, on the doorframe—the excommunication mark Cowboy had made.

I stood there and shivered a moment, studied the door. It was cracked open. Reason for that was the lock had been busted. I wasn't going to need my crowbar.

I pushed the door with my shoulder and went inside. Using my butt, I shoved the door shut. The house felt empty and sad, like a lost romance. I went through the living room, past the cheap furniture. The whole place smelled of old urine, wet fur, and musky hormones.

I paused, pushed the raincoat hood off my head, and stood dripping water onto the already warped wooden floor that swelled and wobbled beneath my feet.

Searching the house didn't take long. There wasn't that much of it. In the bedroom I found a bed with no sheets on it and a slightly rusty-looking stain on the wall that made me nervous. I ran my foot over the floor. It scratched my shoe and felt like a day at the beach. Kevin obviously wasn't much for cleaning. To get a place this nasty took time and determined neglect. There were some wrecked chairs and a busted dresser. Home furnishings by Demolition Interior Design. There were a few dents in the drywall. The mattress had a large stain in the center that might have been a water stain turned rust-colored, or maybe Kevin had spilled Kool-Aid in bed.

I noticed there were footprints in the dust. Next to the bed, it was less dusty where Kevin walked from bed to bathroom and out into the living room.

On the far side of the bed, on the floor, close to a window with time-tinted blinds raised crookedly above the sill, there were more footprints; some were from shoes or boots, a couple were the tracks of bare feet. The prints were smudged and overlapping.

There was one chair pulled up to a small table near the far wall. On the table were some yellowed books, one about Y2K, the other having to do with the end of the world according to the Mayan calendar. There was a stack of hardcover graphic novels. I didn't pick up either book or the graphic novels, but I studied the covers. Kevin was most definitely a prime candidate for end-of-the-world conspiracies. Or had been until, amid the smell of greasy donuts and powdered-sugar fog, he had opened that window he had talked about and seen the light.

The bathroom was off to the side and barely large enough to turn around in. It had a peeling tile floor and a toilet with a crusty pee-stained interior thick enough for turds to build lakeside condos on. Last time it had been cleaned was the day it came from the factory.

The interior of the sink was stained too, had a dark ring around the drain. There was no tub, just a shower with a blue plastic curtain that separated it from the rest of the bathroom. There was a small rim of plastic at the bottom of the shower, but it didn't look as if it kept the water inside the shower in any substantial way.

Back in the living room, I walked across to the corner that served as a kitchen. There was a bar there that took the place of a table. The refrigerator was bullet-shaped, made in the middle years of the past century. The cabinets contained glasses with cartoon critters on them, sort you get from fast-food joints or that were inherited from nerd parents who still had their *Back to the Future* lunch boxes. The plates were thick as Olympic throwing discuses and could only be broken by artillery fire.

I sat on the couch and tried to figure out if I was missing a clue. I decided I wasn't. And then I noticed that in front of the couch, and not just where my feet rested, the floor was very clean. It had a rectangular shape without dust. A rug had been there.

A cold tongue licked up my spine. It didn't take a great leap of logic to determine that Kevin had been wrapped up in it like a burrito and burned, his car taken out and dumped.

The house shook and some dishes rattled in the cabinet above the sink. I nearly jumped to my feet before realizing it was a train charging down the nearby track.

I pulled my hood up and went outside into the rain. It was nice to get away from the stench. Climbing into the car, I tossed the crowbar onto the passenger seat. I wrestled off my raincoat and gloves and sat in the puddle of water the coat had formed. It made my butt wet and cold. I removed the flashlight from the pocket of the raincoat and returned it to the glove box.

I backed the car out, slipped up to the tracks, and watched the train race by. Right then I wished I were on it.

When it finished clanking by, I drove across the tracks, back into May Town. The streetlights were working. Lights were on in buildings. Either the electricity had automatically kicked back on or some poor civil servant out in the rain had repaired the problem.

I parked in front of the donut shop. I could make out the neon sign through the window. It was enjoying its revived voltage. The sign said CLOSED.

That was all right. I didn't want a donut and I didn't know of anyone I'd want to talk to if it were open.

In my rearview mirror, I could see the bank across the street. There was a sign on the door that was too far away for me to read, but I doubted it read COME ON IN. Not in this weather and uncertain electricity.

I took out my cell and called Cherry. I was surprised I had service. I got her answering machine. I left a brief message, sat and thought about things, listening to the rain slam my car and wash the windshield. I had decided to give up and go home when Cherry called.

"I could use Grover's address, if you don't mind," I said.

"Where are you?"

"In my car."

"Out in this?"

"That's right. Look, Cherry, I'm not on the stand being cross-examined. Do you have Grover's address?"

"Why?"

"I'm putting him on my Christmas-card list."

"You and Felix keep thinking you're a couple of smart-asses. But you're pains in the ass is what you are."

"May I have the address?" I had activated the GPS on the Prius, and I punched the address into it as she gave it to me.

"You're not going over to see him, are you?"

"Why I asked for the address, Cherry. I don't actually have a Christmas-card list, you know."

"Grover told us what he told us, and that's all he's got to tell. He's an old, sick man. You should leave him alone."

"I said I was working on getting us in the warehouse, and a visit with Grover is a big part of that."

"Thought we were going to wait until the rain was done. You should go home. And why do we need to involve Grover? The whole thing is embarrassing to him. He's still getting over the death of his wife, the immersion in the cult. Besides, it's crazy-raining. East Texas is under a flood watch. You shouldn't be out in that."

"Murder doesn't care about the rain."

"That sounds like an old-time paperback title," she said. "And it sounds dumb. What murder? Meg's? You don't know. Felix is just guessing. She might have run off to join the circus. I'm telling you, Charlie, don't be stupid."

She had forgotten Kevin, but I didn't bother to remind her. I figured poor Kevin was forgotten a lot. I didn't mention his e-mail or my visit to his god-awful house.

"Stupid is as stupid does," I said.

"Isn't that the truth——"

I punched the phone off with Cherry still talking and drove over to Grover's place. I did this while thinking about Kevin. About what he had gone through. Obviously, Cowboy and Mr. Biggs had been back for a second visit, and Mr. Biggs had dismantled Kevin like a cheap action figure. Then there was the rug, a bit of toasting, and leaving his car to be found. They wanted him found. They were sending a signal to nosy folks like me who were messing in the Saucer People cult.

I kept that in mind as I drove over to see Grover.

(21)

Grover's place was simple, made of brick, with a new roof on it. The garage was closed up with an aluminum door that would slide up and down. The house and garage were on about three well-kept acres. It was a sharp contrast to Kevin's joint down by the railroad tracks.

I struggled into my raincoat and rushed across the spongy yard to the large porch that surrounded the house. I was wet and shivering from the cold, and the wind was making my raincoat rustle like a cheap tent pitched in the Himalayas. I leaned on the front doorbell.

Grover answered. He looked a lot better than he had in the office. He actually had some color in his complexion and was walking with a cane. He smiled some new dentures at me; I wasn't sure they had been worth the money. He had a small automatic pistol stuck in his pants pocket as if it were a holster. The butt of it hung free for easy access.

"Had a feeling I'd see you again," he said.

"Looks like you might have been expecting someone else."

"I always am. I feel they might come eventually. Read the news feed about the kid that was burned up. Worked in the donut shop?"

"Yeah."

"You talked to him, right?"

"Yeah."

"Figured."

"I shouldn't have come."

"It's all right, Charlie. I probably can't tell you much more than I already told you. But as for being scared, I'm inches from going down the greasy slide anyway. I'm past caring or worrying about the Saucer People. Time and genetics are collecting their dues. Still, I would shoot one of them if they messed with me. Let's have some coffee."

Grover helped me out of my raincoat, hung it on a hook by the door. The floor was concrete, which I loved. Easy to tend. Water from the coat pooled beneath where my coat hung.

I took the polite route, though. "Maybe I should leave it on the porch?"

"Water will wipe up. Come on in."

As we entered the dining room/kitchen, Grover motioned me to a chair at the table. I sat down.

"You look better today than the other day," I said.

Grover was going about making coffee. He didn't use pods. He was old-school, like Felix. He scooped coffee from a can, put it in a paper filter, put the filter in the coffee maker, and turned it on. "Some days aren't as bad as others. But the day is fresh. And I got some teeth replaced. That cheers me up a bit. I can eat without pain now. Might as well finish out my days being able to tear a steak apart."

Okay, not dentures.

"Later, I won't feel so good. Long as I take it easy, stay home, take my meds, it's not so bad. A trip to the store can be so tough, I want to put a gun in my mouth. This one in my pocket, to be exact. At your brother's office the other day, and driving over there with Cherry, talking, thinking back on things, it wore me out emotionally. Strangely enough, knowing I'm dying is a comfort. You'd think it would intensify me wanting to believe in an afterlife, but it's just the opposite. Like your brother, I've come to the idea of just being gone, and that sounds all right. Sugar? Milk?"

"Black is fine."

Grover took down two cups and set them beside the coffeepot. The pot was making a noise like a dead gopher draining through a sewer pipe.

"There's a young lady investigating this business too. Came to see me, said she was from the newspaper here. I didn't believe that. I know this town. I know the newspaper. It's an older couple keeps it going. Write about lost dogs and swap meets. They're not going to run an article about the Saucer People that's negative. They don't want to mess with the donut business in town. They don't even want to stir milk in coffee too briskly. Not their style. Newspaper hangs on by a frayed thread. People aren't waiting breathlessly for a once-a-week paper to show up in their mailboxes, unless it's to cut ads out of it for the local Dollar Store, maybe the Kroger or Walmart or Brookshire's over in Nacogdoches. My guess is they lose money every month. More of a hobby, I think. Bottom line, I knew that girl was lying."

"Did you talk to her?" I asked. "This young lady that came around. I mean, really talk to her?"

"Wanted to, just because she was attractive. Might have been nice to have coffee with her just to look at her for a while. But I didn't know for sure what her game was. Was she working for them, trying to see what I knew? Wouldn't be surprised if the Saucer People knew I'd been to Nacogdoches to talk to you, Cherry, and your brother. This town, you take a dump, someone's nearby to flush the toilet. I was polite. Talked a little, but I didn't tell her anything of any importance. I don't know I have anything important."

I told Grover about my talk with Kevin, his mention of a female reporter, it probably being the same person. Then I told him what I had found in Kevin's house after he was murdered. The place where a rug most likely had been. The various footprints in dust. The mark on the doorframe. All of it.

"Maybe he was just a rotten housekeeper."

"Certainly that's part of it. But I know he was visited by a fellow named Cowboy and his chimp, Mr. Biggs. My guess is he was visited a second time along with someone else. Someone to drive Kevin's car, help out with this or that—cleaning up a little, wrapping and burning, disposing of the body."

If a face could clabber like spoiled milk, Grover's did. He leaned on the kitchen counter, watched the coffee percolate for a moment.

"Cowboy. What a horror. Weaseled in with Bacon. Just a saucer guy at first. Later he rose in the ranks. Was promoted to a position of protecting Bacon and the cult. Likes to dress up like Clint Eastwood or some such. You remember Jim Jones and the Peoples Temple?"

"The poisoned Kool-Aid. All those people committing suicide in Guyana."

"Flavor Aid, actually. Right before my wife and I bailed, Saucer People were starting to have that same vibe. Jim Jones wanted more control over his people, his tribe, so he moved his followers from the U.S. to Guyana, built what was supposed to be a self-sufficient community there. Started screwing the womenfolk, menfolk too, married or not. Mistreated the children. Wanted to constantly be praised. In the end, he had his own set of enforcers, like Cowboy and the Managers, and when things started coming apart, Jones had them help his people commit suicide by drinking poison to go to the Promised Land. There's some evidence he talked about their spirits arriving on another planet to live in paradise. Sound familiar?"

"From what I learned from reading about this stuff, there are quite a few flying-saucer utopian-planet cults."

"Like the Heaven's Gate people. Waiting for the flying saucer coming with the Hale-Bopp comet to pick them up. Figure their leader realized that when the comet came, he'd have to deal with humiliation, because I'm sure he knew the saucer wasn't coming. He decided to convince them they could catch a ride in spirit, if not in person. Persuaded them to commit suicide. All of them had a nice lunch, bought new tennis shoes to wear, for some reason. Never figured that one out. They took the killer drugs, pulled plastic bags over their heads, and checked out. I'm snide about it now, but some of that is me feeling my own stupidity. I bought into a similar viewpoint for far too long. Then it was like cataracts were removed from my eyes. Suddenly, I could see."

"Kevin compared it to looking out a window and seeing the world as it was."

"I've given it a lot of thought. Maybe too much. I have too many theories. Maybe it comes down to the middle class believing in nothing but slogans, therefore it's easy for new slogans with better promises to take over. We're constantly bombarded with ads for bigger cars and larger houses and bigger dicks and hotter sex. We all think everyone else is having more fun than we are. But mystical rewards, they can't be measured the same way. Bacon gives us a chance to think of ourselves as warriors and eventually happy spirits, all of us equally rewarded.

"It's so enticing, we don't even stop and listen to ourselves and how ridiculous we sound. In fact, the idea is to destroy the thinking part of your brain. To think of the intellectuals as fools, and they can be, and the nonintellectuals can be smart as they come. But the idea is to let your common sense loose of your thoughts so you can be seduced by a mania that puts you among the in-crowd. At least as they perceive it.

"My guess is next on the agenda is prophesying the saucers' arrival. 'The saucers will be here Tuesday. Cancel that hair appointment and don't shop for next week.' Then the prophecy date arrives. Nothing happens. And that's when everything can go south on a bullet. And before you go, maybe you'll decide to take others with you."

"Then why would Bacon make such a prediction?"

Grover poured coffee from the pot into our cups, placed one in front of me, then sat down in a chair across from me.

"I don't know he will. But it's a vibe I get from the true believers that I still know. Though it may be coming from his Managers instead of him. They could be creating that vibe because they've had enough. I bet the Managers know there's no fish in the pond. I think they have long lost faith in the saucer business, if they ever had any. What I think they haven't lost faith in is all that money they've been packing away. Some really rich people turned over their life savings to that bozo, Bacon. Some not so rich—and I raise my hand here.

"They know their followers are becoming anxious, and they're figuring out an exit strategy. Suicide, but maybe not suicide for all. Like in that book *Animal Farm,* where the pigs say everyone is equal, but some are more equal than others. Do you know Cowboy's history?"

"No."

"Ex-con, and he wasn't in for stealing cars. His real name is Jack Pleasant. Should have been Jack Unpleasant. I read about him quite a bit once. Studied him when I was still a cop. I had left the cult by then, but I was on the fence, you know. Cowboy came around, so I was curious about him.

"Shitty childhood where his father raped him regularly and his mother didn't care. One night he broke into an animal shelter and killed a bunch of dogs and cats, spreading his anger around. Tried to set the place on fire, succeeded in burning a desk up; a few more animals died of smoke inhalation. He got caught trying to start another fire at a department store. Knocked the window out, set fire to the clothes on a mannequin. He did some juvie time.

"Got out of juvie, had some other scrapes. Mostly starting fires and causing explosions. He likes fire and explosions. Can make a bomb out of a bag of fertilizer and a few odds and ends as easy as baking a cake.

"Later on, as a young man, he and an associate stole a car in Lufkin, invaded a house somewhere around Houston. They shot the husband to death, tied the mother and daughter to a bed, raped them, then set the bed and house on fire. Neighbors saw the fire, heard the screaming. Saw Cowboy and his buddy shagging across the yard to the stolen car. Cowboy had a VCR under his arm. He and his partner got eighty-five dollars, that VCR, and a handful of VHS videos. They sold the VCR and the videos, used the eighty-five dollars to buy crack. Murdered three people for that good time."

"How the hell is he out?"

"His excellent lawyer worked it so the other guy took the big fall and is all set for a needle in the arm. The partner had an IQ of fifty, if you gave it a boost with a step stool. Cowboy talked first and got a lighter sentence. How he managed that defies common sense, but then again, we are talking about the legal system. I think Cowboy is the one that hatched the plan, and when they got caught, he made sure his accomplice was thought to be the instigator. The jury didn't have information about his previous crimes, as that was considered prejudicial. Also, he got Jesus in prison, as is not uncommon for people on the con. He's smart, narcissistic, psychopathic, and wily.

"When he got out of prison, I think he got some relief by joining the Saucer People. Mostly he got a place to stay—three squares and a cot—for being of assistance out there. He worked his way into the position he holds now. Power. It's all about power. Got him a gun and a cowboy hat and a goddamn monkey. Do you know about the monkey?"

"Chimpanzee."

"You do know. Started calling himself Cowboy, and now he's the ramrod. Thing about Cowboy, whatever he's involved in, he's looking for the teat of the thing so he can suck the milk out of it until there isn't any more or he's tired of the taste."

I told him what Kevin had said about the warehouse, that they had been buying food and guns for years, and wouldn't the warehouse be full?

"I've thought about that."

"When you were at Felix's office, you said you did security for their warehouse?"

"Did. Sold the business. I see where you're going. My former son-in-law, Ansel Walton, is who I sold it to. Daughter moved off to California and he didn't. We have a fair relationship, though."

"What I'd like is to get in that warehouse, see what's actually there."

Grover sipped his coffee, narrowed his eyes like a gunfighter at high noon, said, "Let me think about it."

(2 2)

Ablack SUV was behind me for a time, and just as I was becoming nervous, it cut off and went another way. It was like seeing the shadow in the trees that night; it made me skittish. Only it was there for sure, but instead of it being a version of the Men in Black, I concluded it was just someone as dumb as me, out in the blasting wind and the pouring rain.

By the time I got to the cutoff to my property, the storm had stopped, and the sun had decided to abandon evasive action; it was out and warm. Rainwater was fleeing into ditches and dripping off trees along the narrow road to my house.

I stopped at the mailbox and pulled out a fat brown package that had Kevin's name on it as the sender. It was the package he'd told me to expect.

When I got to the house, there was a blue pickup with a blue and white camper fastened over the bed in the driveway, and there was a slim, ginger-haired woman sitting at the table on my deck with her blue-jeaned legs crossed, swinging her foot, as if I were late for an appointment.

I considered I might be having another ghostly visit of some sort, but only for an instant. I got out of the car with my package under my arm, went and sat down at the table, and looked at her. She was nice to look at.

"I came out in the storm," she said. She had a voice like honey inside of steel. "I waited here."

"Sorry, didn't know I was late."

"I don't mean it like that."

"Sounds like you do."

"I'm saying I decided to sit on the porch. It was still raining when I came. It's nice here."

Of course, by this time I knew who I was talking to: The lady Kevin and Grover had mentioned. She was like the girl next door, if the girl next door was not only pretty but had a stare like Supergirl about to let loose with her heat vision.

"Let me ask you this, lady. Why would anyone be out in a storm like that?"

"You were."

"You have me there. Since no one really sells door-to-door anymore, I assume you're here for another reason. Let me show you a mind-reading trick, okay?"

"Okay," she said.

I touched my forehead, right where I was developing another mild headache. "Your name is Amelia Moon."

"That's not a mind-reading trick. That's you talking to people I've talked to because you're trying to find out the same thing I am."

"And you're not, like you've been claiming, with the May Town newspaper, are you?"

"I used that off the top of my head. Made it up. I'd been to see the newspaper folks in May Town, see what they knew about the cult. You know, look at stuff in back issues. They didn't have any back issues. Said they didn't worry about the nice folks out there at the Landing Pad, because their donut shops ran ads in their paper. That paper is a zero. You could find more information on toilet paper. That's a joke."

"I hope so."

"Since I was going to use the newspaper gig, I should have said the Tyler newspaper. That's where I'm from, Tyler. Well, to be exact, Chandler. Little burg outside of Tyler."

"I know where it is."

"I visited Grover because I heard he was the police chief once. I thought he might have some inside poop. He told me he had been a member of the Saucer People, but he and his wife jumped. Saw it for what it was. Dogshit on a stick, I think he called it. That's all he told me. Nice old man. Real sick, he seemed. I could tell he didn't believe me about the May Town paper. Might as well have tried to tell him I was his daughter living in the back room. He was polite about it, though. Didn't say I was lying, but I could tell he thought I was full of it. I did try to work for them once."

"Who?"

"Newspaper. I almost got the job."

"The May Town newspaper?"

"No. The Tyler newspaper."

"You changed gears a little fast. Tried to work for them means you didn't work for them?"

"Correct."

"Almost working for someone doesn't count as a worthy mention."

"I'm writing a book. I've read your book, by the way."

"You say."

"Wordy. But it got its point across. Our East Texas is full of odd stuff. It's got Aryan Nation kooks, weird religious cults trying to raise people from the dead, and then you got these guys. What was it Flannery O'Connor said? 'I know weird when I see it'? But a lot of folks don't know weird anymore. Or won't admit they do."

"Me, I'm starting to be like my big brother. I'm losing sympathy for the happily stupid. Those that have good sense but choose to be stupid."

"I admit I was going to take a more thoughtful and sympathetic route with my book, even if I think these people are just fucking idiots. Today, whatever is wrong with you is someone else's fault. I know I blame a lot of people for my problems."

"That's the free pass, all right."

"You and I could combine our books, our information. I could make you sound a lot better. I promise you that."

"That's sweet. But I didn't say I was writing a book about the Saucer People."

"Snooping around like you are, you're hooked. You're a lot better-looking than I expected."

"Was that flattery to get you something or just a note?"

"Both."

"Okay. You're better-looking than I expected."

"I know," she said.

"Let's put aside our appreciation of our physical attributes, accurate as they may be, and you can tell me why you're really here."

"I said it. I want to write a book. I've been interested in this flying-saucer cult since I was a kid. Cults in general. I wanted to write articles about it, but I couldn't get a job on a paper, an assignment from a magazine. Until recently, I was a dental hygienist in Tyler. Went to school for it. Did it for a whole month or so. Wore me down, looking at teeth all day, breathing in garlic and beer breath. People showing up without brushing their teeth or gargling with something. I quit. Been living off my not-so-substantial savings for a while. While I'm working on my book, I live in the back of my truck, in the camper. I will say this—I'm sick of ramen noodles and tomato soup. Though sometimes I splurge on a granola bar."

"How much of this book have you written?"

"Just notes right now." She stood up, reached in her back pocket, pulled out a cell phone, said, "This isn't mine."

"Okay."

"It belongs to Kevin. You know who Kevin is."

"How do you know I talked to him?"

"Because I talked to him and he told me about you. I think he thought he might bring his camel into my tent. Phone has your name and number in it."

She placed the phone on the table. The rubber guard around it was charred.

"Went out where Kevin died, was looking in the ditch so I could describe the place for my book. And I came across it. It was just lying there. Either the killers threw it there or it fell out of his pocket. I don't know. It's burned a bit. Must have been close to his body when they set him on fire. They didn't notice. And the cops don't seem to have put a lot of energy into securing the scene. Phone still works. Rain and fire didn't kill it. It was easy to get into. He didn't have any pass codes. I just turned it on, and there was all his stuff."

"Kevin seemed like a pretty open guy."

"Your phone number and e-mail made it easy for me to find your address. Kevin had mentioned you to me, said you were a writer, so I felt a connection. The cult has a dark side, Charlie."

"You haven't actually read me, have you?"

"Confession time. I have not."

"But you said you did, and that it was wordy."

"One comment was a downright lie, the other an assumption. There are photos on Kevin's phone."

"I got photos on my phone."

She leaned forward to look at me more closely. Her ginger-colored hair looked to have been combed with a garden rake. It brushed her shoulders. It was quite appealing. She had gold eyes with little brown flecks in them. I'd never seen eyes like that before. She had little strawberry freckles that roamed over her nose and across her cheeks. Her former career as a dental hygienist was confirmed by her excellent teeth. Unlike the bad breath she had talked about, hers was minty sweet. There was no hint of perfume, just a pleasant aroma of simple soap. A nice smell, as Kevin had described. She seemed to be studying me for cancerous moles.

She said, "But do you have photos of the compound?"

"That shouldn't be hard to find online. You can take a tour out there, visit the gift shop."

"It's a lot of photos, Charlie." She leaned back.

I knew she was playing me. I wasn't sure I minded. I said, "How about we go in the house, have a cup of coffee?"

"In trade, I show you the photos, and then why don't we open that package you have together, see what's inside. I see Kevin's name on it."

(2 3)

I f we're going to be friends," she said, sitting at the kitchen table, studying her cup of coffee, "you should call me what my friends call me."

"We're going to be friends?"

"I think so."

"Then what do your friends call you?"

"Scrappy."

"Like Scooby-Doo's pal?"

"The pal was Scrappy-Doo, technically. And he was Scooby's nephew. But no. 'Scrappy' as in 'feisty, determined.'"

"'Patchy. Piecemeal. Not finished.'"

"Nope. I don't consider those definitions. Just the one I told you."

"How old are you, Scrappy?"

"Older than I look."

"So, forty-five?"

"That better be a goddamn joke."

"You against middle age?"

"You can bet when I get there, I'll be happy with it. But I'd rather be happy at the age I am while I am that age."

"Okay. You look twenty-three, -four."

"Ha. Twenty-six. You're thirty-four. I found your birthday online."

"You are Miss Resourceful," I said.

"I am."

"I'm guessing you weren't given the name Scrappy at birth."

"Amelia Moon. But the nickname stuck. I'm guessing you went to Kevin's house, like I did. And before you ask, I wore gloves."

"It was you that took down the crime tape?"

"Doubt the cops noticed. I don't think that bunch could find their ass with both hands."

"You spoke to them?"

"Told them I was writing an article on small towns, sneaked in a question about Kevin's murder. You know, 'Even small towns have crime,' I said. Then I gave them a song and dance about how I would only mention it in passing in my article. Like driving by an acquaintance's house and tooting my horn once. They didn't buy that. They wanted me to focus on the donut shops and the jalapeño festival, which is next spring. Did you know they had a jalapeño festival?"

"You talked to the chief?"

"No, one of the deputies. I think his name was Duncan, something like that. Talking to him was like trying to get a gnat's attention using semaphore."

"Did you find anything of interest at Kevin's house?"

"Did you?"

"Asked you first."

"Fair enough," she said. "I think they killed him there, stuck him in the rug. No real detective work needed for that conclusion."

"Yeah, me too," I said. "I think the chimpanzee—Mr. Biggs, he's called—rearranged Kevin's body parts as well as some of the furniture, and then Cowboy and an accomplice did a hasty cleanup, rug-wrapped him. Someone drove out to that ditch in Kevin's wreck, and someone followed. One of those someones was Cowboy.

Mr. Biggs would have been with him. They burned the body there. I think Kevin got special treatment because they were mad at him for being so talky."

"Kevin mentioned Cowboy to me," she said. "He sounds unpleasant. Are you scared?"

"Starting to be."

"I don't know if I am or not."

"Might want to consider it. Could be time to go back to Tyler and see if that dentist will hire you back."

"I wouldn't go back to that. Construction, maybe. I worked construction a summer when I was young. I think I was too young to be there legally, but they didn't think so. Or didn't know. I think that was it. Possible I lied about my age. I don't recall."

I bet she did recall.

"I wasn't just a flag girl, as they are called. I worked the real stuff. I could lay the shit out of concrete. I could do most anything needed to be done. Interior work, not as much. I couldn't hang a cabinet straight for the life of me. Fell through a ceiling once, you know. That cost me my job. I didn't think that was fair. I had those two faults . . . well, I couldn't do drywall that well either, but everything else, I was your girl."

"Seems to be quite a few things you couldn't do," I said.

"It's all in your perspective. I could tell you some more fascinating facts about my life, but the only one that should matter is I want to write a book about all this."

"Being dead slows the typing fingers."

She shook her head. "Nope. Sticking with it. Look here." She showed me photos on Kevin's phone. Several were of the great mound with the trench around it, the spot where a ramp of dirt had been formed that led up to a dirt wall. The mound was enormous. Another photo showed Bacon's house on a hill overlooking the mound. It was a huge house. Long and high-roofed with buildings off to the side, a few large oaks that had been around since Euro-peans took their first crap in the New World. Maybe before. There were lots of other trees. There were photos of a tall chain-link fence with pines growing close to it. There were photos of chicken houses and of a large pond taken from a distance. A few shots of a small sawmill.

There was a photo of an extremely large man in a cowboy hat. He had a face only a chimpanzee could love, and the chimpanzee was with him, on a chain. It sat on the ground beside him. They both had the same poisonous look in their eyes. The photo seemed to have been taken with the man's full awareness. I could imagine Kevin thinking but not saying: Hey, let me get a shot of you and your prom date.

The photos were good. They didn't really tell me all that much. But it gave me a sense of the place.

"Okay," I said, "now we know what Cowboy looks like, as that must be him, but you're not showing me anything all that special."

"Oh, come on, we'll write together."

"I don't need a collaborator."

"I'm a hell of a researcher."

I thought that over. I had in fact decided to write a book about the cult, just as she suspected. The idea had been growing since the moment I discovered Meg was in it. I had lost interest in the book I'd been writing. And I could use help with research.

Scrappy was eyeing the package I had placed on the kitchen table. "All right," I said. "You're in. I'm in. We're in. But if I think you're going goofy or you're a nuisance, the deal is off."

"Goofy?"

I gave her the phone back, got up, and went to the butcher block. It had scissors in it, along with chef's knives, an assortment of paring knives, and some serrated blades that I had never used. I didn't really know what they were for. Tree trimming?

I used the scissors to cut open the package. I pulled out the contents and dropped them on the table.

A stack of paper. A thumb drive.

Scrappy was on the papers like a duck on a June bug. She started rifling through them. She passed the pages to me as she finished. It was the printed bank statement for the donut shop where Kevin had worked. It contained daily sales and it was all added into the weekly sales on another sheet. Last, there was a list of dates and times when money went into the bank. And there were receipts.

"Is there a note?" Scrappy asked.

I picked up the package and shook it. No note fell out. I looked inside. No note.

"What's this about?" she said.

"I thought you were the intrepid researcher."

"I'm not an accountant, though," Scrappy said. "I'm sure it's important or he wouldn't have sent it. I'm guessing the thumb drive has the same information. Probably printed it out to make it easier to handle."

"I know someone who might be able to make heads or tails of this."

"Who?"

"My brother's girlfriend, Cherry. She's a lawyer, and a good one. She knows about this kind of stuff. She's done all manner of law and was also briefly an accountant. She knows people who know people, so even if it's beyond her evaluation, she can find someone who knows what we're looking at, other than the obvious."

"Should we call her?"

I did that. Cherry didn't answer. I left a message.

"She'll call back eventually," I said.

"Eventually?"

"Reasonably soon."

We had pretty much discussed all we knew about the Saucer People and Kevin. Finally, it was time for me to mention Meg and

Ethan. I didn't have to, but there was something about Scrappy that put me at ease. And I had decided to make her my partner. And Meg and Ethan were part of the story.

When I finished telling her about them, Scrappy said, "You still love her?"

"I don't think so. I still care about her. I worry about what's happened to her. Shit, okay. I got feelings. It might be love."

"And her husband?"

"I don't wish him dead, but he's not someone I worry about. Thing is, whatever happened to her most likely happened to him."

"You imagine the worst, then?"

"Sometimes. Other times I think she and Ethan just went off somewhere and one day soon I'll hear from her. Find out she's living in Northern California running a pot farm. She'll have probably divorced Ethan by that time."

"Is that wishful thinking?"

"Call it experience."

I didn't mention my ghostly interlude with Meg. I felt it best to leave that out of the mix.

"I had a boyfriend once," Scrappy said. "He got hit by a car."

It was like she was referring to a cat she'd had a mild interest in.

"I'm sorry."

"He drank a lot."

I thought another shoe might drop, but it didn't.

"I don't know I got much else," I said. "Truth is, I don't know what to do next. Sitting here talking to you, I'm starting to wonder. Should I put myself in the path of Cowboy and the Managers to find out what I suspect? Then again, Meg may be out at the Landing Pad with Ethan, selling Saucer People merchandise in their gift shop. Can you believe that? They got a gift shop."

"Boyfriend that got hit by a car, he'd been out there, bought a key ring. I still have it. That's how I got seriously interested in the whole thing, that and reading about it. He gave me the key ring, and I got to thinking there might be a real story there. I wasn't expecting all this murder and monkeys and shit."

"Chimpanzee."

She dug in the pocket of her blue jeans and brought out a silver key ring with four keys on it. The key fob was in a saucer shape with a chain loop fastened to it, the keys on that. The key chain and fob looked like it cost ten cents to make in China and five cents for an eleven-year-old to make at summer camp.

"Did I mention that the car that hit my boyfriend killed him?"

"It was implied. Did he believe in the Saucer People?"

"Nah. He just went on a tour. Later I found out it was with another girl. The girl, she was with him when that car killed him. She got run over too. She lived, though. Walks with a limp. Bought a cocker spaniel and lives off Broadway in Tyler."

"How do you know all that?"

"Followed her ass around for a while. Guess I was mad. Like it was her fault he cheated on me. Stupid. But I was kind of a stalker for about two weeks after she got out of rehab. Got to thinking on it, decided I was better off without Billy. That was his name. And she was better off with the cocker spaniel. I don't know its name. We both dodged a bullet. Billy, he didn't dodge that car, though."

"You weren't driving the car, were you?"

"Don't be ridiculous. I'd meant him harm, I'd have beaten him to death. He did get the key chain for me, though. That was sweet. Or maybe the girl he was with didn't want it. Sent it from May Town by mail. All in all, it balanced out kind of all right—except for Billy, I mean. Sad news, that. I didn't mean to imply otherwise. I want that understood."

"Of course," I said.

(2 4)

Scrappy moved to the couch and looked through the pages
Kevin had sent while I ran a glass of cold water from the
refrigerator unit. I sat at the table and sipped the water. From there
I could see the back of Scrappy's head. She had pulled her hair up
and bound it with a bright blue scrunchie. I was surprised at how
attractive I thought the back of her neck was.

My phone buzzed. It was Cherry.

I told her about the pages from the donut shop but not much else.
I slid into the bedroom and told her about Scrappy.

"You trust her?" she asked.

"Hard not to. She knows a lot already, and she's in my living
room sitting on my couch reading the printouts from the donut
shop. I don't know that she's getting any more out of it by going
through it twice."

"I'll take a look."

"Want to come out?"

"I'd go to a public stoning even if I was the one being stoned as
long as it was a change of pace. But why don't you come in? I can
grab Felix and we can go somewhere to eat."

"Where?"

"Meet us at the Jalapeño Tree, and we'll have a late lunch. We'll talk there. Bring the girl. I can call ahead. I've got a friend who works there, so I can get us a semiprivate booth, I bet."

"All right."

I went into the living room, said, "Scrappy-Doo, we have a lunch invitation."

She turned and looked over the back of the couch. "Just Scrappy. I'm not a boy dog. That's Scooby's nephew."

"Neither is he a boy dog. He's a cartoon."

"Who's paying for lunch?"

"I guess we go dutch."

"I don't go dutch or Irish or whatever. I only got enough money to exist on the not-so-delicious stuff I got in the camper. Lunch out, that's not happening."

"My treat."

"Let's go."

(2 5)

Cherry couldn't get us that semiprivate booth. For whatever reason, a Stephen F. Austin State University event, perhaps, Jalapeño Tree was packed tight as a daddy pig in a shoebox. There were lots of people standing in line, a line that went all the way out of the restaurant and around the corner.

Turned out the person Cherry knew wasn't there that day, and they didn't hold booths, no matter what. It pissed her off.

We went to Felix's place and called in a pickup order. About twenty minutes later, I drove over to pick it up. Much faster than if we had stood in line.

When I arrived back at Felix's apartment, he buzzed me in, met me at the bottom of the stairs, and helped me tote a bag of the takeout upstairs.

When we walked into the living room, Cherry and Scrappy were laughing loud and talking ninety miles an hour. I had no idea about what.

We ate and talked about this and that. After lunch, Felix made a fire in the fireplace, which had a real draw and a chimney but was fueled by a gas burner that burned paper logs and was easy to shovel out when the pseudo-logs turned to ash. Felix said he sometimes waited a few days, let it cool, and sucked it out with the vacuum cleaner.

I have a real fireplace in my living room and one outside as well, on the deck, designed for outside gatherings, obviously. I have a cord of wood out there waiting. So far, I have yet to build one fire.

Felix made his stout coffee. We sat and sipped and talked in front of the fire while Cherry looked at the charts that Kevin had mailed to me. I went into detail about my visit to Kevin's sad little house. Scrappy told her similar story. We told them about our talks with Grover. I didn't mention Grover saying his ex-son-in-law owned the warehouse's security company, and that there might be a way in for us. I wanted to make sure I had that one in the bag before I revealed it. Of course, Cherry knew I had something like that in mind, due to our phone call.

Felix asked if he could borrow me a minute. We walked across the hall to his office. He closed the door behind us.

"Damn, man. Scrappy, she's something. Hot, goofy, smart. Where'd you find her? I haven't heard you mention her."

"It's not like that," I said.

"How is it?"

"I found her on my porch earlier today."

"What is she, a stray cat? Did you put out a bowl of milk?"

"She was waiting for me. Says she wants to write a book about the Saucer People. With me."

"If that gal is what she seems, you ought to try and nab her."

"She's not a party prize, Felix. It's not like bobbing for apples."

The buzzer for Felix's outside door went off. He turned to the computer on his desk, sat down, and tapped a few keys. I walked around so I could see.

Two men were in the camera eye. It distorted them a little, but they were big. They wore black clothes and dead-dark sunglasses as if it were a sunny day. We both knew one of them. Gogo Simpson.

The other was Black, shorter than Gogo, but wider. He had some serious meat on him, arms and legs like tree trunks. He didn't bother to lift his head. He stood there with his hands in his pockets. The wind shook their coats.

Felix took his pistol and holster out of the drawer, put the pistol in the holster, clipped it to his belt, and arranged his jacket over it.

"Really?" I said.

"Gogo can be unpredictable, and he hangs with unpredictable characters."

Felix turned on the speaker to the door. "Gogo, you old asshole."

Gogo grinned. His face was a slab of slate with narrow eyes cut into it, a flattened nose, and a wide mouth. The smile seemed as if it didn't belong. But Gogo was a smiler.

"Let me in, Felix, you old son of a bitch."

Felix buzzed them in.

(26)

The stairs groaned and nearly puked two-by-fours as the two big men stamped up them. Me and Felix stood at the top of the stairs, looking down on them. It was like watching a golem and his pet boulder climb the stairs.

When they arrived at the top, Felix and Gogo grinned and warmly embraced, patting each other for guns. They both found one.

The other man stood looking at me as if I were a mail-order bride who had shown up and didn't look like her photo. Up close, I could see his features were a combination of Black and Asian.

"We just ate," Felix said, "but I can make you coffee."

"That would be nice," Gogo said, and we all went into the living room, where the fire crackled loudly. Cherry and Scrappy looked up.

"Well, a pleasant surprise," Gogo said. "Beautiful women."

Felix jerked a thumb at Gogo, said, "I found this pile of shit on the sidewalk."

"Flies were gathering on us," Gogo said. "We got tired of dealing with them, all that buzzing, so we rang the bell."

Felix introduced Gogo, said, "We played college ball together. He came out of college ball and went pro. I did a lot of benchwarming back then."

"He played," Gogo said. "Strong, could knock a buffalo over, but he couldn't run as fast as a dead rabbit. You tossed him the ball, his hands were like smoke. Ball went right through them. Me, I went pro for an afternoon and maybe part of a morning."

"Blew out his knee," Felix said, and waved the men over to some fluffy chairs near the fire. "Before he sprung a hubcap, he could run like the four winds were pushing at his back. How he got the name Gogo, ladies. He could go-go."

"I can run all right now, but it's not the same," Gogo said. "Feels fine. Knees are fixed up, but the edge is off. Know what I'm saying? Your edge off, Felix? I mean, you know, one moment you're sharp-eyed, got good muscle twitch, next thing you know, late at night, you got the remote in one hand, bag of Cheetos in the other, living in your sweatpants and a chili-stained T-shirt. Plumped up some since I last seen you, Felix. I take it you let your gym membership lapse?"

"Don't worry about my plump," Felix said. "I could bench-press you like you were a jug of milk and me with my balls nailed to the floor."

Gogo moved his mouth a little. I guess it was a smile. He took off his sunglasses and folded them and put them in his shirt pocket. He sat down. The other man stood where he was. He hadn't removed his sunglasses.

"This is Plug," Gogo said. "He doesn't talk much."

"I can't see he talks at all," Felix said.

"Now and again, he'll ask to have the heat turned up or down. Other than that, he kind of saves himself. Right, Plug?"

Plug said nothing. Didn't make a move that seemed to mean anything. Fact was, he didn't make a move at all.

"Plug," Gogo said, "this is my old friend Felix Garner and his little brother, Charlie. And ladies, I apologize. Don't know you. But you, Red, with that hair, I guess you're a relative."

"No," Scrappy said. "A friend."

"Yeah? A friend, huh? I'd like to have a friend like you."

Scrappy said, "I have a feeling you might have to be slathered in lard to be licked by a puppy, let alone have a friend."

The fire in the room seemed considerably less warm suddenly.

Gogo showed his teeth. "Oh, I can be lovable, believe me."

"You know," Scrappy said, "I can't quite."

Cherry liked that. The side of her mouth flexed. She kept looking at the pair the way she looked at some poor asshole on the witness stand.

Gogo didn't lose his smile.

In the end, the ladies went unintroduced.

Gogo waved a beefy hand at his partner. "Plug here, he was a sumo wrestler in Japan. He's from Hawaii originally. Went to live in Japan for a while to pursue the sport."

"Is he chattier in Japanese?" Felix asked.

"I don't think so," Gogo said. "Might have helped him go higher in sumo ranks had he been chattier. Him being a Black Jap and all asshole worked against him over there. Still, he rose fairly high in the ranking. Was about four hundred pounds at his wrestling weight. He's trimmed down to three hundred and twenty-five now, without his socks. Cut back on the beer is what he did. Sumos drink a lot of beer. Rice beer, maybe. Shit, I don't know. Everything over there is made of rice and fish and fucking seaweed. Anyway, you can only throw big men out of a circle for so long. After that, you got to have a steady job, right?"

"I'll get some coffee for you," Felix said.

Felix left the room. We didn't have a lot to say during the moments he was out. It was as if we were afraid to use our voices lest we start some kind of cosmic avalanche.

Felix soon brought them cups of coffee. Southern hospitality dies hard. Gogo leaned back in the chair, checked out Cherry and Scrappy as he sipped. He looked at them like he was shopping for fruit.

Gradually the air thawed.

Felix and Gogo talked about the old days. Some football games, a couple nights on the town that had been exciting. The rest of us listened. Gogo and Felix seemed as cheerful as Saint Nick and an elf he was bedding. It was hard to tell which was which.

Plug didn't talk. He cuddled the coffee cup in both hands because his finger wouldn't fit through the cup handle. I never once saw him take a sip.

It was all jolly as shit for a while. Sweet cream with razor blades in it. After Gogo finished a banal story that was only funny to him and Felix, one of those you-had-to-be-there stories, his jovial tone grew wings and flew away.

Gogo said, "I hate to set aside the pleasant memories of the past, but I must."

"I didn't think you were here just for the coffee," Felix said.

"You still make a strong cup," Gogo said. "But no. What we got here is a problem. It's easy to fix. It's one of those back-of-the-teeth problems, like you've broken a toothpick off between your molars and you're working it with your tongue, but it won't quite come loose. You know what I mean?"

"My teeth are fine," Felix said.

"This is important to you and Charlie, Felix. Telling you this so something doesn't go wrong, you know? And the ladies here, it could be important to them as well. I want them to stay cute and safe and without problems." Gogo paused to sip from the cup. "That is seriously stout, Felix. I'll say this, that blend will keep your dick hard."

"Get to it," Felix said.

"I have a fellow I'm working for. Peculiar fellow. Has him a big monkey. Calls himself Cowboy."

"Chimpanzee," I said. "It's an ape. Different chromosomes from a monkey. No tail."

"Charlie took an anthropology class once," Felix said. "Can't let it go."

"You're a regular Jane Goodall," Gogo said, smiling at me. "But this fellow, he's nasty. And I mean nasty. Bigger than me. I don't think he's tougher, but he might not have any hesitations. Kind of a firebug. He'd as soon light a match as scratch his balls. Has the conscience of an alligator. I'm here because me and Felix have been friends in the past. Good associates. Maybe that's a better description. I want to give you a tip, Felix. Believe me, it comes from the heart. It might keep you from considerable unpleasantness."

"We wouldn't want unpleasantness," Felix said.

"No. We wouldn't. Thing is, this fellow, Cowboy, he got word, which he passed down to me, that you and your brother and, I believe, these two fine ladies are meddling. Strong word, I know. I wouldn't have used that word."

"What word would you have used?" Scrappy said.

" 'Nosy.' I think that's the word. Cowboy feels it's got to stop."

"What about Mr. Bacon?" Felix said. "Isn't he the big dog out there?"

Gogo ignored that question. "Cowboy didn't tell me how to take care of business. If it was him doing the business instead of him assigning the job, it could be an ugly situation. I like to do things in a tactful manner. A business manner. Less wet, if you know what I mean. Felix, you and Charlie and your lady friends here, you must...how shall I say it? Get the fuck out of Cowboy's business."

"You're not your own man anymore, Gogo," Felix said. "Hate to see that."

"I'm my own man getting paid my own money for a job I've taken on. I'm kind of new out there. Plug here, he's been with Cowboy a while. He thinks more like him, thinks that we ought to get on with it. You know, discourage you. Right, Plug?"

Plug didn't make a move. Didn't say a word. His breathing didn't change.

Gogo tipped his coffee, finishing it off. He scanned his audience.

"I am going to say this, and I really don't want to say it again. I might not be able to take the time for words again. You need to forget all this business about the Saucer People. Cowboy, he's crazy as an electrified squirrel. Him and that monkey . . . chimpanzee. Who the hell keeps a beast that can literally tear your arms off? And on a dog chain. A bad man, that's who Cowboy is. Him and that monkey are probably fucking."

"I heard that rumor," I said. I just thought I'd throw that in there.

Gogo nodded at me. "As for this saucer cult. The aliens are coming, the aliens are coming! There isn't shit coming. But there are business considerations here."

"The donut shops?" I said.

"That and more. You're outmatched, folks. That's the bottom line. They got power and money and they got crazy. I'm done now. Please take heed, Felix. You too, Charlie."

"Before we all start trembling in fear," I said, "might I ask a question?"

"Why not?"

"Do you know a lady named Meg or her husband, Ethan?"

"I've heard their names. But that's all I got."

Gogo leaned down and placed the coffee cup on the floor next to the chair, stood up, removed the sunglasses from his pocket, and put them on. He nodded at Cherry and Scrappy.

"You're shorter than I first thought," Scrappy said.

"Tall enough," he said.

Plug walked gently across the room and placed his cup on the fireplace mantel and picked up the fire poker.

I saw Felix's hand drift under his coat. I glanced at Gogo. He was watching Plug.

Plug let out his breath, held the poker in both hands, and pushed the middle of it against his chest. He took a horse stance, then inhaled deeply to refill. His chest swelled tight against his black shirt. He began to bend the iron poker across his chest like it was a rubber hose.

When the poker was bent into a U, he dropped it clattering to the floor. He looked around at all of us, one by one, then crossed the room light as a ballet dancer.

Felix went over and picked up the poker, grinned at Plug. "So you had a good breakfast, huh, Plug?" Felix pushed the bottom of the U-shaped poker against his chest, pulled back on the ends of it. You could hear Felix grunt and the metal strain. Felix's coat ripped at the shoulders. Slowly, he straightened the bar. It was a little wavy, but straight enough. He placed the poker by the fireplace. He did it gently, as if it were a snake he didn't want to wake. I thought I saw Plug's expression change ever so slightly, like a motorcycle rider that had swallowed a bug.

"Gentlemen, I think we'll call it a day," Felix said. "Can I escort you to the stairs? Kick you down them?"

Gogo laughed. "You haven't lost your style, Felix."

Gogo and Plug moved out of the room and into the hallway. We could hear them thumping down the stairs.

"My God," Cherry said. "Felix. That was amazing."

"Yeah. I think I may have busted a testicle, pulled my shoulders out of place, shit my pants even."

Scrappy laughed. It was more like a bark.

We heard the front door close downstairs.

(27)

Not talking down to anyone," Felix said, "but just so there are no misunderstandings, that was a real threat. Gogo comes at a thing sideways. I think he maybe is truly trying to spare us trouble. We do have a kind of connection. But trust me, that won't keep him from doing what he feels he has to do."

"He had me convinced," I said.

"But neither of you will drop it, will you?" Cherry said.

"No," I said.

"I like that," Cherry said.

"Suits me," Scrappy said.

"Gogo totally knew who Meg and Ethan were," I said, "and I'm pretty sure he knows what happened to them, where they are. He may have seen what happened."

"I didn't get that impression," Felix said.

Cherry reached over and picked up the mound of papers she had placed on the couch, the ones mailed to me by Kevin. She said, "Now, I need some quiet for a while."

Except for Cherry, we adjourned to Felix's office. We talked about this and that, music mostly, then Cherry came in clutching the pages. She leaned on the doorframe.

"These materials sent to you. I've looked them over. It's the same thing on the thumb drive. It's the May Town bank records. All the money from the donut shops goes into the bank. There are other businesses. Gift shop. Chicken houses. A sawmill. A catfish farm, which they seem to have recently phased out. Even that shitty café you ate at with Kevin. Withdrawals are listed here as well. None of the money is seriously withdrawn for guns or storage goods. There's some stuff spent here for things of that nature, but they aren't stockpiling. Some has been spent for food, but a lot of that food isn't storable. You're saving up for a long trip, you're not going to buy meat and loaves of bread or keep it in a warehouse, even if it's in a freezer, for years. That's food they're eating now. Out at the compound. Payroll is listed here too. It's chicken feed, or, more appropriately, it's chickenshit. People are being paid with a few dollars and a promise of righteous war and heavenly energy on a planet beyond the stars. The profit is in the millions, and the Managers are getting healthy salaries."

"Meaning Bacon's likely not waiting for the aliens so he can take them shopping," I said.

Cherry tapped the pages with her finger. "It's hard to tell what Bacon gets out of all this. I don't know how your man got hold of all this stuff, but the power of attorney for Bacon, for the Saucer People, belongs to Jack Pleasant. Whoever that is."

"That's Cowboy's real name," I said. "And I figure Kevin might have been doing a bit more investigating than he admitted to. They might not have toasted him just because he talked to me and Scrappy but because he stole records and maybe some other stuff. Or someone stole it for him, gave it to him."

"Who?" Scrappy said.

"Meg, maybe. She could have finally seen the horse hockey in the barn, become disillusioned, got hold of some information, and given it to Kevin."

"Kevin didn't say that to me," Scrappy said. "I don't think she did that."

"He didn't say it to either of us, but he did mail this stuff to me. So wherever it came from, we have it. Cowboy has taken over. Slithered his way in over time, gained trust, then slunk his way into the cult's bank account."

"I got a friend who can look at this," Cherry said. "Make more out of it than I can, knows how to do some things that might border on illegal and can find out more than the pages say. I'll talk to her."

"Maybe the chimpanzee is behind it all," Felix said.

"Mr. Biggs," I said.

"Fucking Mr. Biggs," Felix said.

(28)

On the way to my house, Scrappy said, "Your brother seems strong."

"Seems?"

"I think both him and Plug did a bit of a trick there. It's like tearing a phone book in half. You got to know how to do it."

"That may be. But knowing how best to accomplish it still requires doing it. I couldn't bend that poker with machinery."

"I believe you," she said.

"One time he backed up to the rear of a Volkswagen, picked it up, and held the end of it off the ground long enough for his friend to change a tire."

"Dang," Scrappy said.

I thought about telling Scrappy something else about Felix I wanted her to know. I hesitated a moment, and then the hesitation sailed away. Scrappy made me feel at ease.

"Felix always says he quit being a psychiatrist due to being worn out listening to people having daddy and mommy issues. Might be part of it. But he kind of had to quit."

"I'm intrigued."

"He had a practice in Houston. Woman was coming to him for consultation, the usual parental issues, and then she shifted into her present life, revealed to Felix that her boyfriend was controlling her and hurting her the way her father had, and she said she knew it was her fault, so she put up with it. Felix tried to give her strength, convince her it wasn't her fault at all and that she had to let him go. And he was very convincing. She did. Let him go. And that man, a husky fellow, put her in the hospital. Terrible beating. Really messed up her face. She healed all right, but she still has some scars on the side of her face, or so I heard."

"Oh. Awful. What a son of a bitch."

"You said it. Felix took it bad. He was the one told her to leave. He didn't like that his advice, good as it actually was, prompted her boyfriend to hurt her. He talked the lady into having him arrested for what he did, and he was, but he got off on bail or some such. Next day, he started stalking her. Didn't manage to get his hands on her again, but she didn't call the law. She called Felix. He found the boyfriend and left him in a ditch with a broken kneecap, a dislocated shoulder, and a face swollen up like the Elephant Man. Guy came out of that with only two teeth. It rained that night and he had to sit there in a puddle of blood and mud because he couldn't walk. He finally crawled out and a passing car stopped and called an ambulance. Don't remember for sure. He said Felix ran him off the road and beat him up. Felix admitted it. They took Felix in and he paid a fine, and it looked as if he might go to jail, but Cherry, who he had just met—they weren't a couple yet, she was just his lawyer—got him off. Sympathetic judge. Judge's best friend's daughter had been murdered by a similar asshole. But Felix had to throw in the towel as a psychiatrist. He quit, he wasn't fired. But it was the same thing. He took an anger-management class. It wasn't all that helpful, but he went through it. He didn't see what he'd done as anger. He saw it as justice. I don't know which it is, but I know I never lost any sleep over that bastard lying in a ditch. Still, got to admit, Felix can be a bit testy now and then. Maybe he did need that anger-management class."

"Sounds like what he did was righteous."

"I don't know. There's an edge to him. I fear sometimes that he might kill someone."

"If he does, they'll have it coming."

"Maybe, but a jail cell, or worse, wouldn't be good for him. I wonder sometimes if I have the same sort of anger in me. I don't think so, but I got to wonder. My father had that. Never did anything bad, and he was a great parent, but he had that same kind of edge. I think he died of a heart attack because he was angry at the world. Only my mother could soothe him. When he was hot like that, she talked to him like a child or like she was calming down an abused pit bull that she had rescued. In a way, from what I've heard, she did rescue Dad. I don't think people should hook up with people because they think they can change them, make them better, but in her case, I think she did just that. Kept him on a short leash, anyway. Felix does fine, but sometimes, it's like someone has removed the shock collar."

"I have a feeling you and Felix are both okay," Scrappy said. "But to change the subject, what are we going to do now?"

"I think you ought to bail on this business."

"I bail, then I don't write my book."

"You bail, you might not end up dead. Write a different book. It's more personal with me. This is about finding out what happened to Meg. That's all I wanted to know in the beginning anyway. Now it's about bringing down these assholes. Like so many cults, they've turned dangerous. When people believe any crazy-ass thing, they'll do any crazy-ass thing."

"In spite of what Felix said, do you think there's a chance Gogo might be all talk?"

"I do not."

"Why not tell the police?"

"May Town doesn't seem a place that's worried about what the cult does. Some of its officers are members or sympathizers. Long as the cult puts money in their pockets, they let things slide along. Some guy like Kevin, he's nothing to them. Just some goofy kid who got murdered, possibly in a drug deal. That's how they'll see it. That's how they'll want to see it. Still, with what we know now, maybe they'll see things different if we tell them. They're not the only authorities in the world. This is bigger than May Town."

"All those papers show is Cowboy runs the business, has power of attorney. They don't have a thing to do with Ethan or your ex-wife. Not directly."

"Sometimes indirectly can get you there."

Scrappy let that sink in for a while. "Tell me about Meg and Ethan," she said.

"Ethan, I don't really know. Met him a couple times. We didn't hang. Me and Meg, we get along well enough for exes."

"And you said you still have a thing for her?"

"I didn't quite say that. Well, I don't know. I know this much: I think about her. I worry about her."

I surprised myself by telling her about the night I saw Meg's ghost. And her car's ghost.

"Do you really think it was her?"

"I don't know. I worry about myself sometimes. I have headaches. Now and again, I see things, but this was special."

"The stuff about the mound in the circle," Scrappy said. "That must be the mound out at the Landing Pad. As for the omelet, that's an unusual warning."

"Think?"

"Okay. Let's put the Saucer People on a shelf. We can't do anything about it right now."

"Okay."

"What do you like to do? I know you write. Hobbies? Interests? Strange pets?"

"So this is the 'I like to take long, slow walks on the beach' part of our conversation?"

"For the record, I can't stand the beach. I get sunburned and I hate sand between my toes and in my underwear."

"I agree with you about the beach. Us redheads burn. I'd like a dog, but I'm too lazy to own one. I read. Exercise. Ride my bike. Walk. Lift some light weights, stretch. Out in the storage unit, I have a hanging bag. I box it from time to time, but not lately."

"What about other boxers? You box them?"

"Not anymore. I've found the bag is less likely to hit back."

"What else?"

"I have a telescope. I like to look at the stars."

"I've always wanted to."

"Wasn't such a cloudy night, I'd get it out and we'd look. It's like looking into your own past. You know, scientists say we're all made of starlight, and there's the past out there. You're looking at the light from dead stars, and we're pieces of stars, of that energy, anyway. If that's the right term. In the end, whatever animates us, or animates reality, will go back to being what it was before. Or some fashion of it."

"So you do that a lot, look at the stars?"

"Yeah. And read. And write. Watch movies, TV shows. Exercise some. Pretty simple life, and I'm not sure I'm doing good by getting back into investigating. But then there's Meg, you know. Where is she? Has something happened to her, and is this cult responsible? It haunts me."

"I think mysteries will always haunt you, Charlie. I know they do me, and I think that's a good thing. It bounces the starlight in me around. Let me ask you something else. Do you have a lot of sex?"

"What?"

"You heard me."

"Not much lately."

"Would you like to?"

(29)

It had been a while, so I felt a little out of practice on how to handle the situation. When we were inside, I locked the door, started to turn. Scrappy pushed my shoulders back and pinned me against the door. She put her lips to mine. They were so hot, they burned. The taste of fire was surprisingly delightful.

From there, it was like the Hansel and Gretel bread-crumb trail made with our clothes. By the time we climbed in bed, we were completely naked.

She straddled me and put her face close to mine. Our noses touched.

She said, "I think we're going to go there, we ought to have some guidelines."

"Guidelines?"

"Here's the thing. I have a list from A to F. I could probably add more letters, but I find these sufficient, and a couple I'm merely curious about. I used to have a G but discovered I didn't like sticky things like chocolate or honey spread on me. I hate sticky."

"Check. No G. No sticky."

"I thought I'd best mention it straight out. Each one of these letters is something I like to do or might like to do. I'll tell you each, and you tell me which ones interest you or might interest you."

"I'm sort of game in general. Maybe we can just find out as we go."

"No. Listen."

She told me the list from A to F. No G.

"Okay," she said. "Which ones?"

"A and B I'm definitely in for. D sounds good and nasty. I have done that one before. F, I don't know. That's on the fringe."

"What's wrong with C?"

"You like C?" I asked.

"I didn't say that."

"Okay. I don't think I'd like that."

"Score it this way. We are definitely going to do A and B. D if time and energy allow, as I'm hoping you're not a wham-bam-thank-you-ma'am kind of guy."

"Depends on the day. And how long this preparation is going to take."

"C is a wobble. Right? Admit it. You thought: Maybe. Right? But you didn't want to be embarrassed?"

"I guess so."

"That elevates C to performance."

"Does it?"

"F is out."

"Out."

"And I've already said about G."

"I'm all with you there."

"Let's start with B, Charlie boy. What do you think?"

"Definitely B."

B was fun, A was better, and D was terrific. C turned out to be damn good too. We even ended up doing F. We saved it for last.

(3 0)

s I was lying there with Scrappy's arm across my chest, she said, "Does this mean we're friends?"

"It certainly seemed friendly to me. Especially the F part. Though I think I prefer B overall."

"Umm," she said. "I like you have hair on your chest."

"Not a fashion statement."

"And I like that you don't shave your pubic hair. I don't either."

"Think you know I noticed."

"Your nose fit right in there."

"It could have been designed for it."

She was starting to drift. I lay there until she fell asleep, then she rolled away from me and pushed her warm butt against me. That gave me ideas I was too tired for. Our lovemaking had been so intense, I had nearly blown a kidney.

My head had started to throb. I eased out of bed and pulled on my robe and stepped into my house shoes. In the bathroom I took a fistful of Tylenol. I peed in the toilet. I washed my hands and tried to see myself in the mirror. It was too dark. I didn't want to turn on the light. My head hurt too much for that.

I decided on some fresh air. I went out on the porch, but this time I sat on the steps that led to the driveway. It was a little too cold, but I sat there anyway. Sat there and looked at Scrappy's truck and little camper. My head hurt so bad, even the thin light from the moon and the stars was like a needle to my brain.

I squinted. I felt the hairs on the back of my neck rise, and my skin bubbled up with goose bumps.

She sat down by me. Meg, I mean. I could smell her perfume, a hint of damp earth. My insides trembled.

She was wearing the same shorts as before. She had on high white socks and white tennis shoes. She sat there and put her hand on my leg. I couldn't feel it. I didn't turn to look at her.

"You've found someone," she said.

"For tonight."

"Could it be more?"

"I don't know. I told her I thought about you. I lied a little. I didn't admit how much."

"It's okay, Charlie. You need to move on."

"You did, didn't you?"

"That's right. I did. In my case it was a mistake. So, how do you really feel about her?"

"I like her. I want to like her even more. I wouldn't mind loving her. But I still love you."

"I'm lovable."

"That you are. I was thinking about the time you found that mudhole that was full of tadpoles, and you had me go to town, buy a fishnet and a bait bucket, come back, scoop them out, drive them out to the lake, and put them in the water."

"The mudhole was drying up. They wouldn't have lasted long."

"That's the kind of stuff I think about when I think about you."

She didn't have a comment for that.

A frog bleated out somewhere in the woods, near the pond.

Maybe he had been out drinking too late and his wife wouldn't let him back in the water.

"What's the thing about omelets?" I asked.

"Watch out for them."

"Did you bring your car this time?"

"I came on the wind."

"There isn't any wind."

"I came on the wind, Charlie. Are you going to find me?"

I had a hard time saying it, but I did. "Are you dead?"

"I don't know."

I had been hesitating to look at her full on, but now I turned to see her face.

There was no one there.

———

There had been no wind, and now there was. It lifted my hair, fluttered my robe, and made me even colder. I had had enough fresh air.

I eased back into the house, locked the door off the porch, and went back to bed. Scrappy was warm. I pushed up against her.

Like Meg, she smelled nice. Meg wore perfume. With Scrappy, it was soap and water. I stuck my nose into her hair. That smelled different than the rest of her. But only a little different. Shampoo. Herbal.

Jesus. Did I really see Meg's ghost? If I did, she had to be dead. Or I had to have had one hell of a hallucination.

She had touched me, and I felt nothing.

I closed my eyes. I could feel the earth moving. I felt the sky shaking and sensed the stars rearranging. I felt my head slowly relaxing. It was like the headache pain was melting into the bed, falling to the floor, and entering the earth like rainwater. It was going away from me, going down, down, down.

When I opened my eyes there was morning light. It came through a slit in the bedroom curtains. I normally kept those closed tight. But I had opened them yesterday and forgotten to close them. This morning the light was good, like a wedge of fine cheese.

Scrappy still lay snoozing beside me. And that was good too.

(31)

I didn't tell Scrappy about my talk with Meg late last night. After telling her about the first event, I thought that might be as much as she could comfortably digest; hearing about the second, she might decide to make an exit while I was brushing my teeth.

We spent most of the morning trying out some different alphabet letters that had gone unlisted, and by the time we were done, we were starving.

After a non-omelet late breakfast, Scrappy, sitting at the table wearing my shirt and nothing else, crossed her legs, said, "I think we need to talk to the May Town police as concerned citizens. Even if they aren't all that capable, it starts there. Right? We don't really know what they will do or won't do until we talk to them. We're working a lot of rumor and say-so."

Me, I was wearing my boxer shorts and a cheap yellow T-shirt with a picture of a black dog on it. I bought it because the money went to the animal shelter. "Last time I talked to the May Town cops, me and Felix were in a jail cell at their station," I said. "Didn't get the feeling they enjoyed our company. Hadn't been for Cherry, me and Felix would be dealing with a breaking-and-entering charge and might be on our way to being some serial killer's dates in Huntsville."

"I have a feeling Felix might make the serial killer his date."

"That's true."

"Don't you think when we write our book, we'll need to put in it that we did what we could to be legitimate? Because the way I see it, we're going to end up going rogue. It might make us sound better to have at first tried to go legitimate."

"I'm not sure that would make us sound better. That whole jail-time thing always looks bad on your résumé no matter what route you take and where you stop along the way to get there."

"I'm thinking of posterity. We can investigate, make our notes, then later write the book. But we have to put ourselves in a positive light, and by going to see the police, telling them our concerns, trying to work with them, trying to truly understand which side of the fence they're on, we can approach things with the correct mind-set. We put that in the book, then we don't seem like two goobers who assumed the worst from the first."

"I tend not to think of myself as a goober, though in the May Town cops' case, I do assume the worst. But you know what? Now that I'm sitting here sexually satisfied, full of coffee and breakfast, I'm thinking maybe you're right. We should talk to the police. We might actually learn something from them."

"We need to find out personally if the chief over there will or won't help us. We don't really know who's who, as we don't have a program that lists all the players. Maybe they are investigating Meg and Ethan's disappearance. Kevin's murder. They could be. They might not be as incompetent as you think. You could tell them about your talk with Kevin. Leave the bank records out of it. They already know you went to Meg's place to look for her. We just might have the right questions. That could be all that's needed, asking them the right way. Not assuming they're working against us, that they're corrupt. We don't truly know that."

"And we might piss them off," I said.

"Always a possibility," she said. "I don't mind taking that chance."

One thing I had learned about investigations: You found out most things by stirring up the hornet's nest. That's when mistakes were made by others that might prove to be in your favor. Inconsistent stories. Easily detected lies. Finding out who did what wasn't as much about clues as it was about being persistent, or even annoying. Of course, sometimes the hornets stung you.

We showered together and tried an alphabet letter that worked well enough in the shower, then dressed and drove over to May Town, looking spiffy and polished and secure in our nobility as well as sexually satisfied.

By the time we were actually in the parking lot of the May Town police station, I was feeling less noble and not quite as spiffy. Nervousness had set in. I still felt sexually satisfied.

We went inside and asked for the chief.

A sleepy-looking cop with B. BREWER printed on the nameplate pinned over his pocket was sitting at a card table making notes on a pad. He had a Styrofoam cup that he now and again spit into. He had close-cropped blond hair, and one of his eyes looked to have had milk poured into it.

An older lady was typing rapidly on a keyboard. I had seen her before, when Felix and I were there for our visit. She looked as if she might have a stick up her ass. We knew she was the receptionist because they cleverly announced it with a desk placard that said RE-CEPTIONIST. And, in smaller letters beneath that, LILLIAN MAINS.

We stood in front of her desk for a moment before she stopped typing, looked up at us.

"I have a report to finish up," she said.

"It says you're the receptionist," Scrappy said.

"I still have a report to type up."

Brewer called us over to his table. He spoke to us with snuff on his breath, picked up a phone, and talked into it for a moment.

He had us sit on the bench where Felix and I had sat when we were first brought in, before we were given accommodations in a nice jail cell.

Scrappy talked about this and that, but I was so anxious by this point, I wasn't really listening. I thought maybe we should have stayed home and practiced more letters.

It felt like we were there for an hour, but when I checked my watch, I discovered we had been sitting for about fifteen minutes. I tapped my watch to make sure it was working. It seemed to be.

The chief came out. He looked like he looked before, but without his hat. The big revolver was still on his hip. He wore an expression like that of a man who constantly battled constipation.

He motioned us to follow, turned, and went away briskly, as if we might have to search for him if we didn't catch up.

In his office he gently shut the door and had us sit down. We nestled ourselves into a couple of uncomfortable chairs in front of his desk.

The office wall was decorated with cheap-looking paintings of ducks flying up as hunters pointed shotguns at them from duck blinds. On one end of his desk there was a taxidermied duck and on the other end what looked like a mangy beaver or perhaps a possum in disguise or a disintegrating hairpiece. A lot of the hair from it was on the corner of his desk. His big white hat hung on a peg on a post close to the wall. His jacket hung from another peg. Next to that, on the floor, were a couple of dog bowls; one was filled with water, the other looked to have been licked clean.

"Where's the doggy?" Scrappy said.

"He's getting his claws trimmed. They have to put him under for it. He don't like it none. I pick him up later. Makes him grumpy for a few hours. I drive him into Nacogdoches and take him through the Starbucks drive-through for a Puppuccino."

Chief turned his attention to me, said, "Weren't you here a few days back? With another redhead? Big man with a beard, looked like a Viking?"

"Yep."

"Drunk charges?"

"Breaking and entering. My brother and I were arrested by accident."

"You fell into the cop car?"

"No, sir." I told him the tale. When I finished, he pursed his lips as if he might whistle, but didn't.

"Oh yeah. I remember. I don't think it was so much a misunderstanding as it was you had a good lawyer, and a good-looking one at that. She threatened us with a lawsuit."

"You could call this a follow-up to a misunderstanding," I said. "We were looking for my ex-wife and her husband. We didn't feel like their disappearance was taken seriously enough. Still don't. Neither does our lawyer."

"Threats from your lawyer to sue only go so far."

"It's nothing like that," I said.

Chief Nelson looked Scrappy over. "She wasn't with you the other night."

"No, sir."

"Hi, I'm Amelia." She was saving her secret identity as fearless crime fighter Scrappy, master of the alphabet, for when she needed it.

"Hello, Amelia," he said.

"I'll get right to it," I said.

"Please do."

"Meg is my main concern. She's disappeared and I can't find her."

"Yep, you and your brother reported it."

"And?"

"Nothing. We figure she and her husband skipped out on their rent."

"It was paid up."

"Next month maybe they figured they couldn't cut it and left."

"They left all their belongings. Everything from furniture to underwear."

"Sometimes folks just pick up and go."

"She had a job."

"She quit it."

"She belongs to the Saucer People organization, a religion. Could she have gone there?"

"Don't think so."

"Came to that conclusion through tossing the I Ching?"

"The what?"

"Not important. Another thing, possible connection. Kid that was found burned up and wrapped in a rug, tossed in a ditch. I knew him a little, and I was wondering if whoever did that has been found."

"Not our jurisdiction."

"He lived in town."

"Found outside of town. Didn't find any evidence at his house to suggest foul play."

"I think we can both safely conclude there was foul play."

"Not in our town. That wasn't our ditch he was found in. We got ditches, but not that one."

"You had a forensic team look over his house?"

"No, I sent Barney out there. Barney Brewer. Deputy. Has a good eye for that kind of thing. Just one, but it's good. His nickname is Barney Fife, but he doesn't like it."

I didn't want to admit I had been in the house, but Barney with the one good eye? Really? He must have just stuck his head in the door with a patch over his good eye. It was obvious bad things had gone on there.

I moved a verbal chess piece.

"Let me ask you something else. Mark this one up to curiosity, Chief. Do you belong to the Saucer People cult?"

"Are you kidding? Those folks are well meaning but on the fucking gullible side. They pay their bills, stay out of trouble, but they're a bunch of idiots. At least in what they believe. One old chief, Grover Nunn, believed that shit for a while. Embarrassed him to death later on, thinking he got conned. There ain't no flying saucer in the ground. The spacemen ain't coming."

"Cowboy," Scrappy said. "Know him?"

"Oh yeah. Who the hell has a pet monkey that big on a chain? I warned him to keep it out of town."

"Chimpanzee."

"What?"

"It's a chimpanzee, not a monkey."

"He's kind of a freelance anthropologist," Scrappy said.

"Is he now?" the chief said. "Let me tell you something. Those flying-saucer nuts, ones that live out there, they're from all over. They buy food and gas and goods in town. They keep their money in our bank. People come out to see the nutjobs and pay for it, and their money comes back to us. It's like May Town is a carnival, has a two-headed calf and a geek that bites the heads off chickens. They're our sweet spot. It's a wonder, back when the original Bacon came up with that stupid shit, someone didn't tar and feather him and run him out of town. Times have changed. People like stupid shit. Kevin was in the cult, and he ended up dead, but that doesn't mean the cult is behind it. Meg and Ethan, they're gone, and we don't have a clue where they've gone. Have I answered your questions?"

"You've moved my questions around a little," I said.

"Don't push your luck, son. Don't enrage the chief of police. It's not good for you. Hear me?"

"I do."

I had been checkmated.

"What about you, Amelia? You hear me? You got an opinion on this matter?"

"I'm just going to hang in neutral right now and contemplate."

"Look," he said, "I find evidence of foul business or just bad business concerning your ex-wife and her husband or something to do with Kevin being murdered, I'm on it. And if the fellow with the big monkey or the big monkey itself breaks the law, shits on the sidewalk, I'll take care of it."

"Chimpanzee," I said.

"Same thing."

"You should go look at Kevin's house yourself, Chief. I think Barney may have been doing some long-distance viewing on the house. Look in there, you get a picture of things pretty quick."

"You been there?"

"Door was open."

He thought about that a moment, and I was wondering if I was going to regret giving him that information, but he let it slide.

"Unless you're going to give a donation to our police charity for widows and orphans, you can from here on out keep your nose out of my ass. I don't want to see you again unless we pass on the street. We do, don't even wave. Now, take yourself out, and please, when you do, close the door behind you."

"Will you keep us in the loop?"

"Only if you get work at this police department, and I can assure you, you won't."

A bluebottle fly big enough to intimidate a sparrow appeared on the edge of the desk, and the chief, working with great speed and accuracy, slammed a plump hand down on it. When he lifted his hand, you could see fly-goo. He pulled open his desk drawer and took a tissue from inside and used it to wipe his hand.

"Got him. I always get pests in the end."

(32)

"Y ou know," Scrappy said as we climbed into my car, "there are people here in town who voted him into office and keep him there."

"There are people these days who would vote for Cowboy's chimpanzee if it wore a Trump cap."

"What Chief Nelson said about not being in the cult. I believe him."

"I think I do too, but I'll hold off on a definitive conclusion for now."

"What the hell kind of critter was that shedding hair on his desk?"

"I don't know. Nutria. Possum. Beaver. Maybe a weasel. Take your pick."

I had just started the car when there was a tap on my window. It was Deputy Duncan Taylor. I rolled down the window. He was wearing a uniform so crisp, a wrinkle would be ashamed to appear. He had an open box of Animal Crackers in one hand.

"May I visit with you two a moment? It's not a professional visit. A personal visit."

"All right," I said.

"May I sit in your back seat?"

I agreed that he could, flicked the door lock, and he took a seat behind me. I adjusted the rearview mirror to see him better, Scrappy turned in her seat to see him.

"I think you could have some wrong ideas," he said.

"About what?" Scrappy asked.

"The Saucer People."

"Yeah?" I said.

"Yeah. I'm a member, and we are not a bunch of crazies wearing tinfoil hats."

"Okay," I said.

"We are believers. There is an ultimate truth, and it has been delivered, and it has been tapped into, and it has been given to us. It is true because the book says it's true, and Mr. Bacon is our prophet."

"If it is so ultimate and true, why do I not know that?"

"You refuse to. There are evils in our world, thoughts and commands from the dark breed from far out in space, and then there are those of the light. And if you accept the light, then the darkness has no hold, no sway. You are free to be one with the light and to think clearly without earthly interference."

"We're talking aliens from another planet, of course?" I said.

"We are talking the ones who have the answers. Does your life seem empty of purpose? Do you want the glory of transcendence, a fine and perfect place to exist forever as delighted energy?"

"Delighted energy?" I said.

"That's correct. You mock. I can tell. It's in your voice."

I wasn't aware of that, but perhaps.

"Even my family is uncertain. But it takes a death to make a life."

"How's that?" Scrappy asked.

"We die and are reborn. Death and a new life."

"Sounds a whole lot like Christianity."

"But this is real," Duncan said. "Even my family listen to the dark ones. They haven't decided correctly. The thought of leaving them here is overwhelming."

"They don't want to board a saucer?" I asked.

"They are uncertain. But let me tell you this: We are people of peace, but peace is sometimes gained through power. Do you understand?"

With that, Duncan opened the door, climbed out of the car, and walked away.

"I don't know about you," Scrappy said, "but that was so weird, it made my butthole tingle. And not in a good way."

"There's a good way?"

"We have a letter in the alphabet that we have yet to discuss."

"Oh."

"Seems obvious to me that Duncan there is missing the yeast in his dough," Scrappy said.

———————

When we got back to my house, Cherry's car was parked there, and Felix and her were sitting at the porch table. Felix had a key, but if the weather was tolerable, he'd wait there. I knew there was something wrong the moment we arrived. I knew my brother well enough, that even with him sitting, I could tell his posture was off.

Me and Scrappy walked up onto the porch and sat down at the table.

"What's wrong?" I asked.

"There's been a murder," Cherry said.

"Two," Felix said.

"Okay," I said. "We're all here, so who?"

"George Howard," Felix said.

"Who?"

"The guy with all the muscles that I slapped around."

"Oh, shit, man," I said. "You didn't——"

"Someone else did," Felix said. "But that's not the problem. Thing is, he was killed in my office."

"It was bloody," Cherry said. "So bloody."

"I spent the night at Cherry's," Felix said. "We went over to my place this morning. Cherry had some law business at the courthouse about two, thought she'd be closer to it at my place."

"Canceled now," Cherry said.

"We go into my office to have coffee and a banana, and it looked like a blind man had given the place a paint job. Blood splattered all over the walls. Brain tissue. A kneecap blown off and mixed with a piece of pants leg was knocked under my desk. One hand was blown off and had landed on my desk as a kind of paperweight. Probably threw his hand up in front of his face as the killer fired. The knee-cap blown off might have happened after, if George was still alive. Maybe whoever shot him again just did it for pleasure. Heavy-gauge shotgun was used. Twelve-gauge is my guess. Had to have been as loud as thunder, right there in the middle of town. No one heard it. At least, no one reported it. But the place is pretty soundproof.

"An automatic pistol of some sort was lying on the floor. Probably George's gun. He was lying in front of my desk. Though, truth is, I didn't recognize him. There was little to recognize. He looked like a pile of rags that had been used to wipe up red paint.

"We called the cops, started for the living section to wait. There was a pair of shoes outside the doorway, against the wall. A short-barrel revolver was in one of the shoes. Just inside the doorway was George's brother. The revolver would have been his, and the killers put it there. He had been shot through the chest. Looked like it had been scooped out with a shovel. When I saw his face, I knew who was dead in my office. Knew the brothers had come together. The little brother bending to big brother's will. The little brother's hands had been nailed to the floor. So had his bare feet."

"I get it. The brothers had come for you, then someone else came for you, found them instead, and killed them," I said.

"Way I figure it. Brothers had worked out how to get inside, override the lock. Probably got in last night, discovered I was gone, and were waiting. They ate the pizza I had in the refrigerator. I was looking forward to that. I doubt they warmed it up."

"It had pineapple on it," Cherry said. "I love pineapple pizza."

"Pineapple, a bit of fruit is the only sugar I can have," Felix said. "Doctor says I've got to watch my blood sugar. Lately, sugar makes me jump high as the sky, then drop like a meteor through the center of the Earth. I'm pissed about that pizza as well."

I said, "About the brothers?"

"People killed them maybe thought the brothers were us, or friends of mine, or worked for me," Felix said. "That's my educated guess. That means it wasn't Gogo or the Sumo. They'd know us by sight. Probably sent over the B team. Kind of hurts my feelings, them sending in the second string. Whoever it was, they tortured the younger brother to get information he didn't have. The killers got in easy, which means they too knew how to override the lock. I'm going to have to seriously redo that dude. We visited with the cops for a few hours, then they cut us loose, Cherry lawyering us out of there. But they don't think we did it. We could tell. Easy to see the Howard brothers broke in to kill me and her or any of us who might be there. Then someone else who wanted to kill us broke in and killed the less capable assassins. Cops know who the brothers are because we told them. But as for the ones killed them, they don't know. But I do."

"The Saucer People," Scrappy said. It was the first time I had heard a catch in her voice.

"Of course," Felix said. "This shit just got real."

"You did tell the police about the threat from Gogo?"

"I wanted to," Cherry said. "But Felix didn't."

"Kind of take this personal," Felix said. "Cops, I tell them about it, they'll call over to Chief Nelson in May Town, have him check on the Saucer People. Protocol, you know. Chief Nelson will go out there, have lunch with the cult, beat Bacon's meat off while wearing a silk glove, then go home."

"We had a little visit with Chief Nelson this morning, and he may be different from advertised," I said. "But you still might be right about that. He's not looking to stir up the cult, that much is certain."

"Figure I decide I need to tell the cops, I will, but right now, I do that, they could drop a turd in the soup."

"They're cops," Cherry said. "It's what they do. I don't mean turds in the soup. They investigate. They find things out. They arrest folks. Sometimes turds in the soup are involved. I think you should have told them. You didn't break a law by not doing it, but it might have been the right call."

"Investigation is also what me and Charlie do," Felix said. "And we'll do it better."

"I'm retired," I said.

"You're not acting retired. We look into this, we can find out more than they can. We don't have the same rules to follow. We put things together well enough to be satisfied, then we'll tell them."

"They don't like that sort of thing," Cherry said. "It's holding back information and interfering."

"I can't tell them I know for sure who it was now," Felix said. "But if I find out for sure, if I give them those nuts on a saucer, so to speak, along with evidence and a steaming side of Cowboy stuffed up that monkey's ass, then they'll be okay with it. I hope."

I was thinking it, but I didn't say anything.

"Chimpanzee," Scrappy said, smiling at me. "Mr. Biggs is a chimpanzee."

(3 3)

moved Cherry and Felix into my upstairs guest room and then I called a locksmith and security team from Nacogdoches. I paid them extra to put bars over the downstairs windows and had them upgrade the alarm system. They took out and put aside the nice glass-windowed doors and replaced them with solid wooden doors with bands of metal on them. It cost plenty. More than it would normally have cost because I wanted them installed right away. I think the locksmith and the carpenter thought perhaps I was one of those end-of-the-world knuckleheads, bracing for when the zombies came to eat me.

In the closet, in my bedroom, I keep a ten-gauge shotgun and a box of shells. I don't like guns, but that one I had inherited from our father. Felix got a pistol from him. Our father wasn't a gun fanatic. He was old-school. A pistol for moderate firepower kept in the house for protection, a shotgun for squirrel hunting, and he was done. It was before every asshole in the world that had a trigger finger felt it was their God-given right to own a firearm that could punch holes in an army tank and shoot enough times to still be firing when the sun went out and the universe went dark.

I got the shotgun out and cleaned it, which it sorely needed, then

I pumped it a few times, loaded it, and put it back in the closet. The closet was six feet from my bed. At night, if I chose, I could move it to the corner of the wall that was less than three feet away, almost behind the lamp on my nightstand, along with the stack of books I was reading. I also had an ASP in the closet—an extendable, flexible metal rod that could lengthen with a flick of the wrist.

The cops had looked around Felix's office and taken his pistol with them. He took the Irish cudgel I had gotten on a trip to Dublin and carried it upstairs. Cherry had a .22 pistol about the size of a lady's compact with her. It wouldn't stop someone like Gogo or Plug the Sumo unless she was right on target, but it might discourage them a little. Thing was, if they came after us, they wouldn't be carrying the kind of weapons we had. They'd be armed with something serious. Though, from what I knew of Gogo, he'd want to do it with his hands. I think Plug was the same way.

After I'd finished with the shotgun, I went into the living room and found Scrappy sitting on the couch next to an overnight bag from the camper. She looked to be in deep contemplation.

I sat next to her. "Sorry you got involved?"

"You think they'll come here?"

"I don't know. But they damn sure wanted Felix and Cherry, and that means we too are on the list. I think we got a second checkmark beside our names when Gogo didn't get an affirmative that we were dropping it. I doubt he thought we would. That's not the Garner way. We like to not only step in horse manure, we like to track it around on our shoes. Gogo knows that about Felix, for sure. Knows Felix is not going to change shoes. He's not going to change course."

"Odd they're friends, and then they're not."

"Some kind of macho competition going on there. Gogo, he's gone to the dark side, but he's got a code of ethics about him, if you can call it that. Maybe the better way to put it is he has rules to his game. He warned us. Now all bets are off. I think the B team, as Felix called it, came in because Gogo didn't really want to hurt Felix or any of us."

"But he was willing to do it secondhand?"

"I think so. It'll be put in Gogo's lap next time. He'll be the one coming to see us, and he won't come with a smile or ask for a cup of coffee. Cowboy, I think he sees himself as the A plus team, but my guess is, guy like that, liking power, doesn't want to get his hands dirty. Not because he might not enjoy it. I think he would. But dictating to others puts him on a higher plane. Then again, who knows? I'm just blowing wind. Guessing. They might send Mr. Biggs with a willow switch. But at some point, they'll send somebody."

"I don't like the idea of having to be holed up here," Scrappy said.

"I think this is base camp. I think this is where we sleep. But staying here, no. We'll just be cautious."

Scrappy said, "I got this out of the camper. I keep it by my bed." She reached into the bag and pulled out a Bowie knife in a dark leather scabbard. She drew the knife from the scabbard. It was large enough it could easily be mistaken for a sword.

"Damn, that looks badass. And heavy."

"It's balanced. I can throw it, and I studied a bit of knife fighting. I can cut your ass."

"Can you cut bullets in two while they're in flight?"

"I'm going to say no."

"Then it might not be as cool an idea as it sounds."

"Well, I can wear it behind my back on my belt under my coat."

"Okay. That's pretty cool."

Felix and Cherry came down from upstairs. "I talked to the cops," Felix said. "They say I can go home now. They let me send some cleaners in, and they've cleaned up the blood and such. Cherry is going to stay with me, and I'm having the place redone. New paint in the office. Locks changed, more secure door put in, same as you.

I'm going to cut business for a while and hole up except when we're chasing these bastards down."

"I don't want to be imprisoned. I just want to lay down reasonably safe at night," I said. "They want in, they'll get in, but they'll have to work for it. I can see anyone coming close to the house on my phone or laptop, which has an alert on it. Hear Jimi Hendrix's 'Purple Haze' playing on it, heads up."

"I think they're going to be more cautious now," Felix said. "They realized they'd messed up with the two they killed. They hung around afterward, had our pizza, got out of there before morning. Thing is, had they stayed, they'd have caught us coming in. They had the door locked back, so had we shown up, we wouldn't have suspected until it was too late. They knew what they were doing, but they didn't have the right idea of when to do it. So they aren't perfect professionals. They took for granted we'd be home. They should have scouted us for a day or two."

"I'm glad they didn't," Cherry said.

Felix and Cherry had both found places on my enormous couch by then.

"It's not all bad," Felix said. "Cherry has to stay with me."

"Thing like this, even being young, you start thinking about dying," Scrappy said. "Really dying. Not way off in the future, but some time closer."

"True enough," Cherry said.

"You start thinking what family do I have," Scrappy said, "because I don't really have any. Parents are dead. No brothers or sisters. A few cousins I wouldn't want to spend an afternoon with playing dominoes. And I think, How will I be remembered? Who is there to remember me, for that matter?"

"Scrappy," Cherry said. "Honey, listen. In the end, it's not important. It's how you live your life. I don't mean to put down anything you said or sound like I think I'm a philosopher. But nearly everyone is forgotten. Maybe if you have kids, you can say you pass yourself on in a way. But still, that's not you. That's some genetic matter that can be reshaped by circumstance and other genes. I became a lot more content about the whole thing when I realized I was going to die, and that was it."

"What happened to the religion you say you believe in?" Felix said. "Lighting candles. Counting beads. Saying Hail Marys and listening to a guy in a funny hat."

"Episcopalians aren't subject to the pope. Beads and candles, sometimes," Cherry said. "Some days I don't believe in it at all. Other days I think eventually I'll be hanging out at the food court in heaven. Have a slice of angel food cake, of course. Then I think, What the hell? I'm going to meet up with my parents? My grand-father? What age will they be? They died old, and what if I die old? We'll be the same age? Or will they be younger? Will that be part of the reward? Will they be spirits floating around? And if so, what's the fun in that? And babies, children who died—are they babies for eternity? I got questions on days like this."

"For me, it's just anger I'm feeling," Felix said. "I don't intend to be killed by a bunch of assholes and their monkey. I'll deal with them. I'm going to die of old age in my own goddamn bed. Okay, maybe a hospital bed or at an old folks' home with a tube in my dick and an IV in my arm. Shit, now you got me talking the morbid stuff."

"You two coming close to being in the wrong place at the wrong time has set us all off," I said. "And they didn't even get you."

"Don't sound so disappointed," Felix said.

Scrappy said, "Sure you want to go home?"

"We'll soon have two forts," Felix said. "Yours and ours. We can swap out, we get bored. Stay with each other awhile. Thing is, I ought to ask something. I want to make sure that everyone understands that no one is tied to an earlier promise, though there is no doubt I will consider you a liar and a chickenshit for the rest of my life if you don't keep your word. We said we weren't giving up, but that was before they made goo out of those brothers at my place. Anyone wants to try and back out of this whole thing, I could maybe get in touch with Gogo, say you guys are out and done. Might matter. Might not."

"You know I'll stick with you," I said.

"Was counting on that."

"I'm sticking too," Scrappy said. "I'm just feeling sorry for myself. Not so much scared as just feeling I don't want to die before I've done something with my life besides ride around in a camper."

"I may regret it later, but I'm sticking as well," Cherry said.

(34)

A few days crept by. Building our Alamos seemed less like a good idea and more like a large, unwarranted expense. Panic had been in the driver's seat. Now it was replaced by complacency. Had to watch that. Either extreme could get you killed.

Maybe the killers of the brothers had a beef with them, had tracked them there. Perhaps it had nothing to do with the saucer cult, was just a coincidence of massive unlikeliness. And maybe the moon really was made of green cheese and turds you flushed were down below plotting vengeance in the septic tank.

Me and Scrappy spent some time at Felix's place, and they came to ours from time to time, always careful to watch for following cars or anyone that might be waiting for us at our own doors.

At the end of that first week, me and Scrappy had watched enough TV to turn our eyes to stone, and we had screwed until our equipment was raw. We had eaten too much food and not gotten enough exercise, and our nerves were a little frayed, though, surprisingly, neither of us had killed and eaten the other.

I still had not had an omelet. I wasn't reading much. Wasn't writing. I looked out the windows a lot and checked the shutters and doors at night over and over. I sniffed the air for the putrid aroma of overheated chimpanzee.

In time, I took to walking on my treadmill again. For a day or two, it was like I had never done it before, and then I got in the groove. Scrappy began practicing yoga poses on a yoga mat from her camper. She practiced in front of the couch. Turned out she was pretty good. When I glanced at her, my spine hurt.

One day when I was on the treadmill, "Purple Haze" played on my phone, letting me know someone was at the gate. I killed the treadmill and checked the laptop on the table. Scrappy joined me. We saw that it was a white police car. I turned the gate camera with a tap of the keys, and I could see clearly who was at the wheel. Chief John Patrick Nelson. A dog big enough to guard the gates of hell sat in the seat next to him.

I hit another key that buzzed the gate open, and the chief came rolling up the drive. I grabbed my shotgun, Scrappy her Bowie, and we went out on the porch and waited. I wasn't sure I could put my trust in Chief Nelson, but I wasn't exactly frightened of him either. We sat at the table and I placed the shotgun on it, in plain sight. Scrappy sat with the Bowie in its scabbard resting in her lap.

Chief Nelson parked behind Scrappy's camper and moseyed over to the porch, his belly pushing a full foot before the rest of him. He was carrying a large paper bag. The dog lumbered after him, walking in what I think of as a stalking posture.

When the chief stepped on the porch with the dog, he said, "Howdy, boys and girls."

"Howdy," I said.

"You get lost?" Scrappy said.

"Actually, I looked up Charlie's place, or had Deputy Duncan do it for me. Unlike Barney, he has both eyes. I come bearing a gift."

"Not our birthdays," I said.

He set the sack on the table near the shotgun and took a seat with the comfort of a longtime boarder. The dog lay down at his feet.

"I presume this is the dog that had his nails done," Scrappy said.

"Yep."

"That dog safe?" I asked.

"Most of the time. I tell him, 'Mess it up,' he's dangerous. I tell him, 'Stop,' he stops. He knows I'm not telling him to do anything now, though. It's about the words and tone of voice."

"German shepherd?" Scrappy asked.

"Malinois mixed with something else. A bear, maybe. Tag can bite through a baseball bat." Chief Nelson pulled a hamburger out of the sack and gave it to the dog. The dog downed it in a few quick gulps, faster than the chief could pull his own burger from the sack. He went to work on it, eating a little slower than the dog. He pulled out an enormous cardboard container of fries and pushed it down on top of the sack to make a kind of place mat. He tore open a ketchup pack with his teeth and squirted ketchup on the sack to use for fry dip.

The chief obviously had not had a mother who taught him that if you ate in front of people, you were supposed to bring enough for everyone.

"So your gift is you're going to give us what's left of your fries?" Scrappy said. "Though it's hard to imagine anything being left. You got you an appetite there, Chief."

"Have to maintain this belly," he said. "It has requirements. My gift to you, minus wrapping paper and a big red bow, is I've been thinking about what you told me. Been thinking too about what I told you. About how the income from the flying-saucer nuts is much appreciated in town, and I don't want to flip over the apple cart. But I got to thinking, which can be a mite painful, that maybe I'm seeing things as I like to see them in May Town. I'm also looking down the road at retirement, and when I think about that, I get a little tingle in my stomach. I'm not one of those that's going to go fishing every day or play golf. I'm just going to sit on my fat ass for a while, then I'm going to go on a diet and exercise and lose weight, and as soon as I'm fit, I'm going to be an astronaut and donate my pension to the goddamn starving donkeys my wife used to give to."

"Starving donkeys?" Scrappy said.

"Maybe they were abused or needed shoes or some such. I forget. Money my wife gave to them, the donkeys ought to start a charity for retired lawmen. Bottom line here, folks, is what have I got to look forward to in retirement? My wife went down with cancer six years ago. The donkeys have gone wanting. Thing is, I haven't done an honest day of lawing in years. Not really. I get reelected by not doing much. I'm thinking now that I'm not running for office and retirement is around the corner, I ought to do some law work for a change. If there's any to be done. I could go on and run again, but the question is why? Doing another term is more than I want to consider. I don't think there's anything to this stuff you're telling me, not really, but it won't hurt to check. You never know what's what.

"Take for instance ol' Butch Chaney. Damn solid farmer outside of town way back when. Was respected. Went to church with his wife on Sunday. Kids went to college and were doing well out of state. When I was a deputy, he found out his wife was servicing their billy goat. Went into the barn to get a rake, and bam, there she and the goat were. Upset him so much he got his gun and shot the goat. Word is, the former wife still grieves. Butch left her, as forgiveness for such didn't seem an option, got a job in town running a filling station. Still there. In the station window he has a sign that says NO GOATS ALLOWED ON PREMISES. You know, like goats are shopping there, buying gas and grabbing soft drinks. Word is, he won't allow goats to even be discussed."

"Is there a lot of goat conversation going around?" Scrappy asked.

"Can't say," he said. "I know I sometimes go entire weeks without hearing mention of a goat."

"Does this story have a moral?" Scrappy asked.

"Besides don't marry a woman that would fuck a goat? Not really. But Butch wasn't willing to let it slide, and he wasn't willing to keep on keeping on the way he had been. Changed his whole life, buying that filling station. Maybe I should get a goat."

That story floated in the air between us for a while. I know I was having a lot of uncomfortable visualization. I was also thinking the story and its connection to the chief seemed tenuous. Probably he just wanted to get that goat story off his chest.

"In some ways you sound like a prime candidate for joining the Saucer People, Chief," Scrappy said. "I mean, with all the life plans you don't have. Except maybe buying your own goat. And with a taxidermied rat on your desk—I mean, you know, I got to think maybe you'll be sitting next to one of the saucer pilots."

"Unlike the true believers, I'm not an idiot. At least a goat would be real."

"Permission would need to be asked of the goat, though," Scrappy said.

"Yeah," he said. "Maybe something in writing about it being consensual. Sealed with a kiss. As for the taxidermy, it's inherited, and that makes it all right. And I think it's a mink. Who ever heard of a rat that big?"

I started to tell him about Gogo and the Sumo, the murders in my brother's apartment. But I hesitated.

"I said I came with a gift, and here it is," Chief Nelson said. "The Saucer People have a get-together planned. My deputy Duncan, he's one of those nutballs, and he invited me. Looking for recruits, as usual. I'm going out there. You two can come with me in a kind of ride-along. Guess they're going to talk about which seats you get on the saucer if you join up, where the vomit bags are, rules about seat belts. Vegan meals heated by ray gun. I don't know."

"We are writing a book about the cult," Scrappy said. "And a ride-along would be appreciated."

"Let me tell you why I'm really going," Chief Nelson said. "I went over to that Kevin's house. Yeah, Barney must be blind in both eyes. That wasn't just a wild party went on there. Another thing, billboards went up this morning around town, signs here and there. There's even a sign in the station next to the NO GOATS sign. Bunch of folks walking the streets, standing on street corners with placards spouting slogans. It's gone from Mayberry to Twin Peaks all of a sudden. I know a lot of those people. Remember when they had common sense. Signs they're carrying say things like JOIN US IN PARADISE and WHAT IS THIS WORLD WITHOUT HOPE? and THERE IS A PLACE BEYOND SPACE AND TIME, AND IT IS GLORIOUS. Whole thing makes me nervous, and it would do me good to talk to someone smarter than a toe wart. You two are at least that. You want to go out there with me, be at my office three thirty tomorrow afternoon. They're having a meeting of members and recruits out there at five. We'll go out there, listen a bit, rove a bit. Look around. See if there's anything fishy."

"Won't you need a search warrant for the looking-around part?" Scrappy said.

"Doubt it. I'm not going up to the house to look under the bed or go through Bacon and his wife's underwear drawer. I've got some warrants in a drawer if needed. Judge I know is fucking the mayor's boyfriend when the mayor isn't. Learned that by accident. No need to get into that. Judge knows I know about it, and him with a wife and four kids and a sickly dog. He knows that kind of information could put him out of a job, so he was kind enough to sign a bunch of warrants for me in advance. I need one, I fill it in how I like. Haven't used one in ages, but he's still a judge and they're still good, and he's still fucking the mayor's boyfriend. His sickly dog may have passed, now that I think about it. But he's still got the wife and kids to worry about. His job in May Town is like being hired to cash checks. Same with mine, really. Those warrants, long as he's a judge, are like timeless coupons for a barbecue sandwich. I take one out of my desk drawer, blow the dust off, write out what I need, and we're good to go. Anyway, I've put the offer to you two."

"We'll consider," I said.

"Show tomorrow, leave the sword and shotgun at home. Might want to bring some supper money. Better yet, pack a granola bar, make a sandwich, fill a thermos with coffee. I don't know they'll be serving out at the Landing Pad or selling anything to eat, and we'll be there at suppertime. Better to have something and end up feeding it to Tag here than not to have it and go hungry."

(35)

Chief Nelson waddled off the porch with his bear and drove away.

Scrappy said, "Think we should have mentioned to him that people are trying to kill us as well as Felix and Cherry?"

"I thought about it and didn't. I think him doing this is a whim. Maybe he's with them on this, and we'll end up in a ditch wrapped up in a smoking rug. We got to consider that. Did he really get bored and decide how about a ride-along out to the Landing Pad with people he doesn't know, or is he setting us up?"

"He sounded pretty sincere. I think we've misjudged him. I think he's lonely. He's played that good-ol'-boy act so long, all he can attract are good ol' boys that want to talk about football, deer antlers, and making their own ammunition."

"Sounding sincere and being sincere aren't necessarily the same thing."

"True enough. When I was a slip of a girl, a boy told me if you kissed a frog, he would turn into a prince. I made him kiss one, and he was still the same asshole he was before."

"It's the frog that's supposed to change into a prince."

"Yeah? Don't remember it that way. Anyway, a bit of my natural trust was lost after that."

"Veering from frogs and back to the question at hand, do we go out there to a meeting of the Saucer People with a man who has a gun and a monster for a dog and a rotting weasel on his desk? Cowboy, Gogo, they aren't fans of ours, and Gogo and the Sumo gave us a warning. We show up in their midst, it's like we've come gift-wrapped. Is that smart?"

"Couldn't we tell your brother and Cherry what we're doing, then tell the chief we told them, just to show we got people knowing where we are?"

"I don't know how much that would scare him, if he needs scaring. Even if he's straight as an arrow, things get sideways, he might not be able to protect us. I wouldn't want to measure his fat ass up against Cowboy, Gogo, or Plug."

We let it stew for a while. Scrappy went back to yoga.

An hour later, I called Felix and told him about Chief Nelson, what he had offered.

"I don't know, little brother. Sounds to me like you're putting your dick in a sausage grinder, standing there waiting for Cowboy's monkey to turn the crank."

I sighed. "You do the monkey thing just to irritate me, don't you?"

"Could be."

"I'm scared, Felix. I won't kid you. Scrappy, she's for it. She's ready to pack a sandwich tomorrow and hit the trail."

"Where is she?"

"Downstairs. Doing yoga. I'm considering working on my will. You get my leather-bound Sherlock Holmes and all my old underwear if I die."

"Yeah? The red leather ones?"

"Books or underwear?"

"I'll take either. Wait. Boxers or briefs?"

"I'm not really making out a will, Felix."

"Oh."

"I called for advice, man."

"I'm not sure I have the right advice, but I have a suggestion."

"Lay it out."

"I go too. That puts me and you and Scrappy and maybe the chief, if he's telling the truth, against them if it all goes south. I doubt the bulk of the congregation is in on murder, so to speak. I think the dangerous stuff comes from Cowboy and the Managers. Maybe Bacon, of course. I don't know about his wife. I think the monkey is a follower. Anyway, I should probably go with you. Might mention we have informed our lawyer, Cherry the Shark, we're going out there. I think the chief and his department might be a bit afraid of her. I know I am."

"Adding you to a possible fatality list doesn't seem like a real solution."

"Little brother, you die, I die. You first, though."

(36)

You can bet with me and Scrappy working on the alphabet come bedtime and me worrying the rest of the night about our upcoming trip, nursing one of my headaches, I didn't get much sleep.

I admit it: Right then I missed my parents. I wanted to talk to them about the mess I was in and how I got into it. I wanted my mother to hold me and say it would be all right.

But my father was long gone, knocked back into the void due to a heart attack. My mother was in Tyler still, but in a rest home with her mind sailing the dark corridors between loss of memory and time, the wind hard in her sails, carrying her onward to her final destination. If I were to call her, she couldn't take the phone, and if she could, she wouldn't know who I was or what I was talking about. I hadn't seen her in over a month. I felt guilty. My only faint consolation was she didn't remember me enough to know when I was gone. Most likely, she didn't miss me at all.

Guilt seemed strong that night, knowing that I might get big-time dead and would leave her without someone to hold her hand. Felix would do that if he could, but I figured we went out there and things went sideways, both of us, along with Scrappy, would have a smoldering rug of our own, be found with gunshots and chimpanzee bites lying in a ditch with disconnected arms and legs.

Scrappy, though, was made of sterner stuff. After we finished practicing our letters, she went directly to sleep, snoring a bit but not moving until morning light.

The morning and the day crawled by. Scrappy slept two hours later than I did. About two in the afternoon, after we'd had a lunch of macaroni and cheese and split an avocado that was maybe a day short of becoming a source of food poisoning, Scrappy was at the counter smearing peanut butter and jelly on bread. She had cut off the crust where it was moldy. I certainly needed to go shopping.

"You're really making sandwiches for our trip?"

"For me. You, you're on your own. I don't want to get hungry. I get pissy when I'm hungry. You have any chips?"

"I do not."

"I always think a sandwich goes better with chips."

"Then you're in for a disappointment."

"We could leave early, stop and get some on the way."

"If we must."

"You sound grumpy, Charlie. Wasn't last night okay?"

"Sorry. Last night was fantastic. I have a headache and I didn't sleep well, and I'm fearful that they're going to give us to the chimpanzee as toys. I think this could be the worst decision of our short lives. Could you make me one of those?"

"I'd be uncertain how much peanut butter and jelly to put on it."

"How about one like yours?"

"Very well, but don't expect me to take over the cooking and the maid service."

"You're not cooking, and your clothes are strung all over the bedroom, so no one in their right mind would accuse you of being a maid. You got toothpaste in the sink. You could scrape those chunks out of there and use them for breath mints. Leave them a few more days, you could maybe stack them together for a little wall for an ant farm."

"I had an ant farm. The ants died. No one told me you had to put stuff in there for them to eat. I guess I thought they went shopping or something. I mean, the ant farm had a little ant town built in there. I remember one of the buildings had POST OFFICE written across it. I could imagine a little ant in a little mailman suit, roaming about with letters for little ant mailboxes. They all withered up and died, though. I felt bad about it, but what're you gonna do?"

"Feed them."

"Oh, by then they couldn't eat."

"I meant before."

"Little late to worry about it now, don't you think?"

"Never mind."

"I'll make you a sandwich, but you're going to want those chips. Wait. Think they sell soft drinks out there? Milk would be better."

"I don't know they got a supermarket, Scrappy. They're flying-saucer nuts, not Kroger."

"Gift shop. They got that. They're bound to sell soft drinks or water. But milk with peanut butter, that's my favorite. I guess buying little cartons of milk when we get the chips wouldn't be a good idea? I mean, it might spoil in the car. Though, in this weather, maybe not. What do you think?"

"I have no idea."

"You're a big guy. I'm going to double your peanut butter. Twice what I have. That okay?"

"Yes. You do know this could be dangerous, don't you?"

"My middle name is Danger."

"I doubt that."

"Do you really want to stay home?"

"Thinking about it," I said. "This is like putting your head in a lion's mouth to check its bite ratio."

"It will certainly be interesting. Wait—I made you a sandwich, so should I make Felix one? We get ours out to eat, and he's there with his bare face hanging out and no sandwich, I'm going to feel bad. Though, I've got to say, men with beards, peanut butter and jelly—not a good combination."

"It makes you feel better, I'll call and tell him to bring his own picnic supplies."

"Hey, ask him about chips. He might have some."

(37)

Felix didn't have any chips, but he had what he called a pocket pistol. He made the pistol live up to its name by pushing it into his coat pocket. He showed it to me before it went back to rest in that loose receptacle of cotton and rayon.

It was a revolver. Felix was a fair-to-middling shot. I'd have a better chance using it to try and beat someone to death.

Cherry had packed up and fled to Houston for a few days to hole up in a hotel room and go deep into those spreadsheets, see what little surprises they might reveal. She had some connections to call, experts in financial forensics. Some of her experts were completely legal, and some were not, but they all owed her favors, Felix said.

We rode over to May Town in Scrappy's camper because she wanted to fill it up with gas. Stopped off at a station/store just inside of town and bought Scrappy her chips and threw the peanut butter sandwiches away and bought some premade ham-and-cheese sandwiches on bread that didn't need trimming for mold, then filled the camper truck up with gas.

In the store window we saw the sign about NO GOATS and one that spoke of saucer redemption or some such. It wasn't really a sign so much as a one-page pamphlet taped to the glass.

We had already seen our first Saucer People advertisement on a billboard placed by the city-limits sign: THEY ARE COMING. DO YOU WANT TO KNOW ETERNAL PEACE AND HAPPINESS? There was also a number to call. Way I felt that day, I was tempted.

In town were more billboards. We didn't see anyone carrying signs.

We found Chief Nelson in his office decked out in a pressed white shirt with his badge shined and his gun prominent in its holster. He was wearing his hat. It looked freshly blocked and brushed.

The shedding mink had shed even more. If the mink were alive, Rogaine would be recommended. The duck on the other end of the desk looked just fine except for being deceased.

The chief gave Felix the once-over, said to me, "Your brother, right? I didn't get his name night you were in jail. Or rather, I did, but I've forgotten it."

"Felix," my brother said.

"I didn't really want to know. It was a brief moment of me trying to be polite. What are you here for?"

"I'm going with you," Felix said.

"You are, are you?"

"We thought one more wouldn't hurt," I said. "It'll be okay, won't it?"

Chief Nelson studied Felix for a moment—trying to determine his character, I guess.

Felix said, "Is that a weasel?"

"Mink."

"Aren't they some kind of weasel?"

"I don't know," Chief Nelson said.

"It's nearly bald," Felix said.

"It was inherited. Yeah, you can go, but no more criticism of my mink. You don't have anyone else outside waiting in the car, do you? A cousin or such?"

"Nope," Scrappy said. "We're it."

"What's in the sack?" Chief Nelson said.

"You said to bring our supper," Scrappy said.

"Yeah, and me telling you didn't help me remember to bring anything."

"Oh," Scrappy said. "Charlie will give you half of his, and you can divide the chips."

I gave Scrappy a look, but she was elusive with her eye contact.

"Tag!" the chief said.

The giant dog came through an open door off the office with the confidence of a lion in a roomful of rats. He sat and licked his jowls with a tongue like a wet bath towel.

"Let's go," Chief Nelson said.

With Tag following after, we went out to the chief's personal car, not a cruiser. Scrappy, Tag, and me were in the back seat, Felix up front in the passenger's, Chief Nelson behind the wheel.

From time to time, as we rode, Tag would turn and study me. I think he felt crowded.

(38)

Chief Nelson's car had an old-style CD player, and there were stacks of CDs in a container beneath the armrest. He was playing a Wagner piece, and somewhere in the middle of it, Scrappy said, "I used to play triangle."

"You mean hit on it," Chief Nelson said.

"That's the view of an amateur," she said. "It takes skill and timing. Lot more complicated than the layman thinks."

"Sure," Chief Nelson said. "I can beat on an aluminum chair with a pencil and get that sound without training. If Tag had thumbs, he could do it."

"I doubt it," Scrappy said, and she decided to look out the window. I think she was insulted that her musical skill on the triangle had been questioned. I was trying to determine if the triangle really did require skill.

Tag had taken to licking my hair. I was developing a dog lick, as opposed to a cowlick. I pulled my pocket comb out and arranged my do, but after a half dozen times, I gave it up. Tag leaned on me. I put my arm around him.

Glancing in the rearview mirror, Chief Nelson said, "He's quite affectionate if you don't piss him off. And I'll tell you this, so you'll know: He's too young to date."

We rode to the music of Wagner's Valkyries flying high, finally drove down a blacktop that looked to have been freshly oiled, then cruised through the thickening woods as the sun set, though there was still enough light not to need headlights.

We continued along the blacktop until it became a thinner road and more of a driveway. There was a wide metal-bar gate, and it was open. Cars were filing in ahead of us. There were people on both sides of the gate wearing orange jackets, waving us in.

By the time we arrived where the get-together was happening, the sun was completely dead, but there were a large number of lights on high poles bright enough to mistake for daylight.

We parked where a lot of other cars were parked on about four acres of concrete lot. From there we could see a great mound rising higher than any American Indian mound I had seen before. There was a hard clay trail around it with a metal railing. In several spots there were gaps in the railing that led down to concrete steps that ended on a lower, narrower trail that ran tight around the mound.

I have to say, it was a stunning sight, those lights and that mound, all the bugs swarming the lights, forming wobbling halos. And out and beyond, tall trees, mostly pines.

People were talking as they walked, descending the steps, strolling around the mound, reaching out with eager hands to touch it, its sides glazed hard by sunlight and time.

I didn't see anyone I knew, certainly not Meg or Ethan. No Gogo, Plug, or any of the Managers who were supposed to exist. I didn't see Cowboy or Mr. Biggs either.

Up on a higher and wider hill above it all, I could see a great three-story house. It had a long porch visible from the front and both sides, and it most likely wrapped around the back of the house as well. I bet that house was ten thousand square feet or more. I couldn't see how far it extended in the rear.

The design was simple, but it was impressive, though a bit of paint wouldn't hurt. The long rows of windows, top and bottom, caught the light from the poles. There was only one light in the house that could be seen. It shone through one of the windows on the second floor.

Near the house, visible to the left, was a row of long, narrow chicken houses. They were made of wood and aluminum with open shutters that let air in through windows covered in wire grates.

On the right side of the house was a long, low row of what looked like barracks. Near the barracks was a sawmill that I surmised had only a short time before thrown its off switch because there was a mist of sawdust in the air that looked like fairy powder under the pole lights.

On a lower tier of dirt than the house and mill was a saucer-shaped building with a sign that said CONTROL CENTER. It had a blinking blue light on its roof. The windows were made to look like portholes; they went all around it and were lit up like a cheap aquarium. I could see people moving around behind the glass like fish. I assumed the Control Center to be the gift shop.

Tag sat beside me as I looked. For a dog, he seemed impressed. Perhaps he might like a flying-saucer key chain? I thought I might ask him. It would look cool hanging off his collar.

Scrappy, who had been wandering, came up beside me, patted Tag on the head, said, "Not what I expected."

"Me either."

Chief Nelson and Felix were still wandering about, but as we stood there looking at the house and buildings on the hill, they joined us.

Felix said, "I don't know if I'm impressed or weirded out."

We all turned and looked at the mound. The folks in orange jackets were answering questions and perhaps giving a bit of information about what was supposed to be under all that hardened dirt and clay. I couldn't really tell for sure; they were too far away to hear properly. They patted children on the head, shook hands, and, in some cases, hugged the adults.

"Cattle," Chief Nelson said. "Shall we join them?"

"Moo," Scrappy said.

We went along with the others, fell into a long line that was buzzy-bee talking. The line moved rapidly. We arrived at a gap in the railing, marched down the steps to where we could touch the mound, and did. It felt like a ceramic bowl.

No one was leading our group, but we all seemed to know what to do. We walked around the concrete walk, which wound about and out through a railing on the other side.

In time, people began to leave the circular path, some wandering up to the gift shop. We went back up as well. A few cars left, people satisfied with having seen the mound and the gathering of nuts.

An announcement was made. It came from a loudspeaker that blasted from the house. There was no one visible, just a voice on a speaker tucked away somewhere.

"Please enjoy our site. Be careful what you touch. The Control Center gift shop is open. Simple food is sold along with memorabilia. An announcement will be made in half an hour. The gift shop will close temporarily, and Reverend Bacon will speak to you. This is a rare moment. There will be a treat for all of you who remain after his announcement."

"Reverend?" Felix said.

"I guess they could have called him Professor or Grand Poopoo," I said, "but instead they settled on a title East Texans have grown up with."

"Asshole might be a better title," Felix said.

"Grand Asshole," Scrappy said.

"Super Grand Asshole Reverend," Chief Nelson said.

"Tag," I said, "an option?"

Tag was silent on the matter.

(39)

Trying to absorb all of it, we made a trip up to the gift shop. You got up there via a long flight of twisting stairs with railings. There was a ramp on one side for wheelchairs. There were a few of those rolling up the ramp, all the chairs motorized. We arrived there with Chief Nelson huffing.

"Need to drop a few pounds," he said.

"Maybe more than a few," Felix said.

"Better hope I never pull you over," Chief Nelson said. "Because I'll remember that."

You couldn't get much kitschier than that gift shop. It had key rings and earrings and dog collars and cat collars, a thousand other useless trinkets.

Tag stayed outside sitting next to a bench that Chief Nelson was occupying. Maybe that was because Tag was the kind of dog that wanted that collar, a key ring, some knickknacks. Perhaps he could be expensive. And who was going to tell him no if he asked for something? Or maybe they sat out there because Chief Nelson had waddled himself into a nearly collapsed lung.

We looked around for a while, watching the workers behind the register cheerfully ringing up sale after sale. You'd think with Armageddon on the way, they'd just give that stuff away. But nope.

We sat on a circular bench inside to consider whatever it was that we were considering. Above us, attached to wires, was an air-filled balloon in the shape of a flying saucer. The walls blinked lights: blue and white, red and yellow.

There came a brief alert from the loudspeaker that the moment had arrived for us to be addressed by Reverend Bacon. The gift shop was closing.

We went outside, where a guy in a nice orange jacket pointed us down the hill. Chairs had been rapidly set up in long rows with wide spaces between the rows. They were arranged quite deep, almost to the slope of the mound. Orange jackets were still setting some up, making deeper rows.

We found a spot near the center of what would become the front line. Tag sat down right beside me, leaned on my leg.

I saw a large woman dressed in black standing on the porch of the house. She had features like the faces on Mount Rushmore but less animated. Later, a man in black came out and sat in a glider on the long porch and looked down on us like one of the Olympians.

Managers.

There was a bit of soft music crackling over the speaker. "Fly Me to the Moon." I almost laughed, but no one else was laughing.

A young fellow came over, said, "Chief."

It was Duncan. Almost hadn't recognized him without his uniform. He seemed even stranger than that time he had sat in our car. As if he were walking on eggshells and trying not to breathe razor blades. His face was dotted with beads of sweat, and his hair was damp. He had a look in his eyes like a man that had suddenly realized he had crapped out his innards in the toilet.

"Duncan," Chief Nelson said. "Thought we'd see what it was all about."

"Yeah. Yeah. It's wonderful, Chief. I see you two and this big fellow are here to see what it's all about. You will be transformed."

I could smell liquor on Duncan's breath. People in New Zealand could have smelled liquor on his breath. One more drink, and astronauts in the space station could have smelled liquor on his breath. He was sweaty and wobbly and his hand trembled as he raked his fingers through his sweat-wet hair.

"Your family here?" the chief asked.

Duncan eased close to Chief Nelson. "They aren't believers. I tried to get them to come. They wouldn't. I told them there was to be a big announcement. They used to come out with me, you know. We could have all been saved. But now they got other ideas. I think it's the TV, you know. It distracts. It'll just be me."

"What ideas do they have?" Chief Nelson asked.

"Mary, she said just this morning that I was full of shit."

"Ever wonder if you are?" Felix said.

"What?"

"Wonder if you're full of shit?"

"No. I mean, sometimes, yeah. But what else is there? What is out there besides this?"

I thought that was a sad way to look at things. And it was obvious that Duncan seemed a lot less certain than before. Or maybe that day in the car he had been desperately certain, like a drowning man in the ocean grabbing at floating straws but knowing full well they were unlikely to support him.

"Prepare to listen" came a voice. Everyone went silent. I looked up at the porch, but there were only the two Managers. The voice had come through a hidden speaker.

The speaker crackled, then there was a rustling. Eventually the voice continued.

"There comes a time when all bad things must become good. There comes a time when the flesh of the body must melt away.

There comes a time when bones are nothing but the lumber that frames our house. There comes a time when the skin that fits the frame must rip and fall away. There comes a time when the soul must be released like a flock of birds. A time when we must win a holy war through force of spirit to be happy and free and eternal. Are you ready for that time?"

The response from trained followers among our group came so quick and loud and in unison, I nearly crapped my pants. Tag did a little hop.

"Yes!"

Glancing back, I could see there were plenty in the crowd as startled as I was. Like us, they were here for the amusement, not religious conviction.

When the words came over the speaker, they were sharp in my ears: "Three days. Three days until our glory. Can you say it? Three days!"

"Three days!" came the crowd's reply.

"You're ready?"

A blast of voices came with "We're ready!"

"This is not a drill like before, when some thought the prophecy failed. That was a drill. To count the faithful. To lose those with doubt. But now, the moment is truly nigh. The skies will soon illuminate with the lights of our liberators. We will enter our ship of assignment, and we will go to the fight. And then we will go to paradise. Paradise. Say it."

"Paradise!"

I thought: Doesn't this sound silly to them? Then again, there were those who believed in the Rapture. That God would jerk the righteous out of their clothes and pull them to heaven, leaving the wicked behind. It all seemed sad to me.

The voice from the speaker said, "In three days' time, you must come here in the early morning. You need only the clothes on your back. Well, perhaps a change of clothes and some toiletries. Weapons and food that we have been gathering for oh so long will be here. We will meet and send our blessings to the sky, await the arrival of our redeemers, perhaps by midday, perhaps by nightfall. The craft in the mound will break free of its earthly containment. Its doors will open. It will be filled with food and weapons by the Managers. Three days' time. Say it!"

"Three days' time!" came the cry.

"What has needed to be said has been said. What is next is next. The great moment itself. Let us offer to you our earthly nectar and ambrosia and feel the reverberations of the soul of our original visitor, down there in the spacecraft, waiting. Feel the soul of my father, feel my soul, feel the cries of need that come from across the universe. You will be transformed with the power and insight of their souls, and you will be with them soon. Inside the ship you will fall asleep until arrival. And then the just will make all things just, and our paradise will be permanent. We have a great and glorious journey and adventure ahead of us. Let us heed it. Let us rejoice. Let us accept that some we care about will be left behind. And we, the true believers amongst this gathering, will pay our dues to live forever in paradise."

From atop the hill came at least a hundred men and women in orange jackets. They carried foldout tables. Some had stacks of cardboard boxes on pushcarts, and there were shiny metal urns. Down the concrete ramp they came, carrying tables, pushing carts.

Tables were placed in front of the chairs and mounded with the boxes and the urns. It happened fast.

"Enjoy this treat. Be blessed. And return in three days' time."

Duncan sat in the row with us. Tag was still sitting on the ground next to me.

What was in front of us on the table were open boxes of donuts, paper plates, cups, and urns of coffee. We were poured coffee. Donuts were put on our plates. Tag sniffed the air.

"Their version of loaves and fishes," I said to Scrappy.

"I wouldn't drink or eat anything," Scrappy said to me. Added: "Remember Jim Jones."

Duncan leaned out, looked down our row. "I heard that." Duncan picked up a donut and bit into it. He picked up his paper cup of coffee and sipped. "See. I'm fine."

Everyone was digging in. The donuts did look good. They smelled of hot dough, sweet glaze, grease, and sugar.

"I like donuts," Chief Nelson said, and took one and bit into it. "Damn. That's good."

Gradually, all of us except Felix, who was off sugar, took a donut.

The donut smelled so good, and no one was dying. The smell pulled at me. Duncan tossed Tag a donut. It landed on the ground beside him. Tag gobbled it in two bites.

I thought that if this group was to be poisoned, it wouldn't be now. It would be three days from now. And it would be the true believers that showed up for that. Not just us curious lookie-loos. Frankly, I just convinced myself a hot, delicious donut was worth it.

The grease was greasy and the sugar was sweet. I ate and sipped coffee, and pretty soon, I realized I had eaten three donuts. I rarely eat donuts, and never three. More boxes were brought down and loaded on the tables. More hot coffee was brought. People ate and drank and chattered. The pole lights that brightened the sky flickered like torches, and the bugs that had circled them became the sky. The sky buzzed.

Looking down, I saw the table was crawling and my donut-glazed hands resting on it were huge and white, like Mickey Mouse gloves.

I peeked at the others.

Scrappy and Felix and the chief were melting like candle wax. My chair bucked me onto the ground. I rolled over on my back among my melted friends, realizing I too was melting. Tag was eating donuts that had fallen on the ground. His jaws chomped like a wood chipper as he dissolved into a hairy doggy goo. I could hear the bugs in the sky working their wings, clicking their mandibles, farting their gas. I thought I could hear dying stars scream.

I tried to roll over and get my hands under me. It was hard. Then I was lifted to my feet. My legs were rubber, yet I was moving, the toes of my shoes dragging along the ground. An alien had me, and the alien was strong.

This dragging went on for some time. We came to a space-craft, and the door opened. Tag, full-on doggy now, leaped inside ahead of me.

I was lifted inside. A door was shut. Tag opened his mouth, stuck out a damp, pink rag, bathed my head with it. His eyes were large and the stars were in them.

Time skipped along. I saw Scrappy and the chief through the front-view glass. They were un-melted. They were being supported by a monster with a face made of flaming hair. The monster was between them, an arm around each.

Another door opened in the craft. The door banged shut.

One more door, one more bang.

In a short time, another door, another bang. The monster slid into position in front of me.

I could see over the front seat of the saucer, see the ship's rearview mirror. In the mirror, at an angle, I could see our alien pilot. A bulbous head with a mass of squirming tentacles and a hairy face.

As I watched, the tentacles went away and the head became less swollen but no less hairy. Jesus. Was that Tag driving?

No. Tag was beside me. In fact, he had his head in my lap. I could feel his hot breath blowing against my pants, warming my balls.

I could tell who the pilot was now. I felt strong and proud and smart because I knew it was Felix.

"You stupid assholes," Felix said. "You don't go to the witch's house and taste the cookies she's baked."

"Donuts," I said.

"Go to hell," Felix said.

My porthole banged. I turned and saw some kind of monster looking in, beating on the glass with his fist. The face shifted, and the mouth seemed as large and open as a manhole. The eyes were huge and shattered. The monster's greasy forehead seemed as big as a parking lot. Some part of my mind thought: Duncan.

"Hi," I said. Or I think I said.

"They smell like the end of the world. They stink on fire."

"What?" I said.

But we were moving, leaving Duncan to stagger about as if he had tree stumps for legs.

The spacecraft roared. It turned among the swirling bugs and the bright pole lights. I leaned my head against the porthole so that I could look out and up. I could see the shiny moon and the silver stars from there. The stars had stopped screaming. They swung about as if on wires and looked as if they belonged in a grade-school play.

I saw the tips of the pines against the dark, framed by moon and starlight, and wondered if they were celestial Christmas trees.

(40)

We were at my house. It was late at night. Except for Felix and Tag, we had all taken turns with the showers, downstairs or up. I took mine cold. I needed it.

Gathering in the living room, Felix having made us all hot cups of coffee, we sat on the enormous couch. Tag lay on his side on a rug in front of the couch. His legs were paddling the air. His tongue was hanging out. His eyes were partially open.

"No shower, no coffee for Tag," Scrappy said. "Will he be all right?"

"He's either dog-paddling the Styx or swimming amongst the stars," Felix said.

"He's tough," Chief Nelson said. "He'll be all right."

"A vet might be a good idea," I said.

"No," Chief Nelson said, "he'll be all right. My guess is he ate more donuts than the rest of us, them having been knocked on the ground. But he'll be all right. Once, on a drug bust, he ate a small baggie of dope. He seemed strangely content for a few days and humped a leg of my desk off and on, but he got over it. He'll get over this."

"Had to be a hallucinogenic," Felix said. "Filled those donuts to get his followers in the mood, make them think they were communing with a spirt of a long-dead alien. An out-of-this-world experience. Sure, some knew it was bullshit, the nonbelievers. But the solid believers, that stuff just deepened their belief. Felt as if they had been masturbated by the space gods. The obvious reason they went mind-sailing wouldn't even occur to them, or if it did, it would be rejected. Nothing stops the true believer from believing."

"I'm assuming their donuts aren't always like that," Scrappy said.

"They are not," Chief Nelson said. "If they were, May Town would be full of car wrecks and people camping out at the donut shop. Man, I thought I was a giant slug. I was happy being one. Crawling all around, with the lights on fire. I could crawl really fast. I wouldn't mind a couple of those donuts right now. They'd go good with this coffee."

"Just drink your coffee," Felix said.

"All I got out of it was being sleepy like a moose," Scrappy said.

"How sleepy do moose get?" Felix said.

"Real sleepy. Oh, I did think about the sandwiches from the gas station. I lay there thinking, 'Are those sandwiches going to be wasted?'"

"In the refrigerator," Felix said.

"Eat 'em later," Scrappy said.

As we continued to decompress, an hour seemed like a minute, then one minute felt like an hour. When it was three in the morning and much coffee had been drunk, the floor quit moving, and all the lights stopped looking like signal fires. But for a long time, I had Mickey Mouse–gloved hands.

Tag quit paddling, began to breathe evenly. I wished he could talk and tell me about his experiences. I have to say, I wasn't one of those who liked their trips into the light fantastic. I felt scared and paranoid and hungry.

Come six a.m., the chief, defying caffeine, crashed on the couch. I remember that Felix called Cherry to say all was good, not mentioning the rest of us had eaten hallucinogenic donuts. After that, he went upstairs to sleep.

After making sure all the window shutters were closed, the jail bars in place, the cameras and alarms still armed, me and Scrappy went to my bedroom, followed by Tag. He had finally come around. He looked as if he were walking on tippy-toe paws. His head drooped, too heavy to lift.

Scrappy and me stripped naked and went to bed without examining the letters of the alphabet. Tag climbed up there with us, and even though he snored quite vigorously, we were easily able to sleep way down there in the far-below wetness of a mystical sea. Stayed there until two o'clock in the cold afternoon.

(41)

When I woke up, I dressed and left Scrappy and Tag sleeping. In the living room, I discovered the chief had gone home.

He left a note on the kitchen table.

You're out of eggs. I ate the last ones. You need cooking oil. The spray oil just doesn't cut it with eggs. Remember, you need grease to make a turd. I left the frying pan on the stove and didn't clean it. When you come over to get Amelia's camper, bring Tag. Oh, and you folks are right. Something is major disturbed out there in Saucer Land. We'll talk later today. I haven't had as much fun as I did last night since my car broke down in front of a Mississippi whorehouse on payday.

I checked the front door to see if it had locked back automatically when the chief left. Then, uncertain which door he had used, I checked them all. Maybe he had crawled out of a window, slipped through the bars. That would be like a hippo turning to smoke. Right then, I felt anything was possible.

My stomach was messy, but I knew I needed to eat to help it out.

I put some raisin bread in the toaster and got out the olive oil butter and started the coffee. By the time that was done, so was the toast. I buttered it up and took it and the coffee to the table.

Before I sat down to eat, I opened all the shutters and let the light in. For a while it felt as if I had let in laser beams. They went deep in my eyes and noodled my brain, but it didn't take long before I felt okay.

The toast and the dark roast coffee, no sugar or cream, did the trick. I decided I was safe enough for the time being. I put on a coat and went outside with another cup of coffee and sat at the table on the porch. It wasn't cold, but it was a little chilly.

No chimpanzees, sumo wrestlers, Gogo, Cowboy, or any of the assholes dressed in black came out of the woods or out from under my porch to kill me. Meg didn't drop in for a ghostly visit.

The morning was off to a good start.

I looked out where the chief's car had been. Last night it was a spaceship for a while.

Finally, the door to the porch opened and Scrappy came out wearing one of my shirts, a coat, sweatpants, and my gym socks. She had a cup of coffee and a granola bar.

Tag trotted out after her. He had a kind of embarrassed look, I thought. A dog like Tag, he likes for you to think he's on the job, in control of things, and last night he had proved as gullible as the rest of us, betrayed by his doggy instincts to eat anything offered to him.

Felix had acted like he was less of an idiot than the rest of us, but he had only come out all right due to watching his blood sugar. Maybe we all suffered from doggy instincts.

When Scrappy was seated at the table, and Tag was lying at her feet, she said, "I gave Tag the sandwiches in the refrigerator. I decided we didn't need to eat them."

"Good call. Felix up yet?"

"Didn't see him. Was last night as weird as I thought?"

"You mean the threesome with you, me, and the dog?"

"Ha-ha."

"Yeah. It was weird out there."

We sat and listened to the wind rattling gently through the trees. We talked very little. The sound of our voices was too loud.

Felix came out. He too carried a coffee cup. One of the big ones. The steam rolled off the top of it like mist from a mosquito fogger.

He sat down at the table, said, "I hate everybody, and I didn't even have a donut."

"I feel you," Scrappy said.

When we eventually convinced our bodies that it was time to start moving about, I called the chief, told him we were coming.

Felix drove us over in my car. I sat up front by Felix, and Scrappy sat in the back with Tag's head in her lap, his tongue dangling. I figured inside his head, he could hear the sunlight yodel.

I know I could.

(42)

In the chief's office, we noted immediately that his balding weasel—mink, whatever—was missing a head. There were framed certificates with the glass broken out lying on the floor. There were bullet holes in the wall. Even Tag seemed surprised.

Chief Nelson, sitting behind his desk, said, "Left your place early. Got here, suddenly felt bad. Had to take one of my pills. Heart problems. Lay down for a nap right there on the floor. Sun bleeding through the blinds finally woke my fat ass up. Saw the mink, its eyeball looking down on me. I panicked, thought it was going to jump. Drew down on it."

"Good shot, shooting the head off it like that," Scrappy said.

"I was trying to hit dead center. Fired five shots. Knocked shit off the wall before I accidentally hit the mink. A family heirloom gone on a bullet. Lillian and Brewer nearly shit themselves. Tag, ol' buddy. Come here, boy."

Tag didn't move.

"You've spoiled my goddamn dog," Chief Nelson said.

"Just a hangover," Scrappy said.

"Fair enough," Chief Nelson said. He looked at his watch. "Right before you came, I listened to my messages. Got one from ol' Grover's ex-son-in-law, Ansel Walton. He's a kind of officious prick. I've had a few dealings with him here and there. Not anything big. He's going to come by in about ten or fifteen minutes and tell me stuff. That's what he said on the message. Tell me stuff. He felt Grover's request was funny, so he wanted to talk to me about you, Charlie. You're here, and he soon will be. Charlie, would you go out to reception, grab a couple extra chairs?"

I did that, and about the time I got them into the office and sat down, Grover's former son-in-law had showed up and was brought in by Lillian, the receptionist. The receptionist looked around the wounded room with distaste and went out.

"By nature," Chief Nelson said, "she's a lot neater than me."

Grover's ex-son-in-law was a man in his thirties. He wore a nice pair of slick blue Walmart off-the-rack pants and an almost white shirt. He took a seat.

Tag was still sitting in the same place. He could have been on Space Mountain at Disneyland or on a sinking ship, and to him, it would have all been the same until the ride ended or his feet got wet.

"What happened in here?" Ansel asked.

"Weasel hunt," Scrappy said. "It got ugly."

Ansel gave the headless beast on the chief's desk a long look.

"Forget that," Chief Nelson said. "You wanted to talk to me. Had to do with Charlie Garner and your former father-in-law. As fate would have it, this is Charlie."

Ansel checked me out, then the rest of the gang.

"It's all right," Chief Nelson said. "They're okay."

"Grover asked if I might help him out, let this Charlie fellow get inside the warehouse the Bacon family owns. Cut the cameras and alarms. Let him look around. He said it had something to do with the flying-saucer yokels, missing persons. Who are we talking about? Who's missing?"

"Police business," Chief Nelson said. "On a need-to-know basis, and now you know all you need to know."

"I have an obligation to my clients to protect them, and my thought was I was tipping you off about being asked to do something illegal. Grover, he's all right, but I don't know if he's asking me to do the right thing. Then I come to see you, and you got this Charlie fellow here. These other two. Who are they?"

"Special deputies working for me. I'm getting them some badges. Tag, of course is a K-Nine operative. You monitor Bacon's storage inside and out?"

"Outside only. That's what they requested. They wanted privacy when they're in there . . . is that dog okay?"

Tag was sitting like a statue, eyes glazed, mouth open.

"He had a big night," Chief Nelson said. "I'm going to ask you to help these folks out on the warehouse. Police business."

"I don't know, Chief. This doesn't sound like police business. I'm feeling a little ambushed."

"How do you know what police business sounds like? I said do what they ask because I agree with what they want, and I'm the goddamn chief of police. Do you get a lot of traffic out there at the warehouse?"

"That seems like a security question I'm not supposed to answer."

"What part about 'This is an investigation and I'm the goddamn chief of police' do you not understand, Ansel?"

"All right, then. Now and again there's traffic."

"Now and again," Chief Nelson said. "Just now and again?"

"That's right."

"Okay. What I want you to do is quit the bullshit and arrange for us to get in there tonight."

"Us?"

"Everyone in this room. Tag may be optional."

Tag decided to lie on the floor.

"Don't you need a search warrant? You had a search warrant, that would distance me a bit. I mean, I got to do what a search warrant asks so I'm not just letting you in. You being law or not, that could come back to bite me on the ass. I know it's about missing persons, but still."

Chief Nelson opened a desk drawer, pulled out one of the search warrants the judge had supplied him with, slapped it on his desk, picked up a pen, and began to fill it out. "I got your goddamn search warrant right here."

"I didn't fall off the hay truck this morning, Chief. Judge would have to sign off on that."

"That's his signature at the bottom of the page."

"Just trying to be safe, legal."

Chief Nelson finished filling out the warrant, reached across the desk, and handed it to Ansel. "It couldn't be any more sound than if it were a sermon written by Jesus in His own goddamn blood. We'll see you, oh, say, seven p.m. Out at the unit. Got it?"

"I suppose."

"No supposing. You be there and you have it so the cameras are off before we arrive. Couple minutes before."

"They got a setup out at their place," Ansel said. "If they're paying attention, and they will be, they'll know the cameras are off. Cameras go offline, they'll be squirting shit. They'll call first, show up second. And frankly, they may not call at all, just show up. They have become an unpleasant bunch, what with all those new folks in funeral duds."

"The Managers?" Chief Nelson said.

"Yeah. And the monkey."

I contained myself.

"They ask what happened out there when things go black," the chief said, "you'll say there was an electrical bump, a raccoon chewed a wire, someone plugged in one blow-dryer and a toaster too many. Whatever you like. I get word you warned them, told them what I've asked you to do, and me with a certified search warrant, then I may have to check out your business close up. See you're following all the regulations to the letter, fire codes and so on. Want that? Might shut you down a few days, force your cameras and alarms to go offline for all your clients."

Ansel nodded. "I'll see you tonight."

"You bet your ass you will."

(4 3)

We left out of there with Tag still tripping the light fantastic, the decapitated weasel perched on the chief's desk, the chief still seated behind it. Ansel had departed before us. I suppose I should mention that the taxidermied duck remained in his original position.

"You think Ansel will squeal on us, let the Saucer People know?" Scrappy said.

"Hope not," Felix said. "I'd rather not fight Gogo, Plug the Sumo, Cowboy, and Mr. Biggs."

"I think you might fight anything," Scrappy said to Felix, "and come out pretty good."

"Depends on the day," Felix said.

We were on our way back home to wait until nightfall. We would then gather our burglar tools, which might be a crowbar, gird our loins, have a small bite to eat, and go out and see what there was to see.

About halfway home, Felix got a call. He transferred the call to my car speaker. It was Cherry. Felix said, "I'm in the car with Charlie and Scrappy. We can all hear you now. Don't mention all the sexual pleasures you expect from me later."

"Dress as a forensic accountant. I've had a sexy day visiting with my gal pal," Cherry said. "You'll need a white shirt and a black skirt and some sensible shoes. That's what my forensic pal Sally Farmer wears. She took a look at the spreadsheets. Discovered some interesting things that if you don't know how to look for them, do the research, you'd miss. She's looking further for me, thinks there's more to discover, but she verified a lot of what I thought."

"Who's she work for?" Felix said.

"She once worked for the CIA."

"Once? So this isn't legal?"

"Not exactly, and therein lies the flies on the fruitcake. But Sally owes me a favor or two, and she doesn't like to see people like this get away with what they're getting away with. Duping folks. But considering how and where we got this information, we have to find some other way to reveal things or we'll be sharing gruel in Huntsville. Well, I'll be in the women's unit. But perhaps we can bribe a guard to pass notes."

"Please tell me you discovered from those spreadsheets that the saucers are actually coming," I said.

"Even if they are, a lot of money is being shifted and mixed and dodged, so I have concluded, as we suspected, not everyone involved with the Saucer People are true believers. Bacon doesn't own anything, not even the property and the house he lives in, any of the businesses. It's all been shifted to Jack Pleasant, aka good ol' Cowboy. The donut shops have been sold, and the new owner will take charge of them at the end of this week."

"Interesting," Felix said.

"At first glance, it looks legal," Cherry said. "It seems like Bacon has signed the right papers to make the shift, given Jack Pleasant the power of attorney, but Sally says the signature, the papers, would have to be verified by Bacon to be certain. Perhaps a handwriting expert. Maybe it's legal business going on, maybe not. Would you like to hear about the certainly not-so-legal stuff Sally did?"

"We would," Felix said.

"Sally got into the May Town bank's computer system."

"You can do that?" Felix said.

"If you're Sally, you can. Again, it might be a tad unlawful."

"A tad?"

"All right, lots of tads," Cherry said. "Looks as if a few other accounts, ones not belonging to the Saucer People, are being tapped. I mean, hell, the crooks own the bank, and crooks will be crooks. Large accounts are losing money, but it's being siphoned off cleverly, so no one can see it in the personal accounts, not right away. But Sally sees it. Either Cowboy is smarter than we thought, or someone in his employ knows how to do the dirty work. Could be he's paying some outsider to do it. Another day or two, Sally should have enough info to prove it. Right now, she can see the markings but not the absolute. When she has that nailed down, she'll drop that information to the right authorities anonymously. Then it's up to them."

"It'll turn out that Mr. Biggs is a computer wizard," Felix said. "Wait and see. And another thing—Sally's conclusions and anonymous drop may come too late."

"How's that?" Cherry asked.

Felix told Cherry about our trip out to the Landing Pad, about hearing the prophecy from Bacon over the loudspeakers, our experience with the doped donuts.

"Did you actually see Bacon?" Cherry asked.

"No."

"When the prophecy fails and news gets out about the bank thefts, they'll lose core followers and will find it difficult to attract new ones. Which validates further that Cowboy might be thinking all good things come to an end and it's time for him and Mr. Biggs to buy a condo and set up house in the Cayman Islands."

"With a jungle gym, of course," Felix said.

"Who knows if that voice you heard over the speaker really was Bacon," Cherry said. "Or it could have been recorded by him, maybe against his will?"

"To what end?" I asked. "They're losing their piggy bank once the saucers don't show."

"Let me give you my psychiatrist version," Felix said. "Cowboy as well as Bacon are fucking nuts in different ways, but at the bottom of it all, at least in Cowboy's case, it's intense lack of self-worth. Shitty home life. Abuse. Though there are plenty of folks that have had the same things happen to them, and they don't choose to cheat, steal, or kill.

"Someone else might turn those impulses into something benign, like an obsession with neatness, maybe become a real estate thief or a shady used-car salesman. Cowboy has chosen a darker, different path. And it is a choice. He's a con man. Gets his happy moments from displays of power. Money is power. Controlling people and killing people is power. But those moments don't last. He's constantly looking for something to fill that unfillable hole. He's the kind of guy that if he thinks his string is running out would maybe take everything down with him. Or hurt everyone he can, run off with the money. The others—Gogo, Plug, any of them—they're just pawns in his game, and at some point, you can bet he'll take all of them off the board. That includes whoever helped him computer-rob the bank. In a short time he'll be back to his old tricks in some form or another, desperately trying to fill that hole again."

"Damn, you actually did graduate," Cherry said.

"Bottom of my class," Felix said. "I might also add that when it comes to Mr. Biggs, he's a follower. Perhaps has some intense anger issues over abuse, circus tricks gone wrong, too many green bananas, but all in all, at the end of it, he's just doing what he's told."

(44)

When we got to my house, Felix dropped us off, moved to his truck, and went on to his place to gear up for the night. The spacecraft would rise in three days, supposedly. This was day one.

Exhausted from the night before, Scrappy and I took a nap, woke up in time to drink coffee, eat a bite, and hang out. Later, we dressed in black, because that seemed to be the thing to do when you were breaking into someone's warehouse.

Felix showed up and I drove us off in my car as the late-autumn night fell and the moon glowed high in a clear night sky. We arrived at the address of the warehouse with five minutes to spare.

The warehouse was on the outskirts of May Town on a patch of about three acres, and the building stood on at least an acre and a half of that. It was tall and there were bright lights all around it and a chain-link fence that could have contained a rhino.

We had only been there a few seconds when the lights went out at the warehouse up the street. Ansel was doing what he had been asked. So good, so far.

About the same time, Chief Nelson drove up in his personal

vehicle and parked behind us. When he got out, Tag got out right behind him.

Chief Nelson wasn't wearing his uniform. He had on a blue work shirt and blue jeans and lace-up boots and a dark coat. He wore his holstered gun. He was carrying a large bolt cutter. Tag wore his fur suit with his usual dog collar, no hat, no shoes, and seemed to have brought an attitude.

We greeted one another politely, and with flashlights in our coat pockets, gumption in our hearts, we began to walk over to the warehouse, Tag trotting along with us.

"I ended up having Ansel come by my house," Chief Nelson said. "Decided I didn't want to have a chat out here with him in case someone saw us and that put him in danger. I've brought a padlock that Ansel says is a duplicate of the one I'm going to cut. Same key configuration. We have thirty minutes, then the lights and cameras go back online."

"You'd think they'd do their own security business and have a backup generator," I said.

"This was set up long ago, before things got so mysterious, so they trusted the local security. After all, back then, Grover was one of them."

"Think Ansel might warn the Managers?" Scrappy asked.

"Threatened to pistol-whip him if he did, give him to Tag for a snack. Tomorrow I'll fill out a search warrant for the Landing Pad. One I'm using here is for Ansel. I didn't want the Saucer People to know we were going to do it. And I'm not truly sure how legal all this is, warrant or not."

At the fence, the chief applied the bolt cutters to the padlock, snipped it off. He tossed the bolt cutters on the ground and pulled the gate open.

Inside the fence, Felix guided us with his flashlight.

There was a huge sliding door at the front of the building, pulled down and secured. We didn't try it.

Chief Nelson said, "I have Ansel's instructions for the best place to go in."

We took brisk steps to the side of the building, stopped in front of a normal-size door. Chief Nelson used his lockpick and went to work. The door clicked open quickly.

Inside, the air was stale and dark. Felix waved his flashlight around as the rest of us got hold of our own lights.

It was creepy in there. I felt as if something were crawling up my spine using an ice-cold rock hammer and ice-spiked shoes.

Our flashlight beams danced around the place, and dust motes moved in the light and made it hazy.

We all focused our lights on an enormous shape.

I won't lie. I felt what we might be looking at was the shadowy shape of an alien spacecraft.

(45)

A moment later I felt the weight of disappointment, like a kid expecting a tricycle at Christmas, only to end up with socks and underwear with happy animal characters on them.

I knew too that such a thing as a spacecraft had never crossed Felix's mind. He saw it for exactly what it was: A long military vehicle. Some version of a black Humvee. It took me a moment to readjust my wishful thinking.

I flashed my beam through the dusty glass on the driver's side. There was nothing to see but car seats and a steering wheel. I tried to open the door, but it was locked.

Parked near the Humvee was a black pickup, a forklift, a backhoe, a dozer, and a couple of enormous orange tractors, along with their attachments. Hitched to one of the tractors was a disc plow, its blades shiny and menacing in the flashlight beams. There was also a front-end loader up on a trailer. It was a pretty big one, with ladder steps.

There were a half dozen large blue steel toolboxes on as many plank tables, and there were a few loose tools lying on the tables as well. Hanging on the wall closest to us were shovels, hoes, axes, sling blades, chain saws, hammers, and so on. Near the tables and under them were bags of fertilizer.

All of this made perfect sense, of course, as the cult grew its own food. And it looked as if they did their own construction as well.

Scrappy climbed up on the trailer and then up on the loader. I put my light on her.

"Left the keys in it," she said. "Wanted to, I could drive it."

"No, you couldn't," I said.

"Yes, I could. I can drive anything in here. I worked summers for that construction company, learned to operate lots of machinery. You don't know everything, Charlie Garner."

She climbed down, and we walked around some more.

Against the far wall there was a row of chest freezers. Maybe they held food for their imaginary trip to paradise. If so, a handful of freezers seemed a little light in the pants to contain enough goods for a long journey across space and time, though I guess if you were in a vaporous state or whatever it was, you wouldn't need much in the food department. But once those souls were reconstituted as flesh, ready for the war, regular chow would be desirable.

We didn't see any canned goods or ammunition stacked anywhere. There was a microwave and a table with a coffeepot on it near the freezers.

Chief Nelson said, "Maybe they're just planning on a weekend trip."

Scrappy went over and opened one of the freezers. There was a rise of cold steam. Tag reared up on his hind legs, curled his forelegs over the edge of the freezer, looked in, sniffed.

Scrappy gave a short whistle, said, "Do you guys, when you freeze meat, pack the head with the eyes still in it?"

We all put our lights where Scrappy's was. There were some bags of corn, okra, peas, and under them was a body, the head facing us. We moved some bags and could see the body was nude and withered and had its knees practically under its chin. The wrinkles on the face had filled with streaks of ice. The hair was thin and pale. The eyes were frosted over, like windows on a cold day.

"You know," Chief Nelson said, "I haven't seen him in years, but that's Ben Bacon, one who inherited this whole doodle from his father."

"Maybe got onto the Managers and their schemes," I said. "Was going to cast them out, but they did him in. Could have died of natural causes, I guess, and they just decided not to let anyone know."

"Why would they keep him, though?" Scrappy asked.

"Probably killed him here," Felix said. "Bacon might have insisted on seeing the contents of the warehouse. Same thing that occurred to us may have occurred to him. He came here to look, Cowboy had him done in. I think he's been here a while. If so, means stuff we heard over the loudspeaker was recorded some time back, or it was an imitator."

"There's a body under Bacon," I said. "I can see some teeth under those frozen pea bags."

We lifted Bacon up, moved some bags of vegetables. It was a nude older woman. Her hair was plastered to her face with red ice — frozen blood. She appeared to be smiling or gritting her teeth. Her body was in the same position as Bacon's.

"It's his wife," Chief Nelson said.

There was something hairy at the woman's feet. It was a frozen white dog, one of those little things that looks as if it ought to have a stick up its ass and be used for a mop.

Tag sniffed as Chief Nelson lifted the dog out by the hind legs. Behind the dog's ear was a dark spot. Bullet hole was my guess.

"They eliminated the whole family," Chief Nelson said, "because, far as I know, Ben Bacon never had children." Chief Nelson dropped the dog back into the freezer, closed it up.

"And we're not out of freezers," Felix said. He walked to the next one and opened it. "Bingo."

We all moved after him. In that freezer was a nude middle-aged woman who looked as if she'd lived on the weight machine in a gym.

She was curled up the same as Bacon and his wife. Underneath her was another body.

Felix lifted her up slightly. The body underneath was a nude man. Half his head was gone. It wasn't Gogo or Plug. These were the two we had seen on the porch of the Bacon house on donut day.

"Cowboy is eliminating the help and the split in profit," Chief Nelson said. "Got them here on some pretense and killed them. Probably told the others these two bailed for some reason or another."

There were still two more freezers. I thought of Meg and Ethan. We looked.

Duncan. The chief's deputy. He wasn't nude. Was still wearing civies. The clothes he had on when we had last seen him.

"Oh, hell, not the boy," the chief said. "Shit, why?"

I moved ahead of the others, lifted the last freezer lid, fearing what I might see inside.

It only had a few frozen TV dinners in it. Managers probably came here for some free time, eat a bit of this and that, hang out, maybe smoke some dope, drink coffee, talk about the best way to dismember a body. Even stone-cold killers need relaxation.

"Goddamn," Chief Nelson said. He sat down on the concrete between freezers, his back against the wall. I put my flashlight on him. I could see his face was beaded with sweat. Tag was sitting beside him.

Chief Nelson reached in his coat pocket, pulled out a bottle of pills, opened it up, carefully took one, put the bottle back. He sighed, put his arm around the dog. Tag licked his face.

"Poor Duncan," Chief Nelson said. "A goddamn Popsicle. He was all right. He was quite all right. His poor family. Move the light, Charlie, it's making my eyes water."

(46)

Our time had grown short so we left out of there and went quickly back to the gate. Chief Nelson replaced the padlock with the identical one under the close scrutiny of Tag, then recovered the bolt cutters and the old lock.

We walked down the street toward our cars, and right before we reached them, the lights at the warehouse popped on. I assumed the cameras did too.

"What are you going to do about Duncan?" I asked the chief.

"I'll tell his family, but not before I go out to Bozo Land with a search warrant. I don't intend to tell anyone at my office. I hate to say it, I don't know I can trust them. Except Lillian. She's all right. I can tell her anything. I won't kid you. I'm mad. That kid was an idiot in some ways, but I bet he came out of that stupor he was in, thought about losing his family for some imagined space trip, challenged someone out there about their horseshit, and that's what got him killed. He said something. Saw something. Cowboy couldn't let him throw a wrench in his plans this close to being out and away with his fortune. Damn. I'm a shitty chief of police."

"You're all right," Scrappy said.

"Don't kid yourself, girl. I am shitty. But I don't have to stay that way. I'm going to go out there and search that place. Along with Tag, of course."

"When are you going?" Felix said.

"I want to catch them when they're unprepared, slightly before their doomsday moment. But not when all their supporters are there."

"Managers could be tough," Felix said. "You might need some help."

"Well, they're short a couple Managers, and I got a gun and I got the law on my side. For what it's worth. Thing is, you've done more than you should. I've let you do more than I should. It's up to me now."

"Got to tell you, Chief, with all respect, you look pooped," I said.

"You're not wrong."

"Change your mind, let us know," Felix said.

The chief adjusted his gun belt where it had fallen down over his fat ass, and he climbed in his car with the bolt cutters and Tag and drove away.

(47)

I was lying in bed, early morning, propped up on pillows, hoping Cherry was having some luck convincing someone with a lot of law and a lot of guns to go out to the Landing Pad, look for some explosives, Cowboy, and his helpers.

I was also wondering how long it would take for me to put a foot out of bed and pull the rest of me after it, make some coffee, toast some bread.

Scrappy was already up. She had slipped out before I cracked an eye. We had returned to our practice of the ABCs last night, so not all was doom and gloom.

I finally got up, bare as the day of my birth, slipped on my pajamas that lay crumpled on the floor, slid my feet into house shoes, shuffled into the kitchen. Scrappy had opened all the shutters. The light made my head hurt. Almost anything made my head hurt.

Scrappy was standing in front of the hissing Keurig, watching it pee coffee into her cup. She looked at me and smiled.

"Think we need to cut F from our lessons," she said. "It leaves you lethargic."

"I like F."

"Who the hell doesn't, but your health has to be considered."

"Know what I dreamed last night?"

"Something nasty, and I was in it?"

"Not exactly. I mean, you were in the dream. Naked, driving one of those big machines in the warehouse."

"Where was I driving it?"

"I don't know, but you were driving like hell was on your heels."

"Where were you?"

"I was kind of in the ether. But I was watching, you know, omniscient-like."

"What happened?"

"That's it, you drove the machine around. It wasn't exactly a sexy dream."

"Okay. Well, I dreamed I was at a book signing."

"Yeah?"

"Not really. But I wish I had. Wish I'd done the real thing. To be at a book signing for a book I've written, or we've cowritten."

"I've had that dream, and then it came true. Thing was, first book signing I had was sitting at a card table in a Barnes and Noble in Tyler, and they forgot to put the sign up that announced I would be signing my book that day. They said they used social media. I don't know. Maybe they did. Lot of people came by, looked at the book, looked at me, said, 'You write that?' I was tempted to say, 'No, I sign for the author while he's in the toilet.' I sold three books that day. My brother bought one, Cherry another, and some elderly lady who I think felt sorry for me a third. Somewhere she too has a son that's a failure."

"You're hardly a failure," Scrappy said.

"Later on, I sold more. It's been all right. Just trying to warn you, don't expect people to be falling all over you. Those card tables hold a lot more books than you usually sell."

"Right now, selling one would seem pretty exciting."

We had our coffee at the table, though I had to get up and find the device, which I sometimes confused with the TV remote, to close the shutters to spare me the raw rays of the morning sun. I placed the remote on the table next to my coffee.

Devices. Technology. It made things better, and it made things worse. With or without technology, I had come to be of the opinion we were living in a dystopia. It had snuck up on us like a lion on an antelope, and we hadn't noticed. Now it was gently and slowly devouring us.

I went upstairs and worked awhile. When I came down a few hours later, Scrappy was at the dining-room table, writing furiously in a composition notebook, kind you buy when you're in high school and college. Her ballpoint pen scratched across the paper rapidly. Her laptop was open on the table, out of ready reach but accessible.

I leaned into the kitchen counter and watched her write. This went on for about fifteen minutes.

Scrappy looked up, saw me, said, "I like to get my notes down on paper, then write on the laptop. You?"

"Mostly straight to the word processor. How's it going?"

"Good. I think we can combine our take on all this, you know, to get our book done. Want to look at my notes?"

"Okay."

I sat at the table and read them. They were a lot of notes and they were very concise. Dealt with our visit to the Landing Pad, the drugged donuts.

"You did all this this morning?"

"Yep. I remember good."

"Seems that way. Okay. I'm impressed."

"Wait until you read my actual writing."

"You have examples?"

"Yep."

She showed me some articles she had written freelance. One had been published in *Texas Highways*, another in the *Texas Observer,* and there was one she had tried to sell to *Texas Monthly* without success. It was a good article on a crime that happened in Tyler, Texas. Had to do with a gun-collecting preacher murdering his wife. Guess if you're going to be a preacher, you need to sin so you can tell other folks how bad it is.

It was a really well-researched and well-written article. I couldn't figure what the editors that had passed on it had been thinking. Maybe her writing style was too stylish for that sort of magazine, but it damn sure wasn't too stylish for a true-crime book.

"Thing is, Scrappy. I don't know what you need me for. You can write. And your notes are good."

"I need your experience. You can shorten my learning time."

"You think?"

"I do."

I extended my hand across the table.

"We already agreed," she said.

"But we didn't shake on it. I believe in a handshake deal."

She shook my paw vigorously. "Deal," she said.

(48)

In East Texas, unlike the more barren North and West Texas, the stars are harder to see due to the trees, but my backyard was clear of trees, though it was surrounded by them.

Sitting on a tall stool with an eye to the telescope, you could hear insects scratching at their fiddles, frogs working on their bass notes, and you could eyeball the universe through a tube.

I had set the telescope up in the backyard again, positioned it on Venus so Scrappy could have a look. She made little squeaky noises, she was so excited about the view.

"This is wonderful, Charlie."

"Yep. It is. Now, climb off the stool and let me adjust it on a cluster of stars."

We did this for a couple of hours, moving the telescope and stool, taking turns having a look. The air got cold, and we finally gave it up. I locked the telescope up in the storage room off the carport.

In the house, I picked my phone off the dining-room table.

There was a message.

It was from the chief's phone.

But it wasn't from the chief.

I listened.

"Lillian here, the chief's receptionist. He wants to see you. He's in the hospital. Heart attack. They've moved him out of the ICU and he's doing a little better, if not good. It's the only hospital in May Town, so it shouldn't be too hard to find. He says come soon as you can, but thing is, they've got him sedated. Come if you want to chance it, though maybe tomorrow would be better. I'm up here with him, going to sleep in a chair. He told them I was his fiancée. Isn't that funny?"

That was it.

"He must have gone out to the Landing Pad," Scrappy said, "and it didn't go well."

"Maybe." I was thinking about those pills he took, the heart problems.

I called Felix, told him about the message.

He drove out and we all drove over to the hospital in Felix's car, or, rather, one he had borrowed from Cherry. She had three. This one was a white BMW.

So far, no word from Cherry about the FBI, Texas Rangers, highway patrol, or any such law enforcement.

Wasn't much left of the three-day countdown, and I wasn't feeling optimistic about the law.

Things were about to shift.

(49)

The hospital was pretty basic-looking, three stories high. Chief Nelson was on the second floor. They let us in, said we were expected but a short visit was all that was allowed.

We walked into his room, pulled our coats off, stood around the bed with the coats in the crooks of our bent arms, and looked down at the so-pale chief in the so-white bed in the so-white room. His eyes were closed. A monitor was nearby. Little lines danced on the screen. An IV bag hung on a metal rack next to the bed and a tube from it went down to where it was taped to Chief Nelson's arm.

Lillian sat in a chair by the bed. She nodded to us as we came in but didn't speak. She looked rough. Her hair was a mess and her face, sans makeup, was red and cracked.

Tag was lying on the floor, but when we arrived, he came over and sniffed my pants leg, then Felix's, and finally Scrappy's. He pushed his head against her hard enough, it moved her a bit, then he sat down close to her. Scrappy gave him a pat on his massive head. Scrappy said, "They allow dogs?"

"They do now," Lillian said.

After a moment, Lillian stood up and leaned over Chief Nelson. "John. Can you talk?"

There was a moment where Chief Nelson's eyelids fluttered like snagged window shades, then the shades came unsnagged and he opened his eyes, but not wide. He looked at us. A smile cracked his face and went away.

"Hey," he said. When he spoke, his lips made a smacking sound.

Lillian picked up a plastic bottle containing water. It had a straw in it. She used a button on a cable to lift the bed up so she could give him a drink. He sucked on the straw, heaved a deep breath, and turned his head slightly to see us better.

Scrappy reached out and touched his arm. "Hey, you," she said. Me and Felix nodded and smiled as if seeing a man recovering from a heart attack was nothing at all.

"Had to be on oxygen awhile," the chief said. "Glad they got that off my face. After I started breathing good, I mean. When I was having trouble there at first, I thought that oxygen mask was my bosom buddy. Listen here. I meant to go out there to the site, though I was having some hesitation. I was a little scared, if I'm being honest. Lillian, do you mind if we talk privately?"

She nodded, slung her purse strap over her shoulder, went out, and closed the door.

"Don't know what I'd have done without her. But some things I'd prefer she not know, though I'm sure she knows more than I know she knows. She always does. Rather not involve her more than necessary, okay?"

"Sure," I said.

"I was in the office, making plans, filling out a search warrant. Things started spinning and I was sick to my stomach. I took a pill, and it helped, but I didn't feel jump-started, you know? Next thing, I smelled something like toast burning, and then I was here. Lillian heard me fall out of my chair, called the ambulance to come pick up my fat ass. Did it just in time."

"You seem to be doing okay," Felix said.

"'Seem' sounds accurate. Doctor, short time ago, she kind of waltzed around it, but I think she was saying I have about as much chance of recovery as I do of growing a third arm. I may have had a little stroke along with the heart attack."

"You sound all right," I said.

"My brain is working as much as it ever worked. You know, I haven't had a truly good day since my wife died. Until you three came along. We had a little adventure. I felt like a real cop. Just to be honest, I hated all of you on sight. But Tag liked you, so I gave you a second chance. Now I feel closer to you than anyone but Lillian and Duncan. And he's gone. Goddamn them."

"Don't get worked up, Chief," Scrappy said.

"You know same as me that those bodies in the freezers are gone now."

"Of course," I said.

"I just wanted you to know why nothing is happening, that I'm in here and may not recover. I don't know if I care if I do. Lillian, though, I'm thinking she might be worth it. Recovering for, I mean."

"That's good," Scrappy said.

"Yes, young lady. It is. Only thing I want to do with my time left as chief is nail these fuckers did Duncan in, and here I am lying in bed with a tube in my arm and a tube in my dick. I did get my replacement for chief set. Fellow's forty-five, I think. From out of town and he has a lot of law enforcement experience. Started in the highway patrol, lot of other things after that. He applied, and since the town lets me recommend my replacement, I did. They hesitated slightly when they found out he was Black. Still got some holdouts, you know, but they saw his credentials and citations for bravery, a lot of other stuff, and they agreed. I get through with my run, end of year, he's in and, thankfully, I'm out.

"But that's not why I called you over. There's another bit of a hazard, by the way. I thought there wouldn't be, but there is."

"What?" Felix said.

"Ansel. They hadn't no more than put me in this room when he came in yesterday. I'd have called you then had I not had a bit of a relapse from his news. Guess he felt he had to tell me, as he knew I'd find out. Wanted to have a clear conscience or something. I don't know. I know if I could get out of this bed and had the strength, I'd put a foot up his ass."

"He told them we visited the warehouse?" I said.

"Morning after we went out there, Cowboy and his monkey came to his house early for a little sit-down and a chat. Monkey was wearing a tuxedo jacket with a white shirt and a big-ass diaper. Cowboy said something to the monkey, and it grabbed a chair and beat it damn near to sawdust against the floor. Chattering and hopping around. Ansel said he didn't know what to do but figured a lie wasn't the way to go. Expected to end up like that chair the monkey busted up.

"Ansel tried to lie a little at first, he said, but Cowboy kept looking at him, and the monkey came over and leaned on its knuckles in front of him. Ansel said the lie died in his mouth. He told him — Cowboy, not the monkey — that I had asked for the cameras to be cut, had a search warrant for the place. Ansel could have at least kept you three out of it, but he didn't. He mentioned us all."

"Son of a bitch," Felix said.

"Ansel said Cowboy thanked him politely; the monkey took off its diaper and shit on the floor, and they left."

"Damn," Scrappy said. "They've gone feral."

"Yep. Lillian went over to my house to get me some things and said it smelled like a zoo in there, though she didn't see anybody. I think Cowboy and the monkey came looking for me, and the monkey left its stink. Maybe had I been home, I'd have shot them both, I don't know, but I was here.

"I don't trust Barney, the others. Only Lillian and you three. What I'm asking is maybe you three could kind of watch after me for a few days. Lillian is doing her best, but she may not be enough. Not like I can do much from here. I don't mind dying, but not by their hands or ripped up and thrown around the room by a monkey—that lacks a certain appeal."

"You got it," Felix said.

"Ask Lillian to tell the hospital folks I want you three here off and on or at the same time. Death can have me under normal circumstances. But lying here in bed like an offering on a plate, that doesn't appeal to me. I advise you folks to carry a gun. Bazooka or anti-monkey gun if you got it."

"I have a pistol in my pocket," Felix said.

"Lillian, she brought my pistol in. It's in the nightstand drawer. She told the doctors and nurses, the administration, that, as chief of police, I had the right to have it nearby. Of course, it would only do me good if I'm awake and can reach it. I don't feel like I could wrestle a teddy bear to a draw right now, even if it was two out of three and the teddy bear was leaking stuffing. Could you maybe politely send Lillian home? Tell her I asked for you to work in shifts so she could get some rest."

"Done," I said.

Chief Nelson nodded a little. He closed his eyes and was immediately asleep. That might have had something to do with what was in the tube running into his arm, or he may have just burned up all his firewood, so to speak.

We went out in the hall and found Lillian sitting on a couch in the waiting area. I told her what the chief had said.

"I don't like it," she said. "He hardly knows you three."

"You're right, but he knows us well enough to ask us to tell you to get some rest and for you to make sure the hospital knows that the chief of police wants us here, and he's calling it police business."

She nodded and stood up from the couch. "He's a good man, you know. Really in love with his wife, and during that time, and now, I was really in love with him. I think he just realized it. I'm thinking maybe he gets better, he'll want to change up his life some."

"And you'd like to be included in the change?" Scrappy said.

"I've thought about it. I don't know if he has."

"I think maybe he has," Scrappy said.

"You know, no kids for either of us. Nothing but a job, and we're not spring chickens, so we ought to consider something other than what we're doing. Together, if possible. If not, still something other than what we got. I don't think being chief is working for him anymore, and I don't think he wants to retire to an empty house. I know I don't. Says he's going to run for office again, but that's just because he doesn't know what else to do. This town. I hate it. I think I will go and get some rest. I'm feeling a bit washed out. Thank you."

"Sure," Scrappy said.

"I know him sending me home, asking you to stay, there's more going on than he's letting on."

"No comment," Scrappy said.

"You know," Lillian said to Scrappy, "you are the cutest thing."

"Thank you, ma'am."

"I'll call the powers that be when I get home, tell the administrator that the chief says you three need to be here."

"Oh," I said. "Chief doesn't want you mentioning any of this business to Deputy Brewer or anyone else."

"He should know I won't." She opened her purse, took out a card. It had her name on it and her phone number. She handed it to me. "I only give this out now and then, as I don't really want people having my number. But, you know, sometimes."

"Sure," I said.

"I'm going to get some rest, do some thinking. I might have an idea or two to make him a little safer, because I know he's not safe here."

We didn't respond to that.

Lillian walked away then, a little woman with big uncombed hair shuffling toward the door, thinking of something she hoped would happen between her and Chief, knowing full well it might not.

(50)

Felix stayed in the chief's room. He had the .22 pistol in his pocket, and he had the chief's gun in the nightstand drawer as backup.

We drove home in Cherry's car to get some self-defense tools, grab a toothbrush and toothpaste, some odds and ends. We thought too we might pick up supper, come back, and relieve Felix when it got dark.

As I drove us, Scrappy said, "It was all you could do not to mention the monkey business to the chief, am I right?"

"I figured a sick, maybe dying man ought to have the right to call a chimpanzee a monkey right now, call a woodchuck a beaver if he liked."

"He does call a weasel a mink."

"There you go."

At the house I picked up my ASP. I left the shotgun. Seemed like a bad idea for the hospital. Scrappy stuck to her Bowie knife.

We gathered up a few things, ordered some food to go from Nijiya, one of my favorite restaurants. Sushi for us and, for Tag, teriyaki chicken, no rice or vegetables. We drove into Nacogdoches, picked the food up, and drove back to May Town.

At the hospital we all ate dinner except the chief. He was eating morphine dreams or some such thing. Just looking at him, you could see how deep he was under. But he was breathing steady. The machine showed lines and bumps of light, made beeps that indicated he wasn't dead.

I put the takeout box for Tag on the floor and opened it. Tag made slurpy short work of his chicken, then eyed us with a look that said "Where's mine?" I believed he had eaten so fast, there hadn't been time for him to form a memory of his meal.

As we ate, keeping an eye on the door, Felix said, "Change of plans. After you left, room phone rang. It was Lillian. She got home and got to thinking she had to get the chief out of here. She knows somebody that knows somebody, and she was able to arrange for a private ambulance coming from Tyler to pick him up, take him to a hospital there. They won't bother to sign him out here, and they'll sign him into Tyler under a false name.

"Lillian told the people here at the hospital they were moving him to Longview. A bit of subterfuge there, just in case Cowboy has contacts here. We wait awhile, the ambulance will be here. By now, Cowboy and what's left of his crew — Gogo and Plug, for sure — most likely know the chief is here, so she wants to move him."

"Think they'd actually hit him in the hospital?" I said.

"I don't think so, but it's hard to figure a psychopath. Moving him is a good preventive option."

The wait seemed to go on forever, but shortly after nightfall, the ambulance arrived. We were sent word it was outside. Felix took the chief's gun from the nightstand, wrapped it in a hand towel from the bathroom.

The EMTs managed Chief Nelson out of his bed and onto a rolling gurney, pushed him outside to the ambulance with one of the orderlies carrying his IV bag, holding it high.

Tag trotted along with us.

Mr. Biggs didn't come in hot, driving the Humvee and hooting with excitement. Nobody showed up except Lillian. She left her car in the lot.

When Chief Nelson was loaded in and the gurney was fastened down safe, she said, "Thank you," and climbed into the ambulance. The back door was wide open. Lillian sat on the bench near the gurney, reached out, and held the chief's plump hand.

Felix leaned in and held out the towel with the gun inside. "From the nightstand," he said.

Lillian nodded understanding. She reached out and took it and placed it in her lap.

Tag jumped inside. One of the EMTs, a stout-looking lady, tried to take hold of his collar to pull him out. Tag growled like a lion. She let go of his collar. At that point, she would have let Tag drive.

"It's okay, Tag," Lillian said. "Go with our friends here."

Tag looked at her, then at us. Guess he was trying to decide how good of friends we were. Perhaps he remembered our shared donut adventure, the time he slept in our bed, and maybe he did remember that teriyaki chicken, because he jumped out of the ambulance and came to sit by Scrappy. He didn't look happy about it, though. He was being a dutiful servant.

"Take care of him, please. Chief loves that dog."

"We will," Scrappy said. "You take care of the chief."

They shut the back of the ambulance, and away it went.

(51)

On the way home, Felix driving, Scrappy in front, me in the back with Tag, I thought we could try and interest the FBI in what we knew, but the information we had was obtained illegally. At least a lot of it. That wobbly search warrant might end up biting us in the ass. Not only us but the chief who'd issued it.

We were no longer guarding the chief, and I felt uncomfortable with that, but if Lillian's subterfuge worked, he would be all right. And as vengeful as Cowboy was, would he bother working out where the chief was. That might take more time than he wanted to waste.

Or was that wishful thinking on my part?

When we came up my long drive and parked, standing by a black SUV in the glow of the night-light that shone out from the overhang in the garage was Gogo. He was holding his hands in the air as if he were about to cry out, "Praise Jesus."

Felix parked behind the SUV, stepped out of the car with his .22 pistol in hand. We followed suit. I had my ASP, Scrappy her Bowie knife, Tag his teeth; his hair rose up in a kind of Mohawk and he growled.

"Easy, Tag," I said.

Gogo said, "It's just me, Felix. No one is with me. All alone here."

"Good," Felix said. "I won't have to waste but one shot."

"You sure Plug isn't waiting in the car?" I said.

"If he were," Gogo said, "you can bet that twenty-two pistol wouldn't bother him much. You might as well throw gravel at him."

"I can shoot his eye out," Felix said, "even with just a night-light."

"I doubt that," Gogo said. "But I didn't come here to argue with you or insult your marksmanship."

"If this is another polite warning, or one that's less polite," Felix said, "either way, consider yourself shot in the head."

"Come on, man. Can we talk?" Gogo said.

"Do we have to?" Felix said.

"I think we ought to. I think I might want to see you don't get dead."

"That's a switch," Felix said.

"I never wanted that. I didn't think I'd scare you off, but I thought it was worth a try. Got nothing against you, Felix."

"What will we talk about?" Felix said.

"Cowboy. Money. Maybe an enormous explosion and a bunch of dead folks."

(52)

Felix had Gogo lie facedown on the driveway and I searched him for weapons. All I found was a ballpoint pen. Right situation, right person using it, a ballpoint could do more damage than just writing a hot check. I took it and dropped it in my coat pocket.

When I finished patting him down, Gogo got up and dusted himself off, said, "Needn't worry about me."

"We look worried?" Felix said.

"No, but you're worrying me."

"Come to my place, drink my coffee and criticize it, have that fuckhead bend my fire poker, that's not polite, Gogo."

"For the record, I didn't ask him to bend the poker."

"You brought him there for intimidation," Felix said. "Close enough."

"I reckon that's so. Talk?"

We ended up on the porch sitting around the table. Tag sat between Scrappy and Gogo. He was studying Gogo as if he were trying to decide if biting him in the balls would be as much fun as biting him in the neck.

Felix held the .22 in Gogo's direction.

I had cut on the porch light. It wasn't particularly strong, but it was enough for Gogo to see the gun.

"Can you point that somewhere else?" Gogo said.

"I could. Yeah." Felix didn't move the pistol.

"You sneeze, it could go off."

"Don't know about a sneeze," Felix said. "But I do feel a fart coming on. They make me jump a little."

"Just take it easy."

"I feel quite comfortable," Felix said. "Very easy." He still didn't move the pistol.

"I guess I'll just start in, then," Gogo said.

"That'll be good," Felix said. "Yeah. Why don't you do that? Why don't you start in?"

"Cowboy, he's kind of in the wrap-up phase. Found out you guys were at the warehouse snooping."

"We already know that," I said.

"Cowboy heard Chief Nelson had a heart attack."

"Did he, now?" Felix said. "I don't know that's right."

"Nice try, but he knows, and I know. We know he's in the hospital."

"Okay," Felix said.

"He hopes the fat man dies from it," Gogo said.

"He's Chief Nelson to you," Scrappy said.

"Okay," Gogo said. "Chief Nelson. If he doesn't die from it, Cowboy's thinking he'd like to help him die. But you know, time is not on Cowboy's side. He's about to pull a Jesse James. Rob the bank and head out of Dodge."

"Not telling us any news," Felix said. "Let me see if I can give you some. Do you know there are bodies in freezers in the warehouse? Maybe gone now, but they were there."

"I did not."

"Been missing some of your team lately?"

"As a matter of fact." Then you could see it all coming together in Gogo's head.

"I thought Cowboy had them on a mission. Or maybe they had just gotten tired of the whole thing and gone off. But them being taken care of, it faintly crossed my mind. I didn't like the way Cowboy or Plug had been looking at me lately. Not to mention Mr. Biggs. Plug, he's not like me. He doesn't have doubts. He's all up in Cowboy's ass.

"Cowboy promised the Managers some really good money, and I mean really good. Was to be our severance package. Got to say, been feeling my severance package might actually be considerably less delightful, and Cowboy is probably trying to increase his retirement. Poor old Plug, if he was any more stupid, there'd have to be two of him. You are saying the bodies of our team, a woman and a man, are in the freezers, right?"

"You're testing me, aren't you?"

"Just asking."

"Woman was dark-haired, looked like she could flip a Buick. Other one, he was under her. I took less note of him. And there was Duncan too. You know him? A deputy in May Town?"

"I do. He was trying to be one of the coat wearers, those fools in the bright jackets. But lately, he'd been kind of weepy and maybe starting to clear his head of all that nonsense. Him being a deputy, having a spiritual crisis about leaving his family, maybe beginning to think there was no place to leave to, so I'm guessing Cowboy decided he had to go."

"Bacon and his wife are there too," Felix said.

"I thought they were upstairs in the house. Really did. But Bacon hasn't been a major player for some time. Cowboy runs the show out there, makes the rules. Bacon's wife, she just went along to get along. She got that satellite TV to watch old shows and ordered commemorative plates. Got history scenes on them. Shit like that is

247

all over the house. I never got the impression she thought they were going anywhere besides the front porch."

"Gogo," Felix said. "You had to know what you were getting into with this Cowboy guy."

"Greed got the better of me, old buddy. Easy work. A little intimidation where Cowboy needed it. Seemed all right. And before you go there, no. I didn't have anything to do with that donut fellow."

"Kevin," I said. "His name was Kevin."

"If his name were St. Louis, I still didn't have anything to do with that. That was Cowboy, the woman you saw in the freezer, and Mr. Biggs. They did it. I know that much, but I didn't have anything to do with it. The two dead at your place, Felix. I heard about it after. I wasn't asked to do that. Told Cowboy I wouldn't hurt you or your brother or the ladies."

Tag turned his head a little, as if doubting that statement.

"Still, you know about it," Scrappy said. "You're part of it, directly or indirectly. You were okay hurting people long-distance."

"I don't take any pleasure in it. Just picked up my check. Cash money, actually."

"What I'm thinking," Felix said, "is you might have done it all firsthand had you been asked. I don't know. But I do know this. You don't tell me something I don't already know pretty damn quick, I'm going to shoot you and tell God you died."

"As I remember, you're not religious."

Felix grinned at him. "Call that remark a metaphor. Allegory? Figure of speech. Whatever. Either way, you'll be dead and buried in the back of Charlie's property."

Way Felix said that, I feared he might mean it.

"Maybe I can give you something new," Gogo said.

"Need to," Felix said.

"Cowboy, he's waiting for the folks to come out for the saucer arrival. Should be a pretty good crowd. They'll come and they'll wait for the saucers, and just when they are expecting the saucers from the sky, their world is going to explode."

"Literally explode?" Scrappy asked.

"Shaping up that way. Lots of fertilizer gathered up. Good basis for explosives. I'm talking bags and bags of it. Arranged all over the place. Fertilizer is mixed up with other stuff that'll make it blow. Figure he'll set a timer or some such. In Cowboy's mind, it's checkout time. That's why I quit him."

"I think you knew all about this," I said.

"No. I didn't. Shit like that, blowing people up, that's too much. What put me onto him, chickens aren't being fed. They're dying or dead and buried in the dirt floors of the chicken houses so as to rid the place of stink. Catfish farm has gone to hell. Pond is now home to a couple of alligators and some loud frogs. It's every chicken and fish for himself.

"And, boy, does Cowboy like fire and explosion. Talks about it all the time. When I found out what he did to that family, you know? That was too much. Hadn't known that. But one night, we're setting around, and he bragged about it, like maybe he'd won the lottery that day with those poor people. That's nothing more than cruelty for cruelty's sake. Time comes, for chuckles, he'll blow up the Landing Pad, wipe out as many of the space clowns as he can on his way out. Probably pop Mr. Biggs in the head with a .357. No more bananas. Then he'll catch a private plane to who knows where. Have all that money shifted electronically, waiting. Have his computer guy over for a visit, and that'll be it for him too. I think it's a woman, actually. Whatever, you can bet it's lights-out for whoever it is."

"Might be some real news in there," Felix said, "so for the moment, I don't shoot you in the head, but I'm thinking maybe one of your nuts gets popped."

"Listen up, Felix. I may not be a prime citizen, but I'm not crazy about Cowboy doing what he's done to the team. Plug, well, I can swing either way on him. I don't like him. But there's the people work there. In the barracks. He makes them wrap things up and bed up about eight at night, up at five to take care of things. Or he did. Now, last couple of weeks, he's just had them forget the chores with the chickens and such because none of that matters anymore. Barracks folks, they figure they're getting a saucer ride in the morning. He's got them reading their saucer bibles in the barracks at night, telling each other how cool things are going to be with all their stored food and shiny firearms and the speeding spaceships. But they'll all die in a blaze of fire. I don't go that far, buddy. I'm flawed, but I'm not cracked."

"That's so sweet of you," Scrappy said. "Kill one at a time, but mass murder, that gets under your skin."

"I have my scruples, gorgeous. There's a line I won't step over. I got some ideas on how we can maybe not have the whole place blow up. Make our mark on Cowboy. He has it coming."

"I'm thinking you do too," Felix said.

"Old times' sake, Felix. You and me together."

"It's not like we're going out to chase women, have beer and pizza."

"This is better."

"How do we know we can trust you?" I asked.

"You don't, but you let it go, those space clowns will be smoking up the Landing Pad."

"Cowboy knows you know what's going to happen?" I asked.

"Yeah. But he doesn't know I'm on the outs with him. He might suspicion, but he doesn't know for sure. I told him I had to get away from the place for a bit. Go into Nacogdoches, find something to eat. Get away from the compound. Instead, I came here."

"I hope you're not hinting for a sandwich," Scrappy said.

"What I'm telling you is I can get you out to the Landing Pad without having to take the normal path. We can sneak up on him. The place isn't really that well guarded. It's too big. And some of the folks who might guard it, according to you, ended up in a freezer."

"It's the 'we' part that makes me nervous," Felix said.

"I get that, but that's all I got. Take it or leave it. Tomorrow, that's when it all blows. We can go out tonight. What do you say?"

"We're listening," I said.

(53)

What I think we do is go out to the Landing Pad and disarm the explosives," Gogo said.

"Like we know how?" I said.

"I know."

"Wait a minute," Felix said. "You know how, but you come to us for help? Why didn't you do it yourself?"

"I need someone to watch my back. First, I have to locate the source, you know. I figure Cowboy has the trigger on his cell phone, rigged to blow it all. I saw that on *Veronica Mars* once, a guy using a cell phone to detonate an explosion."

"I saw that episode," Scrappy said. "I loved that show."

"Great characters," Gogo said.

"For heaven's sake, focus," Felix said.

"Right," Gogo said. "Cowboy has ended up on the top floor of the house. Guess you could say that's his lair. I still thought Bacon and his wife were on the second floor, but now I know different. What we do is we go through the woods on the back of the property, out by the catfish pond, ease up on the house."

"Let the people in the barracks out," I said.

"They wouldn't go," Gogo said. "They don't know axle grease

252

from diarrhea. They wouldn't believe you, and they'd make a racket even if they did. We save them without them knowing they're saved. That's how it has to go. It's over, then they can know."

Tag was stone-still, looking directly at Gogo. Maybe he was a natural lie detector. Could smell a lie like stink on death.

"He doesn't like you," Scrappy said.

"Well," Gogo said, "he may be a good judge of character."

"Suspect so," Scrappy said.

"Who disarms the explosives?" Felix said.

"Control the phone, control the explosives."

"If it is a phone detonation," I said.

"Stop Cowboy, stop the explosion. How it's controlled doesn't matter. With me and you three, we got four chances at that."

"I kind of like the idea that you take them out and we wait here for word," I said.

"Like I said, four chances are better than one. And you three wouldn't be expected."

I thought it might be a plan to get us all out there, get rid of us, and satisfy Cowboy's vengeance, give Mr. Biggs something to play with.

"All right," Felix said. "Scrappy and Charlie can do what they want, but I'm coming. You be there."

"I will be," Gogo said.

"Curiosity's sake, what was your payout supposed to be?" I asked.

"One million. But I figure it was actually supposed to be the cost of a bullet, a bonfire with me in the middle of it. I don't know. Maybe an extra banana for Mr. Biggs, if he does it instead. Plug, who knows. He might want a hamburger and some beer and be satisfied. But I know, like me, he's supposed to get a million. Cowboy might have promised him my money as well."

"And you're sure you know nothing about Meg?" I said.

"Just like I told you before. Cowboy keeps a few girls out there.

Barracks folks. Bacon used to as well. His wife, long as she got the dough-re-mi, didn't care. Meg isn't one I've seen there, just at the donut shop a time or two. I'd seen her there, I'd remember her. Nice shorts. Nice legs. That anklet sets the whole thing off. The bow on the package."

"See you tonight," Felix said.

"I can go, then?" Gogo asked.

Felix had dropped his pistol into his coat pocket. "You can, but before you do, Google Map the place for me. But listen to this: You know me. You fuck me, Gogo, I'll kill you. I know you're thinking you can do the same to me, but I'll tell you right now, you can't. You're you, and I'm me, and I'm better."

Gogo pulled out his phone. "We may find out someday, but not this time. I'll show you where to go."

(54)

Felix was acting more rationally than I'd expected, as he could be rash, to say the least. He called Cherry. He wasn't taking Gogo at his word.

The basic idea was Felix asked her to see if she could someway get the information anonymously to someone high up in the FBI, or even local law enforcement, or, better yet, the Texas Rangers. Asked her to tell them some major business was going down. Hell, she couldn't get law enforcement, gather up a troop of dangerous Girl Scouts, maybe a pissed-off Brownie bunch, get them out to the place well before morning when the crowd of true believers were to arrive, tell them to bring guns or, if nothing else, pitchforks, rakes, a hoe, something. Anything stronger than harsh language. Donuts would be served after. Felix talked a lot of angry shit. He did say to exclude the May Town cops, because the chief didn't trust them. That was his proviso.

When he finished speaking with Cherry, he said, "I don't know Cherry will be able to convince anyone, but she can be persuasive. Think about it. We're trying to save fools from themselves. We manage that, it might be a missed moment of righteous Darwinism."

(55)

Felix brought a backup gun he got from somewhere, a .45 revolver. He gave me the .22 to carry, and I gave it to Scrappy and brought my ASP. Scrappy carried her Bowie knife in a scabbard under her coat. Tag brought Tag, and that was plenty.

I had no intention of shooting anyone, but I felt compelled to go. Maybe there was some kind of delusion in that as well. That I could help fix things. That I could make things right. That I was somehow a person of superior ability when it came to correcting things. I had felt that way about my marriage, that I could save it, and now Meg was missing and was most likely dead, a ghost in my head.

That was proof I wasn't an ultimate fixer. Yet the urge was still there, lurking inside of me like a terminal disease.

We decided to use my Prius. It ran quiet as a dead soul. It seemed right for what we had in mind. Gogo had made a point to meet us at midnight, and we made a point to be much earlier.

About ten thirty we started to drift, rode in the Prius to the area Gogo had suggested on Google Maps. Besides early arrival, we had a few switches in mind.

The first had to do with Scrappy and Tag. Tag liked her best and minded her best. I could understand that.

When we were down deep on a dirt road that wound its way into a stretch of looming pine shadows, we stopped well before the spot Gogo had designated and climbed out of the Prius. Felix pulled a long-handled pair of wire cutters from the trunk where he had placed them before our departure. Tag watched him carefully, as if use of the cutters might be turned over to him at some point.

The air was cold and nipped at us. Our breath was frosty. Just beyond a row of pines was a tall fence. It was sturdy and had close netting. It would keep the not-so-serious out. The fence went for a long way through the dark woods in both directions.

Gogo promised he'd meet us at midnight at a back gate, unlock it, and let us in. Maybe he would. Maybe he wouldn't. I felt like one of those curious, hungry fish that looks at a hanging worm, a slight glisten of hook, and thinks: You know, I can make this work.

Felix was cautious as he cut the fence, having us stand back. He thought it might be electrified. It wasn't. He cut a hole big enough for Scrappy and Tag to slip through. She had pulled her Bowie knife by this time. With that big blade in her hand, she would have been a great model for that warrior queen, Boudicca. Tag looked like her faithful war dog. He might have been wishing he was in a nice warm doghouse for all I knew.

"So I creep slowly, cautiously through the woods, and you guys go in and do the commando stuff," Scrappy said. "What is the commando stuff, by the way?"

"We're not sure," Felix said. "Planning too far ahead isn't smart. Locks you in."

"Meaning you have no idea what you're doing?"

"Meaning," he said, "we're going to put the sneak on them and figure it out as we go. Idea is to disarm the explosive and control the enemy."

"This gets better and better," Scrappy said.

"You had some foxy plan, then you should have laid it out," Felix said.

"For a foxy plan, you need more research," she said.

"For a foxy plan, you need more time," Felix said.

"It is what it is," I said. "We get nabbed, maybe you can help, or go for help."

"Meaning the boys get to do the rough stuff?" Scrappy said.

"You are capable, Scrappy, but you aren't as big as a gnat's hind leg," Felix said.

"I'm wiry."

"You're our secret weapon," I said. "You and that sword and Tag."

"What I am is a redheaded lady in the woods with a Bowie knife, a dog, and two nitwits. I don't exactly feel part of the team."

"Just ease up but stay in the shadows," Felix said. "We'll take our time getting to the gate, about a half mile down the road, if the directions are right. We're going to beat Gogo to the punch, get there early. The law might even show up, if Cherry's successful."

"Have a feeling that's about as possible as the spaceships arriving," Scrappy said.

With reluctance, we left Scrappy and Tag to their own devices. They had already begun to move through the trees, using the moonlight and a phone flashlight as a guide. They seemed ready and eager and stealthy.

I heard a mild crash, and then: "Goddamn it, Tag. Watch where you walk."

Maybe they needed a bit more work on the stealth part. Some kind of jungle course or something.

(56)

The East Texas woods at night can be dead dark. One can imagine all manner of things in there. You might even discover a deer is standing next to you.

I had that happen once, while I was on an investigation, sneaking through woods to see if I could get on a property and discover if a suspect was stealing roadwork equipment and hiding it inside a barn.

He was, by the way.

I paused to find the trail I had stepped off of, turned on my flashlight, and there was the deer. Inches from me. We were both surprised.

The deer wheeled and zipped out of there so fast, all he left in his wake was stirred leaves and a slight aroma of damp fur. I wondered what stories he would have to tell his fellow deer about the alien in the woods. Or perhaps he reported me to them as a Bigfoot sighting.

Good luck, Scrappy.

Me and Felix went back to the car and drove down to the gate. It was closed. There was Gogo's black SUV setting on the other side of it, the headlights on, the motor humming, exhaust rising. The woods edged in close to it on both sides. Gogo had arrived early. He had out-snuck us. Predicted what we would do. He was no fool. But maybe we were.

We got out cautiously. I thought about the ASP in my boot, but I didn't pull it. It was scant comfort even knowing it was there. Gogo didn't get out.

Felix climbed over the fence like a giant squirrel. I followed with less squirrel-like maneuvers. We walked around to the SUV, Felix on the driver's side, me on the passenger's.

Felix had pulled the .45. He opened the SUV door, proving it was unlocked. "Shit," he said.

I tried the opposite door. It too was unlocked. I flashed my small penlight in there. Behind the wheel, still as death, because that was in fact the situation, was the chief. His hands were in his lap. There was an oxygen hookup stuck under his nostrils, but the dangling tube was attached to nothing. His throat was cut, and his hospital gown was crusted with blood.

Lying on the seat beside him, her head on his thigh, looking up at the roof of the SUV, was Lillian. She wasn't taking a nap. There was blood all over the seat, and she had what some call the scarlet smile — her throat was cut from ear to ear.

That ambulance ride to Tyler had been shortened. They had been betrayed by someone. My guess, a saucer goon that worked at the hospital. Someone Lillian might have trusted and shouldn't have. I figured that whoever that was had delivered them directly into the hands of the nutjobs, who at this juncture didn't care what they did so as not to be deterred. Some of those jacket wearers, most likely. Replacing the Managers that were cooling in the freezer or by now were in some ditch or rotting in the woods with vultures eating their flesh.

I looked at them for several seconds, took a deep breath. Damn it. I had liked them both. They were looking for a moment together, and what they got was being murdered. I hoped the chief had never woken from his pain cocktail, never knew his throat was being cut. It had happened here, though, that blood being fresh. By then, who knows. Who the hell knows? But poor Lillian, she was awake. Had to be. We had delivered her to that ambulance, and inside were Saucer People, and they had brought them here.

Stunned, I was running all of this through my mind, thinking that maybe letting Cowboy blow the whole shebang up and take those morons with it wasn't such a bad idea. Darwinism at work. A service to the planet. What we might ought to do was go home.

But I couldn't live with that. Not and look in the mirror and shave my baby face, scraping strawberry fur into the sink.

A shadow in the shape of a large tree stump fell over me, silent as mist on water.

I couldn't figure how the stump had been in the trees and moved so swiftly out of them to stand next to me. The stump poked something against my head. I moved my left eye enough to see what was being stuck in me. A long gun. Shotgun, to be exact.

"Cowboy wants to see you," the stump said. It was Plug. He had a high sweet voice like Minnie Mouse during sex with Mickey. Or, if she was promiscuous, Goofy.

No wonder Plug didn't like to talk.

Felix stepped to where he could look over the hood.

"You got some light feet, Plug," Felix said. "Where's Gogo?"

"Cowboy wanted this nice surprise for you," Plug said. "Pull those shits out, get in, and drive. I'll sit with baby brother in the back. Less bloody."

"I thought you might be mute," Felix said.

"I talk when I have something to say."

"You squeak when you have something to squeak, you mean," Felix said. "You might want to get your voice checked. Sounds to me like you could use some oil, maybe find a grown man, jack him up your ass, and have him talk for you."

I thought: Felix, he has a shotgun. To my head. And he isn't friendly.

"Get in, or lose some kin," Plug said. "First, though, slide that forty-five across the hood."

Felix made a point of pushing it hard enough to scrape paint. It fell on the ground on my side of the SUV.

Plug said, "We'll leave it there. And you, brother-boy, pull that ASP out of your boot and drop it on the ground. Didn't think I saw that, did you?"

In fact, I hadn't.

Felix dragged the chief out and dropped him on the ground, then Lillian.

"Sorry," Felix said to the bodies.

Me and Plug got in the back seat. The shotgun barrel continued to be stuck to my head tight as a mole. Felix climbed in the front.

"Goddamn, the seat is sticky with blood," Felix said.

"Go where I tell you," Plug said.

Felix was told to back the car, turn it around where the sandy road widened, head toward the compound.

Few moments later, the shotgun barrel bumping against my noggin, we could see the barracks and the big house in the moonlight; there were pole lights shining on it as well.

Before the house was a narrow strip of land that slipped over a large pond. Water was on either side of the strip. The moonlight made the water look like mercury.

When we came to the land strip, Plug had us stop in the middle of it. He said, "That's supposed to be a catfish farm, but it's a catfish feed for the alligators now. Cowboy has us feed them dead chickens too. I wanted to show you your future home."

"You've grown chatty?" Felix said. "I liked it better when you didn't talk."

"I was thinking how the gators would like you two."

"You're just mad I could bend that fire poker back in place. I embarrassed your ass."

"Drive on," Plug said.

"Where's Gogo?" Felix asked.

No answer.

(57)

We ended up at one of the long chicken houses, and through the cracks in the windows, we could see a dim light.

Plug had Felix park the SUV, and we got out. The shotgun was still against my head. A bump of trigger and I would be gone. It might help my headache, though. My head felt as large and swollen as an over-aired dirigible.

We were marched to the chicken house and through a slightly open door of considerable size. The smell of chicken manure, rank chicken feed, rotting meat, and that musky stench I had smelled at Kevin's house were all knotted up together.

Inside, the small light in the chicken house gave the dusty air a poison-cloud effect. A front-end loader was parked inside. I assumed it was the one we had seen at the warehouse.

Dead chickens were strewn about. There were dead chickens in cages and some that were barely surviving, heads drooping, beaks open. The feed pans and water pans were empty. There were stray feathers in the pans. There was a pile of chickens near the back of the place. There was a door back there, cracked open, letting in outside light, both natural and artificial.

The most obvious thing about the place was that hanging from a chain was Gogo. He had handcuffs on his wrists, and they were fastened to a chain, and the chain had a hook on the opposite end. The hook was fixed through a link on another chain attached to a rafter. Gogo was barely off the ground. He wiggled the toes of his boots trying to touch earth but was not quite able to. Considering his size, it wouldn't be long before his shoulders dislocated, if they hadn't already.

Standing there by him was a large man, larger than Gogo, wearing a white cowboy hat. It was sweat-stained and the faint light in the chicken house made the sweat look even nastier. The photo I had seen didn't do him justice. He was seven foot if he was an inch. He had shoulders wide as a Greyhound bus, legs like the pillars that held up the Acropolis.

He had on a black duster sprinkled with dried chicken droppings and black cowboy boots coated in the same. The duster was pushed back off his right hip, revealing a big old revolver in a jet-black holster with silver conchas. His shirt and pants were black, also powdered with dust and dried chickenshit. He had an electric cattle prod in one hand, was waving it about. I had been hit accidentally by one of those one summer when I had a job working on a ranch. Fellow next to me reached out to hit a cow with it to move it, and he slipped, hit me with the prod. The shock from it made me see all the way back to the beginning of time and feel the pain of all things that had ever died, gave me the shimmy-shimmy shakes, knocked me out for a few seconds. It was not an experience I wished to repeat.

Opposite side of Gogo, sitting on his haunches, leaning forward on his knuckles as if poised for the starter gun in a footrace, was Mr. Biggs.

Biggs was full grown and looked more like a gorilla than a chimpanzee. His black fur was oily and grimy in the light. He had patches of missing fur. He had on a red cowboy hat with a red and white drawstring hanging down from it, pulled tight under his chin. He had on red plastic booties designed to look like cowboy boots. There were little red plastic holsters, one on either hip, supported by a wide belt. The holsters had what looked like cap guns in them. Made to wear that shit, no wonder he had an anger problem.

The smell from Mr. Biggs became more pronounced as we were urged forward by Plug. When we stopped, we were about eight feet away from the trio.

"Nice night, huh?" Felix said.

He just couldn't help himself.

Gogo lifted his head. It took a lot of effort. His face was beaded with sweat. His nose was partly on his cheek, and his lips were bloody, like two worms that had been stomped on. Way he hung there, it caused his lungs to seize up. He kept trying to lift himself by grabbing the chain fastened to his wrist to relieve the pain, but he could manage it for only a few seconds, then had to let go, starting the business all over again.

"I wasn't as sneaky as I thought," Gogo said.

"I can see that," Felix said.

"I want you to know, I talked," he said. "Boy, did I talk."

"Can't blame you," Felix said. "Cattle prod and all."

"Shut up," Cowboy said. "You folks are a pain in my ass for no reason. Chief, that bitch, they weren't even a problem and I had them killed. No one fucks with me, fucks me over and gets away with it. And think about it, they merely annoyed me. You two, I hate badly, and we've only just now met."

"We're kind of stinkers," Felix said. "Of course, nothing to match the stench in here."

Cowboy managed a grin. "I could say to Mr. Biggs, 'Tear them up,' and he could rip off your arms and legs easy as tearing the arms and legs off a child's doll. I can almost do that myself. Off an actual child, I mean. It would take me some work to tear off your arms and legs, but Mr. Biggs, it would be nothing. Ask Kevin. Oh yeah, you can't."

"Mr. Biggs sure dresses cute," Felix said. "No wonder you're screwing him, Cowboy."

Holy shit, shut up for once, Felix.

You could damn near see a cloud forming over Cowboy's head. Mr. Biggs sensed Cowboy's discomfort, stirred a little. The light caught his eyes, and for a moment, it was as if I could see every bad thing ever done to that animal tucked inside of him, ready to explode.

"I had unpleasant plans for you," Cowboy said, "but now I'm thinking I could make them more unpleasant."

Felix studied Cowboy for a moment. "You think you're a Bond villain or what?"

"Always wanted to be a Bond villain," Cowboy said. "A real-life one. Like Dr. No. Here's a Bond villain thing for you: Got this place rigged to blow like Krakatoa shot from a cannon. I want you to know you should have stayed home. I know you're thinking that now."

"This is true," I said.

"Thrills me to think about all that fire," Cowboy said. "I get excited. I can feel my asshole pucker and my dick get hard. Light a match, see a blaze, I get that way. But this, what I got planned, I'll shit myself and blow a wad all at once."

"That sounds messy. But before you do that," Felix said, "why don't you sic Plug there on me. Keep the monkey fresh for a sexual rendezvous."

"Mr. Biggs is a chimpanzee," Cowboy said.

Well, Cowboy had that going for him. The right nomenclature for the right primate. I was kind of impressed.

"Plug's dying for a piece of me," Felix said, "and I'd love to give him some. We're going to go up in flame and smoke, I'd like to have my shot."

"We aren't going up, me and Plug, but you will," Cowboy said.

"Plug said you embarrassed him. Think you're tough, bending a metal bar. But one-on-one, you're not so tough, I assure you. Plug was a sumo. They're a badass bunch."

"Heard that," Felix said. "Haven't seen the evidence."

Gogo could barely speak, his lungs tight from the way he was hanging. But he said, "Felix can take him."

"Well, I'm going to have you hurt bad one way or another," Cowboy said. "I like to think you'll be alive when the explosion sweeps over you. It'll happen so fast, someone else's life will pass before your eyes."

"Find out," Gogo said, and it was all he could do to say it. "Let Plug have a shot at Felix."

"Shut up, Gogo, or I'll let Mr. Biggs pull your face out through your asshole. Want to find out, Plug? Before we wrap things up?"

Plug nodded. For the first time I saw a faint smile on his face. I had faith in Felix, but damn, a sumo?

"I mean, you want to," Cowboy said, "it's all right. I got some time. Still waiting on the true believers to show up."

Felix smiled at Cowboy. That was a smart move. You could see it made Cowboy uncertain.

Cowboy went into deep thought for a moment. "Still, not that much time. Think maybe you people may have someone on the way, so might be best I get this party started. Believers up in the barracks, they've already met the devil. I gassed them while they slept. It was swift and silent. That kind of thing disappoints me. But you see, I thought I'd be where I could see the explosion, see all those saucer idiots vaporized. Then I realized I needed to take them out silently, set some more explosives just right. Hey, wasn't there a girl with you guys? Between prods, Gogo said there was a girl."

"She didn't come," I said.

"I like women," Cowboy said. "Or girls. But I got to agree with an old friend of mine who said if women didn't have a pussy, there'd be a bounty on them."

Mr. Biggs was beginning to rock nervously on his knuckles.

Cowboy reached into the pocket of his duster, pulled out his phone. "Let's give this some stake. You know, like a movie where you see the bomb ticking, the clock inching along. I'm starting the timer now."

He hit something on the phone with his thumb.

"Twenty minutes. Plug, you got to do this turd in less than twenty. Let's say ten. That gives us ten to drive away from here fast as we can go. Then this place, that stupid mound, and, of course, you guys, it's a zap and a flash and you're gone. Better get going, Plug. You got nine minutes."

"He's going to shoot you in the back of the head, Plug," Gogo said, pulling himself up on the chains. "You're not leaving here either. I bet the monkey gets a bullet too. Travel fast, travel light and unencumbered. That's the plan."

Cowboy popped Gogo one with the cattle prod. Gogo jumped, dangled on the chains, gasped for breath.

"No such thing," Cowboy said, as casual as if he had taken a sip of coffee. "Plug is a compadre. Me and Plug and Mr. Biggs will stop by the gate, watch the explosion together. It won't blow back that far. Almost, but not quite. I know my stuff. Plug will break you up, big boy, and we'll shoot your brother's knees out and be gone."

Plug moved away from me, walked over to Cowboy, and gave him the shotgun. Cowboy took it in his free hand, then gently placed it on the ground. He put his hand on his revolver. Mr. Biggs turned his head toward them, inquisitive, anxious.

Cowboy said, "Ungawa, Mr. Biggs."

I think that was Tarzan-movie talk for "Stand your ground." Whatever it was, Mr. Biggs had been trained to understand it, so he stayed where he was.

"Don't try and run," Cowboy said to me. "I can draw fast and shoot the hat off a flea."

"I bet it has to be a big flea," Felix said.

"Test me," Cowboy said.

Felix grinned, stripped off his jacket. Plug did the same. Plug unclipped his holster and pistol, dropped them on the ground at Cowboy's feet.

Mr. Biggs hooted softly.

Cowboy said, "Mr. Biggs, I said ungawa."

Mr. Biggs held his position beside Gogo, who was still attempting to touch the ground with his boot tips. The look on Gogo's face made me hurt.

Felix and Plug moved toward each other. Their arms bulged with enormous knots of muscle. Felix bent at the waist, way he did when he wrestled in high school. His thighs pressed against his pants legs, straining the fabric.

Felix glanced at Cowboy. "I finish with him and you're next, big fella."

Cowboy moved his lips a little, checked the time on his phone.

Felix turned his attention to Plug, who was slightly crouched, arms spread.

Felix said, "Come get you some, honeybunch."

(58)

Felix and Plug came together with a smacking sound followed by grunts, and then they whirled around in a circle, their hands clutching each other's shoulders.

Plug flung Felix away from him. Felix skidded and went to one knee in the grime. He came up quick and they came together again.

Felix smacked Plug over the ear with his palm and it made a whapping sound that moved Plug's head a foot. When his head popped back into place, blood oozed out of his ear.

Plug tried to do the same to Felix, but Felix ducked, and the strike slid over the top of his head and ruffled his hair. Felix pushed Plug back with double palms to the chest, then a right cross to the chin that made Plug do a bit of a dance step. Felix hit him again with a left while he was off balance. Plug grunted, and like Felix had done, he went to one knee, as if he were about to propose.

Felix kicked him in the head and knocked him on his back. He scooped Plug's right ankle up, wrapped the ankle in his armpit, fell backward, threw his left leg against Plug's knee. Felix tightened his biceps on Plug's ankle. He used his right foot to push against Plug's free leg. Felix leaned back farther, looked up and swelled his chest, pushed up with his groin.

There was a sound like a party popper going off. Plug screamed high and long as his knee popped. I saw Mr. Biggs start to move. But Cowboy spoke to him again, commanded him back to his place. This way he could be rid of Plug by Felix's hand, and then it was us.

Plug struggled like a fish on a line but couldn't get loose, couldn't get hold of Felix in any manner that mattered. The chicken mess and dust on the floor had formed a greasy cloud above them as they squirmed.

Out of the corner of my eye, I saw shadows darken the back door-way for a moment, then there was swift movement. The shadows moved in our direction.

A moment later, Cowboy said, "Well, that's some shit, Plug." Then he straightened up suddenly, as if a general had called attention. An involuntary whistle slid through his teeth. He spun quickly to see Tag and Scrappy. As he turned away from us, I could see the Bowie jutting out of his back.

Scrappy said, "Mess him up, Tag."

Tag hit Cowboy. It was crazy. He seized one of Cowboy's ankles, cracked it like a chicken bone, Tag's teeth tearing right through the cowboy boot. But Cowboy didn't fall.

Cowboy tried to reach behind him and touch his back, but he couldn't. Not where Scrappy's Bowie had stabbed him, not where it poked out of his back like an appendage. He spun awkwardly as Tag shifted and went for his balls. Tag ripped right through Cowboy's pants. Blood jumped out of Cowboy's crotch, and I got a glimpse of something wet and meaty.

Tag shook Cowboy like a rag. Amazingly, Cowboy didn't go down. He seemed to be doing a kind of Saint Vitus' dance. He swung the cattle prod at Tag, but the way Tag was shaking him, he missed.

This all happened in seconds. So fast we were all stunned, includ-ing Mr. Biggs. But now the beast hooted and scrambled to Cowboy's aid, his silly red cowboy hat flying off his head and hanging on the drawstring.

Scrappy said, "Stop, Tag. Come to me."

Tag let Cowboy go, ran to Scrappy's side.

Cowboy's snapped ankle had finally had enough. The tendons and muscles that had held him upright let go. Down he went, on his side, flailing the cattle prod about, hoping to hit Tag or Scrappy.

Mr. Biggs was going for the dog, but Cowboy's arm moved and accidentally hit the ape in the leg with the cattle prod.

There was a frying-bacon sizzle, and Mr. Biggs leaped up in the air like a giant fuzzy jumping bean, came down on his silly red plastic cowboy boots, and grabbed the prod. He jerked it from Cowboy's hand.

In pain and blind panic, Mr. Biggs went to work on Cowboy with the prod, using it as a club. It was like watching a rock drummer driving a beat.

Felix let go of Plug, clambered to his feet. Plug lay on the ground, still screaming. His knee poked against his pants at a funny angle.

Felix said, "Enjoy the fire."

By this time Mr. Biggs had abandoned the cattle prod, gotten hold of Cowboy's ankle, and, having lost his shit completely, was swinging Cowboy around, smacking him against the ground like he was thrashing grain.

Mr. Biggs might have meant to help his master, but it seemed to me he was taking out a lot of personal indignities on Cowboy, all the way back to when he had been snatched from his mother and given his first funny uniform to wear. If Cowboy wasn't dead, he was damn close to it. He had lost his hat, his pistol, a boot, and about half his head.

While Mr. Biggs was occupied, me and Felix grabbed Gogo, lifted him off the hook. Mr. Biggs ran around the chicken house swinging Cowboy about like a wet towel. The plastic boots on the ape's feet had come apart and the cap guns had fallen out of the holsters. That was one mad chimpanzee.

When we got Gogo down, Scrappy was already inside the front-end loader cab, cranking it up. Tag, agile as a mountain goat, climbed up after her through the open side on the cab.

"Let's scoot," Scrappy said. Her voice could barely be heard over the roar of the motor, not to mention the roaring in my head; my headache felt like a continual avalanche.

We had to work hard to get Gogo's big ass up there. Him wearing handcuffs didn't help his climbing abilities.

It was a tight fit inside the cab. Felix ended up standing, holding on to the metal doorframe.

I glanced at Tag, sitting between me and Scrappy. His muzzle was coated in blood.

"This baby has some juice," Scrappy said.

"Use it," Gogo said.

I looked back at Plug. He was crawling on the ground toward the front entrance and the SUV. A dead turtle with a hernia and one leg could have moved faster.

Mr. Biggs finally realized his buddy Cowboy had been turned into a bloody tatter of poking bones and peeling meat. He showed his teeth. He let go of what was left of Cowboy, dropped to his knuckles, and started toward us.

I said, "Uh-oh."

Scrappy had been driving the loader toward the back door, but when she looked over her shoulder and saw that Mr. Biggs was going to reach us within moments, she wheeled the front-end loader around expertly. I wouldn't have thought a machine like that could turn the way it did, but Scrappy made it sit up and beg.

"Great suspension," she said. "Nice blade, certified monkey killer."

She drove it straight for Mr. Biggs. He leaped up and grabbed the blade. Scrappy lifted it, slammed it down on the ground, but I could still see Mr. Biggs's dark fingers clutching the top of it. Then his head poked over the blade.

"Time for a monkey scraping," Scrappy said.

Scrappy wheeled the machine all the way around, started right for the chicken-house wall. Dead chickens and pens and the wall collapsed as she ran Mr. Biggs and the blade into them.

There was a splintering of wood and a horrid grating sound. Then we rolled out under lunar beams and pole-light rays. Mr. Biggs was still clinging to the blade. He started climbing over it again.

"Determined, isn't he?" Scrappy said.

Tag was starting to stand. I think he thought he could walk on air out to the blade and bite Mr. Biggs in the face. But bad as Tag was, Mr. Biggs was worse. He was mean and strong and had the smell of blood in his nostrils. He would have ripped apart anything in his path.

Scrappy began to slam the blade down on the ground. Up and down, she rolled along, but Mr. Biggs was not a slacker. He clung.

We came to the catfish pond, still shiny as a big hole full of mercury.

"Get ready to swim," Scrappy said.

We shot out and into the water. Mr. Biggs did not let go of that blade, though his eyes were as wide as saucers and his open mouth looked to be full of wet bayonets.

There was a roar at our backs. The night lit up like a Christmas parade. There was a sound of cracking and breaking, and the fire licked at our backs and tipped us over and down.

There was intense heat, a feeling of weightlessness as we sailed out, then dropped straight down; we hit the pond with an impact that drove the water against us and slapped us out of the cab. I saw a swirl of Gogo in the water, Tag too, and then I was going down, my coat having gotten caught up in something or another on the loader.

Looking up, I could see the fire rolling over the surface of the water, dancing on it. I looked down. The fire was so bright I could see all the way to the bottom of the pond.

Down I went with the machine and Mr. Biggs. The blade hit the bottom, sandwiching Mr. Biggs between it and the pond bed. There was a blast of silt. I felt as if my brain were about to blow out of the top of my head. My coat ripped loose on impact, shaking my teeth and rattling my bones.

I was going up, fast.

The fire had wafted on past the pond, probably blown out.

Scrappy came out of nowhere. She had me by the collar.

When we broke the surface of the water, I gasped for air, then went silent when Scrappy said, "Alligator."

Sure enough, a big one swam right past us, like we were nothing more than bobbing logs. It dove. My guess was chimpanzee meat was on the menu.

Scrappy dragged me a ways, then I got it together and began to swim. I swim like a desert dweller. Me and her made the bank of the pond simultaneously. Felix was there, dripping water. He pulled us out, one at a time. He did it as if we were five-pound bags of sugar.

Tag stood on the bank shaking water out of his fur.

Where all the buildings had been, including the barracks that had held the jacket wearers, there was nothing but smoking lumber and blackened foundations.

Beyond all that, the fire was kissing the woods. Even from that distance, you could hear burning pine bark snapping and green needles hissing. But the bulk of the flames had blown out.

Felix turned and looked at the water. We looked too. There were ribbons of smoke fading over the surface of the pond. The water was coated with debris. Mr. Biggs's red cowboy hat floated in the midst of it.

Felix said, "Where's Gogo?"

"Hard to swim in handcuffs," I said.

"I hope that goddamn Mr. Biggs is dead," Felix said.

"Dead or alive, he is about to provide a very large reptile with a very large supper," I said.

"Bon appétit," Scrappy said.

(59)

I feel weak," I said, holding my aching head. Then I felt a case of the vapors, as they say in those old Victorian novels, and went topsy-turvy into the void.

When I woke up, I was in the back seat of the Prius. Tag was licking my face. It felt good. His breath smelled like spoiled hamburger, but I didn't care.

I closed my eyes and he kept licking. I went to sleep again.

The hospital smelled of disinfectant, colostomy bags, and body odor. I opened my eyes. Helios couldn't have seen a brighter light when he pulled the sun across the sky in his chariot.

I felt so weak that lifting my hand was an effort worthy of Hercules. There was a bandage around my head. I could tell that. I could see a plastic bag on a rack by the bed. The bag was filled with a nearly clear liquid. The room was as white as an empty nowhere.

I closed my eyes against the light and the white.

That was nice.

I liked it behind my eyelids.

I didn't need the bed adjusted. I didn't need a massage, an insurance policy, or a nice breakfast, didn't need anything but that slow drip that was going into my arm.

Meg came to me and sat on the side of the bed. I couldn't see her. I wouldn't, couldn't, open my eyes. But I knew she was there. I smelled lilacs.

She didn't adjust the bed for me.

I think she may have touched my hand. I wasn't sure I felt anything. I just thought she might have touched me.

"One bright stone," she said. "Think about it."

I said, "Huh?"

It seemed as if only a moment had passed, but it had to have been much longer. When I finally opened my eyes, Meg wasn't there. The room was still bright, but the window was touched by morning, and the light there was less bright and golden.

Scrappy was sitting by my bedside.

"I thought you were going to sleep forever," she said.

When I spoke, my mouth was dry and my lips smacked. "Me too, but in a different context. Literally."

"But here you are."

"Yep," I said. "Here I am. Can I have some water?"

Scrappy poured some water into a sippy cup with a plastic straw. That was the best water I ever drank. My throat loved it. My stomach loved it. Even Aquaman would have felt it was the freshest water he had ever been in, though he might want to mess it up with a spoonful of salt.

"Listen here, Charlie. We have enough for one hell of a book."

"Okay. Any news about when I get out of here?"

"Today or tomorrow. You been here, I think . . . let me see. No. Not quite a week. Four days."

"Damn, I must have been hurt worse than I thought."

"It was the brain tumor."

"What?"

"You had one. Doctor determined it while doing other tests and decided it had to go. It was the source of those headaches, Charlie, and it was threatening your health. Your life. So they cut it out. Not cancerous, by the way, but not good to stay put. It could go rogue if left alone. Felix gave them permission to cut on you. He has, like, a power of attorney or some such thing from Cherry."

"Which they made up and most likely backdated," I said. "I don't remember giving them that task."

"Be glad they lied. Otherwise, you'd be cremated and spread over your property like fertilizer."

"Totally content with their lie."

"You'll have a minor scar, but most of it, if not all, will be hidden when your hair grows back."

"They cut my hair?"

I reached up and touched my head.

"Shaved a big patch of it. Looks like a little highway for lice. If you had lice, of course."

"What about Gogo? They find him?"

"Nope. They found some fur and bones from Mr. Biggs, but nothing from Gogo. He may have gotten out of the water on his own, kept going. Seems that way. Felix claims he didn't see him, but remember, he was on the bank when we climbed out of the pond. Felix might have seen him go, though Gogo would have been really weak. If I'd been through what he went through, I'd have needed assistance to nod my head."

"I just want to go home."

"I know."

"I feel sleepy."

"It's the drug. Every now and then it kicks in and shoots sleepy juice into you. Relieves pain too. Maybe something else. You'll have to ask the doctor or a nurse. I really don't have much in the way of medical education."

She said this as if I'd thought she might.

Even though Scrappy was talking nonstop, and I could see her lips moving, I suddenly couldn't have heard an earwig if it farted in my ear through an ear trumpet.

Then, out of nowhere, I heard Meg say, "Shiny. Beware the omelet."

And then, suddenly, I was so far to the bottom, it might as well have been the top. I was pretty sure in that moment I had some answers about some things. They had been in front of me all along, tucked behind my brain tumor, like a misplaced set of keys lying under some knickknack on a shelf.

(60)

A few days later, out of the hospital and wearing a blue ball cap to cover my missing patch of hair, I found out Chief Nelson's out-of-town replacement had become chief. One of his first acts as chief was to ride over and meet me at the apartment complex where Meg and Ethan had lived. I went there alone. Scrappy was home with Tag, who was now our dog.

Chief Stone had a couple of deputies with him I had never seen before. New, I assumed.

The chief was a big obsidian-black man, handsome like a clothes model, only bigger. I doubted he was able to buy most of his clothes off the rack. His uniform seemed to have been tailored for him. His cowboy hat appeared to have been molded to his head. He had on shiny black cowboy boots.

I had been waiting for him and his deputies when they arrived.

He'd brought a signed search warrant along. I wondered if the former chief had told him about the signed ones in his desk drawer.

When I had first arrived at the complex, I stopped in front of the sign out front. It no longer said OOM O ET. It had been filled in with new letters — ROOMS TO LET.

OMELET, it had looked like, but until the hospital I hadn't put it together.

I thought about what Meg had said in the hospital, or perhaps what I had said to myself, giving my thoughts substance by having her be the one to say it.

One bright stone.

Why one bright stone?

Unless it wasn't a stone.

Shortly after the chief came up and we shook hands and introduced ourselves, a couple of hired workers with shovels and such showed up.

Evelyn and her husband were brought out by one of the deputies to stand on the sidewalk. The search warrant was served. Evelyn clutched it in a tight fist. She and the Penis looked weak in the knees.

I showed the chief and the diggers where the flower bed had been made, the one almost in front of Meg's apartment. The one where I thought at the time I had seen a shiny rock.

What could shine in the sun?

A rock? Certain kinds, maybe.

But just one rock?

Gravel? Less likely, but if it did shine, again, would it be just one piece? Lot of rocks and gravel there.

Unless the shiny rock wasn't a rock. Wasn't gravel.

There was another thing that might shine.

A silver heart on an anklet.

There was more dirt in the bed than when I had seen it last, and there were plants, bare rosebushes. Come summer they would grow and bloom, fertilized by what was beneath the soil.

Or they would have bloomed if the diggers that came out with the chief and his search warrant hadn't dug them up and tossed them out. When they dug a little deeper, they released a decaying smell strong enough to support an elephant.

Then part of a leg and a foot was revealed, and something on the chain around the ankle sparkled.

I got sick. Threw up just off the sidewalk. Chief Stone patted me on the back.

I walked out to my car and waited there. I didn't want to see anymore.

(61)

Two days later, at my table having lunch with Scrappy, Felix, and Cherry, Tag watching us eat, I heard a car drive up.

It was Chief Stone.

He was alone. He came in and I set him out an empty plate. He waved the idea away, only asked for a cookie. I had placed a batch on another plate for dessert.

There was some general talk before Chief Stone said, "A bit of news I was told to tell you by one of the old deputies. While you were in the hospital, someone named Grover went into hospice, lasted three days. I presume you knew him?"

"Yes. I'm sorry to hear that," I said.

Cherry, Scrappy, and Felix agreed.

They hadn't got Grover. He had gone out on his own terms.

"Anything on Gogo?" I said.

"That would be the fellow you told me about? Gave y'all a clue on how to get out there?"

"That didn't work out as well as we had hoped," Felix said. "They were onto him. But messy as it was, it did work out."

"Course, there was a barrack full of dead folks," Chief Stone said.

"Yep," Scrappy said. "That's a black mark, but hey, we were trying."

Chief Stone nibbled on his cookie. "You saved a lot of other people from showing up to an explosion. Some came out the next morning, thought the saucers had come early, and them blasting off is what burned all that business down."

"Figures they'd think that," I said.

"As for this Gogo," Chief Stone said, "nothing. He's either in the wind or being digested by one of the pond gators. Gators got a home in the Lufkin Zoo, by the way."

"That's some good news," Scrappy said. "The gators, I mean."

"One morning they might find this Gogo's skull in a pile of alligator poop," Stone said.

"I think Gogo swam out and kept going," Felix said. "That big bastard is tough and crafty."

"Maybe," Chief Stone said.

I got up and made some coffee for us, and then, when we were all settled again, we talked about our maladies for a while. Chief had a slightly bad knee from football. Felix had his sugar problem. Cherry admitted to an ingrown toenail, and I had a recently removed brain tumor. Scrappy and Tag listened to us, probably thinking there had to be something more interesting to discuss, them lacking procedures or diet restrictions.

Cherry was the one who cracked the ice on what we really wanted to know.

"So, Evelyn and her husband, Cletus?"

"Evelyn broke. Talked. Meg didn't do a thing, but Evelyn got tired of her husband looking at her. Said he'd fuck a test-tube hole in case an amoeba or some kind of skin cell was tucked down in it. One night, Evelyn caught Meg coming back from where she would stand at the fence and look at the pool. Meg was sneaking a cigarette. Did it late at night when Ethan was asleep."

"She smoked?" I said.

"What Evelyn said. Some quick puffs down by the pool, then back to bed. Evelyn was tired of Meg and her short-shorts, her husband leering. Evelyn said she had been drinking heavily, her husband was sleeping sound in the bedroom. She was standing at the window looking out and saw Meg by the pool. Said the alcohol took over. She went down and confronted Meg.

"Meg didn't know what she was talking about. Evelyn said she knew she was telling the truth, but she was sick of Cletus ogling her, and she and Meg had some cross words. Stupid words, she called them. Meg tried to go back to her apartment, but Evelyn hit her with her fist, knocked her down. Meg hit her head on the concrete, cracked it like a walnut. She was still alive, squirming on the ground. Evelyn decided she had to finish it. She used a shovel Cletus had left lying in a flower bed he was building."

"Damn," Felix said.

I felt sick to my stomach, but it was a story close to what I had figured out.

"Then here's the corker. Evelyn went and got her husband. Believe that? Kills Meg, then gets her husband to help her dispose of the body. He's already working on the flower bed, so they decide to put her there while it's still dark. Buried her fast and shallow. Figured it was deep enough to hide her until they could order more dirt, have it hauled in. But here's the big ol' sugarplum on top of the shit cake. They use their passkey, sneak into the apartment where Meg lived, and smother Ethan in bed. She said he only knew what was happening for a moment. Cletus did it with a pillow. Thought if they left one alive, there were questions that Ethan would pursue. They didn't take into consideration her ex-husband would be so relentless. Anyway, they both got buried in the flower bed."

"Charlie had it figured all along, just in the back of his thinking, behind whatever else goes on in that head of his," Felix said.

"I think my tumor did all the thinking," I said. "Lately, I haven't seemed to have much in my head besides empty space."

"I can confirm that," Scrappy said.

"The anklet," I said. "I didn't know what I was looking at until later. In the hospital I figured it out. I guess it was me."

"It was you," Felix said. "It wasn't Meg's ghost. And the omelet was something your mind was trying to tell you as well."

"I don't know," Cherry said. "It doesn't shake out all that neat."

Felix grunted.

Stone didn't offer an opinion on the ghost. "Whatever," he said. "Another night, Evelyn not having had a few drinks, it might not have happened. Occurred in a moment of passion. And her husband, who she feared was going to try and seduce Meg, went along with murder, getting rid of the bodies. In a strange way, they have a real love story there. Committing murder, burying bodies, that's some real bonding. All happened because Evelyn was thinking she might lose her man."

"As if Meg would have had him," I said. "And poor Ethan. Collateral damage."

"It's up to a jury now," Stone said.

"And Cowboy and Plug and Mr. Biggs?" I asked, even though I knew the answer. It was just something I wanted confirmed.

"Plug and Cowboy were toast. They did find some of the monkey under the loader. A red cowboy hat on the water. Alligators had been to work on the monkey."

"We saw that gator on his way to supper," Scrappy said.

So far, we hadn't mentioned that Scrappy had stabbed Cowboy in the back. It was kind of minor compared to what Mr. Biggs had done to his master in a fit of rage and what the fire had done to them all.

"You know," Stone said, "that mound was blown sky-high, and there was all manner of shards of Indian pots found, bones, things from back when they were buried there. Long, long ago."

"No spaceship?" Cherry said.

"No spaceship," Stone said. "We're still on our own."

(62)

Meg didn't have any next of kin that mattered. No one who she really was in contact with. I somehow ended up with her ashes after cremation. That was what she'd wanted, to be cremated. She even had funeral instructions and a will. Ethan wasn't mentioned in it.

Young as she was, she was planning ahead. Cherry suggested it was a premonition, and Meg had prepared for it.

I can't say.

But her ashes were given to me. I took them out back of my house one bright winter morning and spread them over the grass, close to where I set up my telescope. Scrappy was with me.

"She's going to be with you as long as you're here," Scrappy said.

"Does that bother you?"

"She's dead, and I'm not."

"You know what I mean."

"You knew her before me. I understand that."

"I do think about her, Scrappy. I won't lie."

"I know," she said. "I am considering on that."

Next morning, after a night without the alphabet, I awoke and Scrappy's camper was gone. Scrappy with it, of course. Tag too.

I felt brokenhearted. I should have told Scrappy that I thought about Meg but that I no longer loved Meg. Shoulda, woulda, coulda.

And then again, was that really true? Some part of me would always love her. She had been my first true love, and she had been smart and silly-stupid at the same time. She was kind and considerate in an unkind world, thinking maybe there was a paradise somewhere where people treated each other better or became sparks of light and energy.

About midday, I stripped and got in the shower. I turned on the hot water and let it run down the back of my neck for a long time, across the raw spot on my head.

It got steamy in the shower, and the glass partition fogged over.

I heard the bedroom door open, then I saw a shape through the fog. It wasn't a clear shape. But I knew who it was.

A moment later the shower door slid open. Scrappy, naked, stepped inside.

"Did you miss me?" I asked.

"We have that book to finish."

"True."

"You can't throw away your past, Charlie. I know that. You shouldn't. Maybe I didn't know it for a minute, but I know that now. Tag is eating the macaroni and cheese you had in the fridge. We don't have any more dog food. That boy needs a big-ass bag of that stuff."

"I was going to have that macaroni and cheese for supper."

"Were you?"

She put her arms around my neck and I put mine around her waist. She felt wet and warm and like all I would ever need. I had felt that way before, of course, but it was good to feel that way again and to hope I was right about it this time.

"No alphabet, just hot water," she said.

"You and that hot water are all I need right now."

"I'm glad. But you will need me when we turn the water off, even if it's just to towel each other off and lie in bed without the alphabet until maybe later tonight or early morning. Then we might work on our letters."

"That sounds good."

We held each other. The shower glass became thicker with steam. I put my head on Scrappy's shoulder while I held her. I thought of Meg briefly, then let her memory go.

I thought of the Donut Legion. Had we arrived a few hours later, had we been dispatched by Cowboy and Plug, those true believers would have gone away in a great draft of fire and explosion.

What were those true believers thinking now, since no ships had shown up?

Among their group they would lose members, but I was certain there was someone already formulating excuses.

Would the Donut Legion rise again?

Sure it would. Or something like it.

We are not a practical species, and we are for sure not nearly as smart as we think. We want to believe we have a place for our souls to land, if indeed we have them. We want to believe in an ultimate truth.

The only way that happens is through self-delusion. I so wished I could accept delusion, and perhaps I was in fact deluded and didn't know it.

Hot water ran down my face. I held Scrappy tight. I tried to concentrate on that. The water tasted salty, like tears.

In the kitchen, Tag barked once. I had no idea what he was trying to say.

ABOUT THE AUTHOR

Joe R. Lansdale is the author of nearly four dozen novels, including *Moon Lake*, the Edgar Award–winning *The Bottoms, Sunset and Sawdust*, and *Paradise Sky*. He has received eleven Bram Stoker Awards, a Spur Award, a British Fantasy Award, and the Grinzane Cavour Prize. He lives with his family in Nacogdoches, Texas.

joerlansdale.com
@joelansdale

MULHOLLAND BOOKS

You won't be able to put down these Mulholland Books.

THE WHEEL OF DOLL *by Jonathan Ames*

FORSAKEN COUNTRY *by Allen Eskens*

EVERYBODY KNOWS *by Jordan Harper*

BLACK WOLF *by Kathleen Kent*

EVERY MAN A KING *by Walter Mosley*

THE DONUT LEGION *by Joe R. Lansdale*

Visit mulhollandbooks.com for
your daily suspense fix.